I0598641

Dark Sanctuary

TRAPPED BY DOUBT

JAYCE CARTER

Trapped by Doubt
ISBN # 978-1-80250-951-9
©Copyright Jayce Carter 2022
Cover Art by Fiona Jayde ©Copyright May 2022
Interior text design by Claire Siemaszkiewicz
Totally Bound Publishing

TRAPPED BY DOUBT

Dedication

To my tarot cards,
who kick my ass more than I think is fair.
Why can't they ever predict naked men
with large dicks?

Chapter One

There was something about the courthouse that Ell both loved and hated. She loved the clear rules and the regimented way it ran. There was never a question about what the next step should be, about what was and wasn't allowed and about how a person went through those steps.

However, another part of her remembered coming as a child and the crushing disappointment that happened no matter how it went. Being there as an adult was different, gave a person a sense of power, but as a kid?

She recalled sitting beside a social worker, trembling, never sure how it would go or what that meant for her. Would they hand her over to her mother? Her father? Some relative she'd never met who wanted good karma points for taking in the poor, destitute child? Or would she take the gamble that was foster parents?

It was terrifying—always.

Which was exactly why Ell handed a closed cup of hot cocoa to the boy sitting on the bench in one of the many long hallways.

Donnie Denton, the first case she'd ever been assigned on her own. She could still remember walking in to see him, black eye but ready to take on anyone he needed to to survive. It had broken her heart to see him like that, to know he'd lived a life where he'd needed that hard edge.

He took the hot cocoa and offered a rough thank you. While other case managers had had trouble with him—they claimed he lied and was disrespectful and labeled him a lost cause—Ell had taken to him right away. She still smiled each time he went to respond with cursing but stopped himself, as if he knew it wasn't appropriate to say in front of her.

At fourteen, Donnie stood taller than her and had started to put on more bulk. Even still, she couldn't help but see the kid he'd been when she'd first met him.

"I'm sorry," he muttered softly, holding the cup between his hands.

"You don't need to apologize." Ell took her seat beside him.

"Yeah, I do. I fu—I screwed up. You shouldn't have to waste your time cleaning up my messes."

Ell shook her head. "I know you—if you got into this fight, you had a good reason, right?"

The color leeched from his lips as he pressed them together, the universal signal for 'I'm no snitch' that he got whenever she questioned anything. Then again, he was going to have to go back to that life, to those streets, and the sorts of people who existed in that world didn't forgive betrayal.

"I'm not trying to find out who it was," she pressed, gesturing at his split lip and his black eye, all signs he'd taken a hell of a beating. "I'm just saying, I know you have a good heart. You wouldn't be out there attacking random, innocent people. So for this to happen, you had a good reason."

He let out a long breath before taking a sip of the drink. He held it in his mouth for a long moment, as if thinking, then swallowed. "Someone wanted me to do a job, but they didn't tell me the real job. When they did? I told them to fu—I told them no. Well, he didn't take no very well."

Ell set her hand on his back and rubbed, knowing there wasn't much she could do for him. It was like his path had been made for him before he'd ever been born, and no matter how hard she tried, she had no idea how to get him off it.

The creaking of a door caught Ell's attention, and sure enough, Jeff Jadzen walked out of his office. Exactly the man she'd been waiting for.

Ell rose to her feet after nodding at Donnie, her way of assuring him she'd handle it.

Jeff took one look her way and walked faster.

Too bad Ell was perfectly fine with running in heels.

"Jeff, I need a minute—"

"Sorry, Ell, but I'm really busy. Set something up with my secretary."

"I tried. I haven't heard anything back in a week, and I've called every day."

"Like I said, very busy." He reached the men's room, then smiled like he'd won some prize. "It was nice to see you. Call the office and we'll try to get together next week." He ducked into the bathroom, his voice floating out as the door swung closed.

Next week would be too late. The pretrial was set for Friday of this week, and she shuddered to think about

Donnie ending up in juvie, of how quickly the rest of his options could float away.

Which was the exact thing that had her walking into the men's room. She'd been in far worse places in her life for far less noble reasons.

"Please tell me you didn't follow me into the men's room." Jeff spoke through a closed stall door, the annoyance palpable.

"I wasn't finished talking with you. At least now, you can't leave."

The longest sigh came from the stall. "Which charity case are you here about this time?"

"Donnie Denton."

"*Him* again? Come on, Ell, you run yourself ragged and for what? Donnie isn't some six-year-old who needs you to save him—he's basically an adult in his world. Stop seeing him as something he isn't."

"He's fourteen—that's still a kid. He isn't a bad kid, either."

"You say that because you didn't see the other person in the fight. Donnie shattered his eye socket with a bat."

That took her off guard, the level of violence new. Still, Ell shook her head, reassuring herself that she knew Donnie. He didn't lie to her. If he didn't want to tell her something, he just wouldn't, but he didn't lie.

"You know what it's like for people who live in that area."

"Yeah, I know, because I see what happens to the victims."

"Some victim. They wanted Donnie to do a job that was bad enough he turned it down once he knew the details."

"Is that what he told you? Well, his 'turned it down' moment ended up being *inside* someone's house as they robbed it. Did he leave that part out? That the woman walked in and saw them there."

Ell cringed at the little detail that, well, yeah, Donnie had left out. Still, it didn't change the rest. "Well, did Donnie touch the woman?"

Silence let her know she was right.

There was the flush of a toilet, then Jeff walked out and headed for the sinks. "No. According to her, Donnie's friend pulled a bat, and when Donnie objected, the two got into a fight. Scared the poor woman half to death, and when Donnie won, when the other man took off, Donnie said sorry and escaped through a window. We caught him down the street."

"You see? He was trying to help."

Jeff dried his hands, then turned to face Ell. "You see the best in people, Ell, and that's great, but it's going to get you killed. These kids you help, they aren't innocent and fragile. By the time they hit their teenage years, a lot of them are already killers. They're dangerous, and they're manipulative, and if you're not careful, it'll end you."

How many times had she heard that sort of warning? People who told Ell that she should pick a safer job, that she should do something else?

It didn't matter. She knew exactly why she did what she did. "Donnie has a shot. If you throw him into juvie, you're just going to solidify this path for him. Prison doesn't rehabilitate kids. It just makes them into better criminals."

Jeff rubbed the corners of his eyes. "What do you want me to do? He broke into a woman's house and put someone else in the hospital. I can't just look the other way with that."

"Community service."

"What?"

"He needs to see there are options for him, that there's a life he can still have that isn't on the streets. Assign him community service hours, and I'll make sure to find him a place to work them where he can do some good, where he can see a different life is possible."

Jeff's expression twisted the way it always did when he was in thought, when he was trying to see all the possible outcomes. His job had jaded him, but he wasn't a bad man.

Finally, he nodded. "Okay. I'll get it all drawn up and present it to his public defender. Make sure he understands that this is it, though. This is his one big shot. If he gets involved in something else like this, you won't be able to save him again."

Ell agreed, thanked Jeff, then exited the men's room. A quick conversation with Donnie outside let him know the details, and even though he wasn't the sort to admit to being nervous, the shuddering breath he released said he had been. He thanked Ell, then took off.

She would have driven him home, but Donnie was used to using the bus system. He always refused when she tried, saying he'd meet her wherever it was.

A glance at her watch told Ell that she didn't have another appointment until later, which gave her time to gather herself. When she slung her bag over her shoulder and turned, however, she ran directly into someone else.

Hands grasped her arms to keep her upright, and Ell glanced up to find a familiar face grinning down at her.

Ethan Jaymes, a detective she'd dealt with more than a few times. He was tall, dark and handsome — all the things that made her certain he was also trouble, especially when he smiled at her the way he always did. His green eyes danced with an amusement that his voice mirrored. "Aren't you in a hurry?"

She pulled away, extracting herself from his strong grasp. "You were the one standing far too close."

"I said your name, and you didn't hear me. Distracted?" He lifted an eyebrow.

"Well, believe it or not, my world doesn't revolve around you."

He let out a soft laugh, the way he always did when she soundly rejected him. It was odd, because sometimes it seemed the meaner she got, the more Ethan liked her.

And, just like clockwork, Ethan's shadow came around the corner.

Clint Faire, Ethan's partner, and an unnerving presence who had always made Ell fidget under his intense stare. He peered at her, no pleasure or surprise showing in his hazel eyes. He had a light brown beard and mustache, both well groomed, but shaved his head. If he weren't dressed so well, she'd no doubt think he was some muscle-head up to no good. "Ms. Hayden," he said, his tone as respectful as always.

Ell nodded back, still trying to calm her racing heart from her surprise at seeing Ethan. It shouldn't have surprised her that much — the two detectives were often at the courthouse — yet they always managed to make her feel out of control.

Which was about the worst feeling she could imagine. Ell was the sort of woman who preferred everything in its place, everything well-regulated and scheduled. Ethan and Clint managed to make her feel the opposite, as if she couldn't quite get a hold of all the pieces of her life, as if she couldn't make sense of it all.

And why, she had no idea.

She'd known the two men for years, though never well. She wouldn't call them friends by any stretch of the imagination, but they'd worked together from time to time—both on the same side and not so much.

"So who are you harassing today?" Clint asked in his matter-of-fact way that always made Ell's cheeks heat.

"I wasn't harassing anyone. I was doing my job."

"And who did your job require you to harass today?" Clint pressed.

"No one." Ell crossed her arms and tapped her foot, trying her best to make her annoyance as clear as possible.

"She followed me into the men's room," Jeff answered as he walked past, not slowing down to talk, seeming more than happy to rush across the hall so he could hide in his office again.

Ethan let out a hard laugh at that, and the fact he accepted her actions without question annoyed Ell. Yes, she was dedicated, but he could have had a second of 'Are they being serious? Would she really do that?' doubt.

"I needed to discuss something important with him, and he wanted to hide in the bathroom."

"You're going to get yourself into trouble one day," Ethan said as he caught his breath from his laughter. "It's good to go to bat for your kids, Ell, but be careful that you don't put yourself in a position you don't want to be in."

His words ran through Ell like they always did, tinged in something she tried so hard to ignore. Why was it that Ethan managed to get beneath her skin like this? His voice was like honey, something sweet enough to draw her closer, but also sticky enough she feared it might trap her.

All the reasons it was a bad idea had gone through in her head on nights when she stayed up thinking about him, even about Clint. She had her life in order. She'd perfectly crafted each part of it, fitting the pieces together, making exactly the picture she wanted. The idea of anyone else coming into that, of them possibly tearing apart everything she'd worked so hard to put into place, terrified her.

Life was hard and scary and dangerous, but if she kept the pieces in their spots, if she made sure everything went where it belonged, she could avoid the pain and fear she'd known so well as a kid.

So Ell offered a quick goodbye before she risked falling any further into either man, before she risked everything she'd built, her perfect house of cards.

The last thing she needed was to let either of these men blow down all the hard work she'd put in.

Clint watched the social worker scurry away, her heels loud against the tile floor. He stared at her ass, at the way it looked in her slacks.

Knock it off, you pervert.

Despite chastising himself, he never fully shook that. Sure, she was *way* too young for him, and there was no doubt she was strung too tight. None of that changed that each damn time he spotted her, his pulse sped and his cock hardened.

Hell, he was pretty sure his cock was like a barometer for that girl—it took notice even before *he* realized she was around.

"She's not interested," Clint said, and yet again, Ethan wished the other man developed some sort of a filter on that mouth of his.

Then again, if he hadn't in twenty years, it probably wouldn't happen now.

Clint said what he thought, no matter the consequences. Teaching him tact was a pointless endeavor.

"Even if she was…" Ethan said.

"She's too young."

Ethan nodded. "Yeah, she really is. She's grown up a lot in the last few years, though. Did you see Jeff all but run away? I can't remember the last person who got him moving like that."

Clint hooked his thumbs into his pockets, staring down the hallway in the direction Ell had scurried off in. "She's got too many hang-ups anyways."

Ethan snorted at the understatement. "That girl has more baggage than could fit on a plane."

Still…

Still what? Ethan couldn't help the fact his brain did that, locked onto her, and each time he came up with all the reasons it was a piss-poor idea, his mind seemed to rebut it.

Not that any of it really mattered. All the whys didn't change anything—she wasn't interested. Ethan hadn't actually asked her out, hadn't tried seriously to pursue anything, but Ell made it clear enough without that. The second their conversations turned to anything remotely personal, when an opening might occur where he could ask her, she shut it down and ran.

He had no idea if that was due to his age, his profession, her background and if she was just so terrified of the world that even the consideration of dating wasn't there.

In fact, he didn't think he'd ever seen her with anyone, or with any sign of dating at all…

Which seemed like a pity.

Ell was the sort of woman who should have a man— maybe more than one.

But since she didn't seem on board with that plan—
and he reminded himself again that neither was he—
Ethan tried to put it behind him. He looked over at
Clint and gestured toward the elevator. "Come on, let's
go get some lunch. We can ponder the direction of our
love life over food."

Clint nodded and followed Ethan's lead.

Why not drown his disappointment in carbs?

Chapter Two

Facing off against full-grown men never really got any easier. Ell had done it enough times in her career that it didn't surprise her, but it always made her heart pound faster.

"You're going to be sorry," the man, Lee, spat out as if he were the first person to ever come up with the idea of threatening Ell to get what they wanted.

He'd come to the hospital to visit his daughter, who he'd put there by crashing the car while drunk. Ell wasn't about to allow that. Still, the back and forth had only gotten him angrier when she blocked his path.

"You need to leave," came a masculine voice from behind Lee.

Lee spun, his eyes narrowed, until he spotted the man who had spoken. Dr. Fox Asher was one of those men who managed to appear intimidating despite not being covered in muscle. It was in the sternness of his expression, in his absolute confidence, in the way his blue eyes stared at a person as if he already knew they'd do as he wanted.

When he spoke, it was hard not to believe that whatever he said was the absolute truth.

Lee moved his gaze between Fox and Ell, then let out a huff saturated in whiskey and frustration. "This isn't over. You can't keep my kid away from me." With that, he turned and stormed off.

Fox didn't look Ell's way until Lee had turned the corner, when he seemed sure that the threat had gone. Once it was, he looked at Ell, the disapproval in his face a normal part of their interactions. "You need to be more careful."

"So I keep hearing." Ell moved back so Fox could come in.

The doctor worked with child protection services, so he cared for many of the kids who needed it. It was how Ell and he had met, why they interacted so often, though always for the worst things.

He'd come into court more than a few times to explain injuries, to talk about how they'd happened, about what the risks had been. In addition, he'd always subtly told Ell what she should do—not just her, though. He had no problem ordering everyone around, though always in the way that made a person think it was for their own good.

She still recalled the first time she'd met him, back when she'd been new to her job. He hadn't struck her as a doctor, not with how handsome he was. He was tall but lean, and always dressed in slacks and a white, collared shirt. His blond hair and blue eyes had made Ell do a double take the first time they'd met, as if he had gotten lost and somehow ended up in a hospital instead of the modeling gig he clearly belonged at.

"Well, you do tend to get yourself into trouble," Fox said.

"I do not."

"You don't believe that man was about to hit you? If you didn't see that, you need to study body language more."

Ell moved back over beside the bed, to stare down at the young girl who had thankfully missed the exchange. "He can get as angry as he wants. This is his fault."

Fox looked over the monitors and machines around the bed. Ell had found that about him, that while most of the other doctors she'd dealt with only glanced at a file, expecting the nurses to keep an eye on everything else, Fox took more care.

He knew his patients personally, knew them by name, could talk about what happened, even what they liked.

Ell wouldn't have considered him overly friendly, but somehow that calm nature of his worked well for kids, tended to relax them.

"I'm going to tell security to not allow Lee in anymore."

Ell nodded. "That's a good idea for the next week or so. Stress like this tends to lead to binge drinking, and she doesn't need to see that when she wakes up, especially since I think they're going to take his visitation."

"Have you contacted her mother?"

"She'll be here in the morning."

Fox nodded as he stood beside the bed and beside Ell. He had lines etched between his eyes, as if he frowned so much, they'd become permanent. "You should rest more," he said softly.

At first, Ell thought he was talking to the girl. When she turned, she found Fox staring right at Ell.

"I rest," she said.

"You have bags under your eyes," he pointed out. "You haven't taken any time off in the years I've known you. You work yourself past the point of exhaustion."

"Coming from you? You haven't taken a vacation that I know of, either."

He let out a soft laugh, one at odds with his normally stern expression. "I'm old, Ell. I rested enough when I was younger."

Ell pressed her lips together, his words bothering her. Yes, he was older than she was, but she didn't think she cared for the way he said it, as if it were a bad thing. She'd never considered him 'old.' Ell was thirty, and while she had to guess, she assumed Fox was in his mid-forties.

"You should go," he pressed. "She won't wake up until morning, when her mom gets here. If anything changes, I'll make sure you're notified."

Ell didn't want to go. She didn't want to leave the girl alone, didn't want to leave her work where she knew her place, where she understood the job. Work always felt safe.

When Fox lifted his eyebrow, Ell knew she had no good argument against him. This became even more clear when she yawned, when the reality of the long hours she worked hit her.

She nodded and squeezed the girl's hand once more.

"You know," Fox said as she went for the door, making her pause. "You really should take better care of yourself." He met her gaze, his bright blue eyes serious. In fact, there was so much intensity, it almost felt like an odd threat.

Not that she could make sense of that.

"I do," she said, even though the moment the words escaped, she knew they were a lie.

He shook his head. "You don't, and I doubt you will, so you need to find someone who takes care of you. Years pass quickly, Ell, and if you keep working the way you do, stress will kill you before anything else."

Ell didn't need to respond — not that she knew what to say — because Fox turned his back to her and pulled the file off the end of the bed, flipping it open as if to review everything was done correctly. It was a not-so-subtle dismissal of Ell, a way to tell her the conversation was over and she should go.

So, with no place else to go, nothing else to do, Ell gave in and headed home.

Chapter Three

Ell pulled at the hemline of her skirt for what had to be the hundredth time as she walked up to Sanctuary, the local BDSM club her friend had guilt tripped her into going to.

"Stop fidgeting." Dean smacked her hand.

Ell gave him a dry look. They'd known each another since they were kids, had spent their childhood watching each other's backs, but that didn't mean they always got along. She figured it was probably the same as blood siblings — they loved one another but bickered constantly.

"Why exactly did I have to wear this?" She tried to ignore exactly how uncomfortable she felt in the outfit. "I had plenty of outfits I could have put on."

"Yeah, but you didn't have one that worked right for *this* sort of event."

Ell gave him a side-eye as they approached the front door. "I thought you said this place wasn't just about sex."

"That's right."

"So why do I need to walk around *looking* like sex?"

His lip curled into a smirk on one side despite him not looking her way. "It isn't *just* about sex, but sex is a part of it. Besides, you needed to relax, and you couldn't do that in what you were wearing."

"It was a perfectly nice outfit."

"It was what you wear to work."

"So? It was still nice."

He let out an exasperated sigh. "It's boring, and you've had enough time in your boring rut of a life. That's why I realized I couldn't trust you to pick your own and got you something. Is it really so terrible to put on a pretty dress and go out with your oldest and best friend?"

Ell wanted to say yes, that it was that bad, but the look on his face stopped her. She knew that Dean wouldn't do anything harmful, that if he was pushing, it was because he cared and wanted the best for her. Sure, that made her uncomfortable, made her want to remind him yet again that she didn't need him looking out for her.

Ell had survived a long time all on her own—she could do so for the foreseeable future and be happy with it.

Unfortunately, Dean meant too much to her. His happiness mattered to her, and she felt responsible for not causing him any pain, which was yet another reason she'd agreed, and had put on the dress.

Dean had bothered her for months about coming with him to Sanctuary, about her needing to get out of the house, about her needing to have some fun. Ell had avoided it for as long as possible until it became *im*possible, with Dean's requests too hard to turn down.

It meant she could come this once, make Dean happy, then crawl right back into her safe little rut.

"Should I know anything special?" Ell asked to hide her nerves.

Dean bumped her with his arm as they paused just outside the front doors of the large building. "Stop worrying so much."

"Why shouldn't I? I'm going into a sex club." Even saying it made Ell's nerves rise. She didn't do *this* sort of thing anymore. It wasn't a part of her life. Sex was something she just didn't think she was capable of, so she'd all but abandoned the idea of it. It wasn't that she was a virgin—far from it. She'd spent time in her teens rebelling, thinking sex and love were the same thing, but she'd grown out of that by twenty. It meant the last ten years had been a very long dry spell.

"Would I take you anywhere dangerous?"

She shook her head.

"Would I ever let you get hurt?"

Again, she shook her head.

"So trust me, Ell."

It seemed simple when he said it like that, so Ell drew in a deep breath and nodded. He was right. She could come here, make Dean happy, then go back her well-regulated and regimented life.

Dean must have been waiting for that submission, because he smiled, then opened the door.

Music filled the space, but not so loud that she felt the need to cringe. The lights weren't overly bright, but also not dark. Then again, judging from the next-to-nothing many people wore, they weren't shy or in need of the darkness to hide.

Dean narrated the whole thing like a tour guide as they walked, explaining each area of the club. He showed her the bar, explained that there was no alcohol, showed her a food table and the different seating areas. Ell filed it all away, made sense of it.

The large room they were in was the most casual. While people still engaged in *fun,* it wasn't as extreme. This was more for mixing and conversation and dancing. Down a hallway rested private rooms, though Dean told her not to go that way. Through another doorway was what Dean had called the more 'interactive' space.

The cry of a woman, one full of passion, echoed into Ell's ears and made her cheeks flush.

"So that's the sex part of the sex club?"

Dean chuckled. "Well, people aren't picky. There can be sex in about any of the areas here, past the reception area, but that's where it's more the whole point. You want to check it out?"

Ell shook her head as quickly as she could. "I think I'll avoid that."

"Dean!" The excited voice of a woman drew Ell's attention to the side.

The woman who had called out wore what looked like a lace body suit, the sort of thing Ell was used to seeing pictures of when companies advertised their lingerie. Seeing her walking around in so little made Ell uncomfortable.

"Hannah," Dean said, a smile on his lips that didn't match his eyes. It was his fake smile, one Ell knew too well. "You look lovely."

Hannah dragged her hands down the outfit, a pink flush on her cheeks. "Thank you. I picked it out because I know how much you like red."

The display made Ell tear her gaze away, feeling as if she were intruding.

"It's wonderful," Dean repeated. "But I've brought a guest tonight, so I'm afraid I'll be a bit busy."

Ell shook her head and interrupted. "It's fine, Dean. I can handle myself."

"I don't want to just abandon you," he said, but Ell could see the desire on his face. Even though his smile was fake, he still seemed to want to go with Hannah.

"I'm a big girl—I can take care of myself. Besides, you wanted me to come here to make friends, right? Well, that won't happen if I spend all night talking to you."

Dean hesitated and stared at Ell for a long moment, as if trying to read the truth. Ell offered him a strained smile, trying to convince him she'd be fine.

At least if he wasn't around, Ell could just get a water and sit in a corner by herself. She'd people watch, and by the end of it, she could say she'd come and realized it wasn't for her. She normally would have read on her phone, but the club didn't want pictures or videos taken inside, so they had people check them, especially guests.

He nodded finally. "Okay, Ell. I'll stay in the main areas so you can find me if you need me. If you can't figure out where I am, talk to the bartender or any of security—they'll help."

"Stop worrying," Ell assured him. "Go on. Have fun."

Dean leaned in and pressed a kiss to Ell's head before he turned toward Hannah and walked off with her.

It left Ell all alone in the club, and she wasn't sure how her well-organized life had landed her here...

Chapter Four

The more time Ell spent at Sanctuary, the more surprised she was to find it calming. There was a level of ease she never would have expected. She wondered if that was partly due to the lack of alcohol.

A few people had approached her over the hour she'd sat at the table, but all had been friendly and quick to accept her 'not interested' and leave her be. As time passed, she'd found herself instead staring out at the others in the club.

They all looked so happy...

It startled her, the way they talked to each other as if friends. Even in a few of the corners, where people were wrapped up in each other, there was a playfulness that she hadn't expected.

Ell had shown up thinking that it would just be sweaty bodies and men who wanted to be called Daddy. Basically, she'd expected a regular bar full of drunken idiots with less clothing and more whips.

Then again, Ell had avoided the more risqué parts, so maybe that was why.

She finished off her drink just as her stomach churned. Drinking a whole can of soda when she hadn't eaten anything today had probably been a bad idea, with the carbonation playing havoc on her stomach. The food tables were there, at the back. She could get a snack to settle her stomach, then go back to people watching.

She had to think Dean would finish soon. Men didn't tend to last long in her experience, and no matter how much she adored her friend, she doubted he was the one exception to that rule.

There were even more people than before, and more streamed in as time had passed. Then again, this was the sort of place people probably preferred after hours, and the clock read nearly midnight already.

Ell headed for the bar, her shoulders back, her chin raised. She'd found it was best to walk as if she wasn't nervous at all, because people tended to pounce on weakness.

She made a plate with crackers, cheese and fruit, then peered back toward the main room. The place she'd sat before was taken, now, and she couldn't spot any open seats.

"There's more tables back there."

Ell turned to find the bartender looking at her and gesturing toward the doorway Dean had said was more extreme.

Ell's cheeks burned. "I'm not sure that's the best place for me..."

The bartender let out a bark of laughter. "Oh, ain't you a sweet thing? Don't worry so much. There are a few areas for scenes, but they don't bite. There's also more tables, though, and those don't get filled as fast since the music isn't as loud in there."

Which sounded pretty good to Ell.

She didn't mind if people wanted to have sex a few feet away from her so long as she wasn't in a splash zone…

She thanked the bartender and ignored the way he'd called her sweet as she carried her plate of food, a water bottle beneath her arm, into the room.

Her feet froze at the threshold. *This* was more of what she'd been thinking when Dean had invited her. The room was large, almost like an auditorium, but longer than it was wide. There were alcoves along each side, and inside each was either a seating area or some weird piece of furniture that Ell didn't recognize.

All the furniture had tie downs, though, which made their purpose clear even if Ell wasn't sure how exactly they worked.

Just like the bartender had said, there was plenty of open seating, but most of the spots for play were filled.

There was a man restrained to what almost looked like a medical bed, with a woman standing above him, staring at him with a surprisingly sweet look on her face given the grip she currently had on his goods.

Ell shuddered. Men had always said that area was sensitive, so what they hell were they thinking?

That wasn't the strangest of the areas, though. In fact, each time Ell saw a new scene, a new couple — or more — she frowned. It all seemed so…chaotic. The sounds, the movements, they felt wild and out of control.

It increased Ell's nausea.

She moved forward, trying to keep her gaze down as she looked for an empty seating area.

She spotted one, near the far end, between a woman in some sort of cage and a man who was being taken by a couple.

As soon as she headed for the spot, the room plunged into darkness.

Startled screams came out, but Ell didn't make that noise. Making any sound when frightened was a horrible idea, something Ell had learned a long time before. Instead, she froze, a tremble to her shoulders.

Something large hit her, knocking her off balance and spilling her plate. She toppled to the side as panic seemed to take over others, as more footsteps said people rushed.

She didn't hit the floor, but the darkness was so absolute she couldn't see anything, couldn't figure out what she'd landed on.

At least, she couldn't until whatever she rested against *moved* and let out a soft chuckle.

"Well, well, looks like I caught something," said a masculine, amused voice.

Which meant Ell had just fallen into the lap of a stranger.

This night was *not* going according to plan.

The weight of a girl in Ethan's lap was surprisingly nice. He set his hands on her waist to settle her as she shifted, to make sure she didn't topple again.

The lights had all gone off, which wasn't the first time he'd been here for a power outage. The club was situated a bit out of town, and power could get dicey from time to time.

Because of privacy concerns, all windows were covered with tinting that prevented anyone from seeing in, but also kept light out. It meant the room was entirely dark. Security had flashlights, but their first goal was to check for injuries, and there wasn't a reason to call them over.

The girl in his lap hadn't spoken, and it took a moment for him to realize she was shaking.

Shit.

"Hey there," Ethan said, his voice gentle. "It's okay. Power never stays off for long."

She still didn't speak, but damn if her breathing didn't turn even more erratic.

He shifted a little, setting her beside him on the booth. Maybe she'd do better if she wasn't right in his lap, but he wasn't all that inclined to let her go wandering in the dark in her condition.

Especially because he'd seen the last power outage, and they'd ended up with a few sprained ankles from people pushing and shoving in panic.

Which struck Ethan as stupid. Darkness wasn't dangerous on its own. If people didn't panic, if they hadn't trampled toward the door, nothing would have happened. Still, his job as a detective had let him see plenty of times just how stupid people really could be.

"She okay?" Fox asked. Even though he probably couldn't see a damn thing either, it seemed he'd been paying attention.

"I think she doesn't care for the dark."

There was a shuffle, as if Fox had moved. "Yeah, her pulse is going crazy. You scared of the dark, sweetheart? Just breathe slowly. Lights go out sometimes, but they never go out for long."

"If she passes out, she won't be scared anymore," Clint offered.

Ethan gave his friend a glare even if he couldn't see it, then went for his one move. "Do you know why you should never fight a dinosaur?"

The woman's breathing slowed a bit, the panting quieting as if the question had distracted her.

Clint let out an exasperated breath. Ethan was pretty sure he hadn't heard this joke before, but then again, neither Clint nor Fox had ever appreciated Ethan's humor.

"Because you'll just get jurasskicked."

There was no response at first, as if it took a good minute to get the joke then deal with just how stupid it really was.

Finally, the woman answered. "You have to be kidding me, right?"

Ethan grinned at her voice, at the sweet annoyance in it. Why he enjoyed being a nuisance, he wasn't sure, but it had always seemed like his place in life. Besides, his stupid joke had managed to pull her out of her distress, and that made it worth it.

"You feeling better?" Ethan asked.

She shifted, brushing against his side. "Yeah. I'm sorry." The apology held shame. Was she embarrassed?

A desire to put his arm around her hit him, but he kept still. Without the lights, he couldn't see the woman, couldn't see her cuffs. For all he knew she wasn't interested in anything, or perhaps she was already taken.

Though, even the desire struck him as odd. He couldn't recall when he'd last had that urge...

"Lots of people are afraid of the dark," Fox said.

"Mostly children," Clint added.

Ethan kicked across the seating area, nailing Clint in the shin.

Clint let out a grunt at the impact but said nothing else.

"Does this happen a lot?" she asked.

"Sometimes." Ethan stretched, trying to ease a tightness in his back from his long day. "But it doesn't stay off for long usually. Still, people start to panic, so it's best to just stay put here until it turns back on."

"You didn't get hurt, right?" Fox asked. "We've had sprained ankles when this has happened before."

She didn't answer right away, and Ethan got the feeling she'd shaken her head before remembering no one could see her. "I'm fine. Sorry about, well, you know."

Ethan couldn't help the smile at her tentative voice. She was sweet, wasn't she? He wondered who she was, suddenly. She didn't sound like someone who came here often, someone he might recognize. There were a lot of members and Ethan hadn't been a big part of the community in a while. There was a familiarity to her voice, but Ethan spoke to so many people because of his job that many voices ended up sounding as if he knew them.

"Hey, I'm not going to complain about a pretty woman falling into my lap," Ethan said, trying to keep the tone light.

He could almost *feel* her glare. So, that meant she was either new or bratty. Otherwise, a little playful flirting wouldn't strike her as so odd.

"I'm really okay," she said then shifted as if to stand.

"You should stay put until the lights come back on," Fox said. "I have a feeling you're new here, and you don't know the place well enough to navigate it in the dark. Just relax here where you won't get knocked over again."

She didn't sit again for a moment, as if deciding. Ethan could all but picture how she'd stare out at the darkened room, remembering everything she'd seen when the lights were still on. A place where people often carried whips and knew how to use blades was probably not the most comfortable when a person couldn't see. Finally, she did as Fox had suggested and sat back down between him and Ethan.

The desire to call her a good girl perched on Ethan's lips, but he kept it in. He didn't know her, so it wasn't his place to say such a thing.

"Is this your first time here?" Fox asked, no doubt trying to ease the situation.

"Yes. I came with a friend."

"Oh yeah? Who is your friend?"

"Dean Havers."

Ethan lifted his eyebrow at the answer. He knew Dean, of course. The man was friendly, and, while they weren't close, he liked him well enough. Dean was still in the phase where he was young enough to fully enjoy tasting every part of life. It meant he went through subs faster than most people had to put gas in their car. He wasn't unkind, but that didn't change that he'd left more than a few broken hearts in his wake.

Was this girl another groupie of his?

"I'm surprised he let you wander around on your own," Clint said.

"Dean isn't possessive," Ethan added. "And he's easily distracted…"

"I don't need a babysitter," the woman said, her tone haughty.

"So you aren't jealous, either?" Ethan asked.

"We aren't like that. We're just friends."

"This is a weird place to bring friends."

Before she could answer, a sound made Ethan frown. It took him a minute to figure out what it was.

Her stomach.

Ethan didn't smother his chuckle before he reached behind him for the plate that Kat had brought for Fox earlier. He didn't say a word and placed it in the woman's lap. "Eat."

The woman took a bite, the quiet chewing telling Ethan she'd listened. After another moment, she offered a quiet thank you.

"So, why is it Dean brought you? Just bored and looking for some place to go?" Fox asked.

"He said I'm in a rut," the woman said. "So I promised him I'd come here so he'd stop bothering me."

And Ethan knew he shouldn't be as happy about that answer as he was. The fact that this woman wasn't with Dean pleased the hell out of him. He had no idea exactly why, but he'd long since stopped worrying about why.

"So what do you think?"

"Hmm?" she made the sound of question around another bite of food.

"Well, you got to spend some time looking around here. What do you think?"

Her answer was slow coming. "I think it isn't my sort of place."

"No?" Ethan buried down his disappointment. Sure, a lot of people weren't into any of this. It wasn't a surprise that she might be vanilla, because that was really the better chance, but it still chafed.

"No." Her tone was sure. "I'm not into some man telling me what to do."

"You know that it isn't just women who are subs, right? There are lots of Dommes ordering male subs around," Clint said.

"Yes, I know that." Even as she answered, the words came a bit slower.

Then again, Ethan had seen this reaction enough times. He couldn't blame women who thought that after how many men on social media all decided they were Doms and were more than happy to pressure any woman they could into what they wanted.

Of course, they weren't *really* Doms. They were just men who wanted their way without the work, who thought BDSM was an easy way to get what they wanted.

Making people understand the truth was hard, though, and often downright impossible. While more people knowing about BDSM was great, the sad fact was that bad information seemed most easily accessible. Talk about a double-edged sword…

"Well, you don't have to worry. No one here is going to force you into anything," Fox assured her. "We're all big on consent, so you're welcome to look around and hang out and not participate in anything you don't want to."

The woman seemed to relax at that, letting Ethan know Fox had guessed right.

But, again, lots of people were nervous in a place like this. It was funny since even if Ethan didn't enjoy it as he had before, it was still a safe space for him. It was somewhere that felt real, honest in a way a lot of places didn't.

"How long have you…" She paused.

"How long have we come here?"

"Yes."

He smiled at the way she asked, at the idea she was curious about them. She was probably just making conversation, just filling the time with something to talk about. "Lots of years. I joined back when it first opened, when I talked to the owner, Toya, when she was still getting everything set up."

"Did all three of you join then?"

"I only joined about eight years ago," Fox said.

"I joined when it opened as well," Clint added.

"So you're pretty dedicated to this whole...thing?"

Ethan grinned at the way she phrased it. "Yeah, I guess so. It's fun because there's always something new."

"New? It feels like whips and chains would get boring after a while."

"Sure, they might, but luckily there's a lot more to it than that," Ethan said, surprised by how much he enjoyed their conversation. "I mean, I think that's what's so funny, how often people decide they aren't interested in *anything* to do with this place without really taking a look. There's a lot of damned stuff involved, and I can't believe there's *nothing* they might like."

"Well, there isn't," the woman said.

"You want to bet?"

She let out a soft sound that implied she thought it was foolish. "A bet? Really?"

"Hey, we're stuck here a little longer, nowhere to go, why not?"

"What's the bet?"

"We'll go through a list. If there's really not a single thing you find interesting, you win. If there's something you are, then we win."

"She'll just lie," Clint said.

Yet again, Ethan kicked him to get him to shut up.

"I will not lie." At least the woman sounded offended by it, meaning she might actually be honest. "What are the stakes?"

Ethan sat back, thinking. "Whoever loses pays for dinner?"

"Do women really fall for that?"

Ethan huffed a laugh at her mouth. She was more fun than she should have been. "Sometimes they do. I guess I should have figured it wouldn't have worked for you. Okay, so you're not interested in dinner, so what about coffee? Whoever loses buys coffee?"

"I've already said I'm not interested in this, so why would I want to have coffee with you?"

"You're friends with Dean, right? And he is into a *lot* of stuff here, but you're still friends."

She didn't answer at first, but when she did, her voice was soft. "That's true..."

"So what's a cup of coffee between friends? Deal?"

Ethan about held his breath waiting, but eventually she agreed.

And Ethan wasn't sure he'd been this excited about anything in a long damned time...

Chapter Five

Ell wished she could see the men she sat with. Their voices felt familiar, but she couldn't place them. It was probably just a symptom of her nerves playing tricks on her.

Really, what were the odds that she'd know anyone *here*? This wasn't her sort of place, so the people who hung out here weren't the type she'd likely know.

The idea of playing such a game, especially without knowing the questions ahead of time, would have normally driven her anxiety sky-high. She had to guess that her willingness had more to do with the darkness, with how she'd already freaked out and how the inability to see the men or have them see her made her feel more relaxed.

Still, she wasn't all that prepared when the first man asked a question.

"Let's make it easy. Say yes, no or maybe to anything we suggest. Only a yes will win for us. You ready?"

"Ready," she said, even though she still had no real idea why she'd agreed.

The silence made her want to shift around, but each time she did, she brushed up against the men to either side of her. The third man was across from her in the booth, though there was no table in front of them.

She expected something extreme, something she would never want to do an internet search for out of fear.

Instead, it was the man who had done most of the talking who asked, "Voyeurism?"

That was an easy one. "No."

"Exhibitionism?"

The idea of people watching her made her shudder. "No."

"Bondage?"

Ell paused as she trailed her fingers over her own cuff. It was strange, because the idea of allowing anyone to bind her made her want to shout an immediate no. Still, she knew damned well she'd woken from dreams in the past with some faceless person and her, her wrists bound behind her. So…was liking an idea in fantasy the same as liking it in real life?

"Are we going to win that easily? Just on number three?" The man let out a soft laugh, one that warmed her.

"You haven't won, yet—I was deciding."

"Deciding?" the man to her other side asked.

"I was deciding if I was actually interested or not."

"And?"

"And…" She drew a slow breath, then shook her head. "No. I can't imagine actually allowing anyone to tie me down."

The man across from them made a soft sound that said he didn't quite believe her, but no one called her a liar.

The man who had done less of the talking, the nice-sounding one, took over on the questions. Ell was surprised that they weren't nearly as graphic as she would have expected, and in fact they were asked almost like some sort of interview. They didn't ask them as if they were imagining it, as if it was foreplay and they were trying to get her to agree. Instead, it felt like a casual getting to know each other thing.

"Role playing."

"That's not a fair question."

"Why not?"

Ell took another bite of the food they'd given her, pleased with how tasty the cookies were. Sure, she should have had something healthier, but she couldn't deny her attitude had improved with the sugar. "Because role playing could mean anything. Teacher and student is a far cry from squirrel and adult baby."

"Adult baby? Maybe you're into kinkier stuff than you want to admit to," the funny one said.

Ell made sure her sigh was just as loud as she could make it.

"Fine," the man who had asked the question said. "That's a fair point. What about good old-fashioned submission?"

Again, Ell was taken to that same old place, where the idea of it might sound nice but the reality was something she couldn't accept or consider. "I don't think so."

"You don't *think* so?"

The darkness made Ell feel safe and more willing to spill her secrets. Why not? She was in a club she'd never return to with men who couldn't even see her. "Sometimes things maybe seem like they could be good, in some vague, never-going-to-happen way."

Silence met her, the sort that made her fidget and want to keep talking. She wasn't sure if they did that on purpose or not, but knowing didn't change that she went on.

"It's like...hang gliding."

"Hang gliding?" the mostly silent man asked as if he couldn't keep up with the conversation. "Hang gliding isn't anything like submission."

"Not like that. I mean that you see hang gliding in magazines, and it looks like so much fun. You think...I could do that. I could be a hang glider. It seems like this wonderful rush that you want to experience so badly."

"So why not try it?" the nice man asked.

"I did. Or, I guess, I tried to. I got tickets, got all the way out to where they took off from, and as soon as I saw the first person take off, I realized that fantasy and reality are two very different things. The fantasy of soaring peacefully was nice. The reality of leaping off a cliff and trusting some metal and fabric turned out not to be my sort of thing at all."

That silence came again, and it was the humorous one who answered her. "So, you're saying that the idea of submission might sound good, but you're sure it won't live up to your expectations, so you won't even give it a try?"

"I don't want to crash and burn. Jumping off cliffs or letting some guy tie me up both sound like quick ways to disaster. There are some mistakes people can't just pick themselves back up after."

"And you're that sure you'll crash and burn?" asked the nice one.

"Maybe, maybe not, but I'm smart enough to recognize that it's not worth the risk."

The quiet one made another one of those soft sounds. It made Ell's cheeks heat again, made her feel as if he could see right through her.

Despite the darkness...

"Does that mean I win?"

"Not yet, sweetheart," said the funny one. "How about humiliation?"

"No. Hard pass."

"Praise?"

"Praise isn't a kink."

"Sure it is. You really trying to tell me you don't want to be called a good girl?"

Ell recalled back to when the man at the door had called her brave, to the way she'd flushed at the compliment. She pictured someone saying those words in a deep, masculine whisper into her ears, the way someone could stroke his hand through hair and look at her as if she'd done well.

She couldn't deny the rush of desire inside her at that thought.

Did that mean she *was* interested?

"Maybe," she offered softly, unwilling to lie but also unable to actually admit it. It wasn't even that she didn't want to lose, so much as she was afraid of saying it. Admitting it felt like the first step down a path she just refused to start on.

"Maybe, huh? Well, that's an interesting answer."

"Who wouldn't like being complimented?" Ell muttered, feeling sullen by the teasing.

If the funny one was sorry, he didn't show it. If anything, he seemed even more amused.

The nice one spoke up, instead. "You know, giving up on something you might be interested in just because you're nervous leads to a pretty boring life."

"I'm okay with boring. Boring is safe."

"Safe is boring," the funny one said.

"Only people who life very safe lives say that."

"Yeah, I'm pretty sure you're wrong about that." All three men laughed, as if in on some joke Ell didn't understand. Was he saying they'd lived dangerous lives? That they had dangerous jobs?

"Maybe other people like the stress and the chaos of new things, but I don't."

"Yet you're here…"

"Because Dean wanted me to come."

"So? Lots of people want things. Why listen to him?"

Ell hesitated, not caring for the personal questions. It wasn't so much that she didn't want to admit it, but more that she didn't care to think about it, to dissect her own feelings about it. Instead, she moved the three items left into equal thirds on the plate. The action helped her to relax, to take a deep breath. "Because I care about him, and I didn't want him to worry."

"So you trust him?" The nice one didn't wait for her to answer before he went on. "If you trust him that much, have you considered he could be right? That maybe you needed to get out of your own way and experience something different?"

If Ell could have erased those words as soon as the left that man's mouth, she would have. They felt like bees floating around, threatening her.

Instead, she tried to let the darkness ease her. Now that she was past the surprise of the moment, the immediate fear that happened when they the lights went off, she had to admit, it wasn't so bad. It was almost relaxing, especially with the warmth of the men beside her.

"Maybe," she admitted softly, trying to allow herself to follow that thought. She had a warmth inside her, one that had grown since she'd sat there between the men.

She would have otherwise said it was alcohol, that same loosening of her muscles she'd felt before from that. Since she hadn't drank anything with alcohol, she wasn't sure what caused it. It was arousal, lust, no matter how little sense that made to her. She hadn't felt this way in so long, so why was it these faceless men could manage it when having a rather tame conversation?

"But Dean's braver than I am," Ell explained. "He's always been braver. We grew up together, and he was tough back then. It's like...a bear is always going to braver than a rabbit because he's bigger and stronger and tougher. So, a bear might be right about advice when giving it to another bear, but if it gives that advice to a rabbit, the rabbit will probably get eaten if it follows it."

"You don't strike me as a rabbit," the nice one said. "I think you're tougher than you give yourself credit for."

Ell thought about her life, about all the ways she avoided the unknown, and she just couldn't see that in herself. "Well, that just shows how little you actually know me."

Silence met her for a moment, before the nice one answered, his voice surprisingly gentle. "You are a mess, sweetheart, aren't you?"

Ell wanted to deny it, but he wasn't wrong. She swung wildly between feeling like her entire life was nothing but chaos and feeling as if she had it all perfectly ordered. Why was it that she hadn't really considered that before?

She recalled Dean watching her as she'd organized the candles on her dresser, the way he'd pointed it out, the flush on her cheeks as she'd realized it. "Probably," she admitted.

"Lights should be back on in a few minutes," came a voice that Ell recognized as the bartender.

What surprised Ell was her moment of disappointment.

"What about orgies?" the funny one asked.

Ell was thankful for the lights still being off, so the men didn't see the flush that no doubt covered her cheeks. "If I wanted to disappoint two people at once, I'd have dinner with my bosses."

The funny one snorted but didn't acknowledge her statement directly. "What else is there?"

"I can't believe you're running out of kinks already. And here I thought the people who came here were imaginative."

"Oh, we're *plenty* imaginative," the nice one said. "We're just being kind and not suggesting things that would make you blush."

Too late. Ell was pretty sure her cheeks had been bright red for most of the conversation already. "I'm not as fragile as you think."

"Oh, so you might be interested in pain play? Flogging? Suspension?"

Ell shook her head no before remembering they couldn't see her. "No. Absolutely not."

"Orgasms," the funny one said.

"That's a noun, not a kink."

"Oh, it can be a kink. Either denial or torture. Having someone else tease you but not let you come, keeping you dangling on that edge?"

Ell struggled to pull in a breath, her heart pounding so fast she was sure they could hear it. In her head, she pictured herself straining, desperate, covering in sweat and unable to have what she wanted. She thought about being at the mercy of someone else, someone who could not only offer pleasure but deny it just as easily. She answered, but the word came out a question. "No?"

The funny one didn't call her on it, just went on. "What about the other? Having someone get you off over and over again?"

"That's just a story men tell," Ell said. "It isn't something that really happens."

"If you think that, Dean was right to bring you here for a little education. Trust me, it's real."

Ell tried to think about that, struggling to accept it. The denial, that made sense to her. How many times had she strained for release and hadn't managed it no matter how hard she or her partner tried? That was easy to picture, but the idea of coming over and over again?

Impossible.

Still, even as she thought that, she couldn't get away from the idea.

"So, is that a yes or a no? The fact you may not think it's possible isn't part of the bet. If it was…would you be interested?"

Ell felt backed into a corner. Yes, she wanted to… The idea consumed her, made her breath quicker, her skin overheated. That meant she was interested, didn't it? She knew she'd lost, but the idea of seeing the men again, of risking her organized life was too great.

"No," she whispered softly, knowing damn well it was a lie.

The funny one let out another of those dark chuckles. "*Right.*" His tone said he knew she was lying.

"That was cheating, anyway. Who wouldn't want multiple orgasms?"

"It wasn't cheating—it was just me knowing more about it than you do. Besides, our little conversation distracted you, right?"

Ell frowned. "You did this to distract me?"

"Sure. You were nervous when the lights went off. We thought a fun game would keep your mind off it," the nice one answered.

Ell opened her mouth to thank them, but the lights flipped back on. It blinded her at first, made it so she couldn't see anything. As her eyes adjusted, she peered at the three men around her, the ones she'd spoken so graphically to.

They weren't strangers, weren't men she'd never met.

Instead, she found the surprised faces of Ethan, Clint and Fox staring back at her…

Seeing Ell just about shut Clint's mind off. They'd talked for what had to have been half an hour, and he'd never suspected it was *her.*

Her voice might have struck him as familiar, but it hadn't even occurred to him that it could have been Ell. This wasn't the sort of place he'd ever thought she'd come.

Though, a glance at her outfit said she wasn't quite so innocent as he'd thought.

Or, rather, she was the sort of innocent he liked…

She wore a schoolgirl costume with a shirt plaid skirt, a buttoned-up white top and a cute tie that he wanted to wrap his fingers around to pull her closer.

Where did that come from?

Clint had heard Ethan drone on about Ell enough times, but Clint preferred not trying for things that weren't possible. Anything with Ell fit into that.

At least, he hadn't thought it possible, but after hearing her answers, Clint wasn't so sure.

"Ell?" Fox asked, as if he couldn't believe it.

"You've got to be kidding me," Ell muttered before rising in a jump, as if she couldn't escape them fast enough.

"Wait," Ethan said, getting to his feet as well. "You don't have to leave."

"I really do. This was a mistake."

Clint stared at her, not rising, not wanting to make her uncomfortable. Too often people couldn't relax around him, something he knew but couldn't seem to fix. Still, he spoke up. "Why was it a mistake? Because you had a good time?"

She offered him a withering glare. "We had a conversation—nothing else."

"A conversation you enjoyed. You said you didn't lie during the bet—are you going to start now?"

She looked defiant standing there, a reminder that no matter how unsure she might have seemed about some of their topics, she wasn't some fragile flower. The girl could go toe-to-toe with anyone. "It doesn't matter. I told you I was only here because Dean brought me."

"So? Why let go of something you're clearly curious about just because somewhere in your head, you've decided it's not a good idea?"

She pressed her lips together, and it made her look impossibly cuter. It made Clint rise to his feet finally, unable to help it. He didn't touch her but stood close enough that they could touch if she leaned forward the slightest amount.

"You're braver than you think, and you're certainly brave enough to give what you want a try."

Ell traced her tongue along her bottom lip, and wasn't that the best temptation? Clint had spent enough time studying body language to recognize that action as attraction, as desire, especially when paired with the pink on her cheeks and the way her breath had quickened.

Clint leaned in, wanting to taste her, to have what he'd dreamed of for *years*. His lips brushed hers, tasting the sweetness from the cookies she'd eaten.

Her lips moved, and for a moment, he thought she was kissing him back. Except, instead of that, he heard a soft word escape from her.

"Red."

Clint pulled back immediately, gave her room, the safe word a slap in the face like it always. The word wasn't a suggestion or a request. It was a full stop that deserved that level of attention.

Ell took two big steps backward, her cheeks even redder, her gaze on the ground.

"Are you okay?" Fox asked, still seated as if to not crowd her.

Ell shook her head, but it was the tremble of her hands that really showed how she really felt. What was going on in her head? What was she struggling with?

Clint wanted to know, wanted to help, but she didn't look all that ready to accept anything from him.

"This was a mistake," Ell said, repeating herself from earlier. "I should go." She lifted her gaze to Clint, as if unsure if they'd let her go.

She really didn't understand, did she?

"We won't stop you," Fox assured her. "You can always go, always stop anything here."

She nodded, then took another step backward.

"Ell!" Dean came rushing from the other room. "I was worried sick. Are you okay?"

Ell nodded, but she made a point to *not* look back at the men, the sort of action that was obvious.

Dean turned, his gaze settling on the three men. There was suspicion there, a reminder that while he might not have a romantic relationship with Ell, he was still a protective Dom. "Everything okay here?"

Ethan smiled and nodded. "We tried to keep her distracted when the lights went off."

Dean narrowed his eyes, then caught Ell's chin.

It left an ache in Clint's chest, a desire to be able to do that same thing.

"Are you sure you're all right?"

Ell nodded then swallowed. "Yeah. I just…"

Fox was the one to answer. "Ell there didn't realize while the lights were off that we all actually know each other. I think she's just a little surprised, maybe a bit embarrassed to have spoken so candidly now."

Dean looked back at Ell. "Is that it?"

Ell nodded, and Dean's expression softened. It was clear he cared about the girl, even if it wasn't romantic or sexual at all.

"I see." Dean released her chin, then gestured toward the front. "Why don't you go collect your coat from the front and sign out? I'll meet you there in a minute."

Ell all but ran, probably relieved to have an out that allowed her an escape.

"We really didn't do anything," Ethan said. "I had no idea we knew her."

"I know. I know you all well enough to know you wouldn't do anything she didn't want."

Clint sat again, relieved at the fact Dean at least trusted them.

"That girl has a whole host of problems, doesn't she?" Ethan said.

Dean nodded. "Yeah, she really does. I was hoping coming here might help her, that she'd find... something. Maybe I was wrong."

Fox shook his head. "I don't think you were. She just might be more stubborn than you expected."

"That sounds about like her. Look, I know she's a lot, that she might seem like a bad bet, but after you get under those walls she builds up, she's a good person."

"I believe that," Fox said. "I just don't know if she's willing to let anyone under those walls."

Dean let out a soft laugh. "This would be the first time I think any of you have given up so easily..." He offered a quick wave. "I better get before she decides I'm taking too long and just drives herself home in my car."

When Dean left, the three men exchanged looks.

None of them liked playing a game they'd lose. They weren't fans of impossible tasks, yet Clint couldn't shake the feeling he had that Ell might just be worth it.

Maybe...

Chapter Six

Ell shook her head as she stared at the building in front of her. *I should go home.* She should stop thinking what had happened last weekend. She should pretend like she'd slept through all those days and nothing at all had occurred beyond sweet, uncomplicated unconsciousness.

Instead, Ell couldn't get her night at Sanctuary out of her head.

Dean had dropped her off without asking anything about what had happened. It wasn't that he didn't care — she was sure of that. Instead, it seemed more like Dean was trying to be polite, trying to not push limits.

Or, more likely, he knew that if he asked her immediately, she'd go off instinct alone. She'd dig her heels in and assure him it was nothing, just a mistake, just a moment of insanity that she knew better than to repeat.

Still, her quiet '*no*' wouldn't go away. Ell was a lot of things, but she wasn't a liar.

So when they'd asked her about orgasms, when she'd known that she damn well was interested, she'd muttered out the lie without even thinking about it. Maybe it was foolish for her to care, but she did.

Or maybe you just can't stop thinking about them…

She didn't want that one to be true, but that didn't mean it wasn't. The reality was that she'd spent far too much time doing web searches on some of the things they'd asked about in the days since.

While some required a very quick back button and a desire for eye-bleach, many others had stirred an interest inside her, one that had made her dreams more sultry than usual.

What did that mean? Did Ell actually want to try any of it? If she did, what did that look like? Would she ask them? Could she trust them?

Ell gave in and forced herself to move. If she didn't do this now, she'd lose her nerve. If she did that, she'd go home and be unable to relax, unable to stop thinking about this.

So, instead, Ell carried what she'd brought into the office building where Fox had his private practice. She'd called first to make sure Fox was there that day.

It was easier to face him than Ethan or Clint, especially since they were together all the time. The idea of speaking to both those men at once felt like far too much stress.

It meant that the safest idea was to see Fox. It wasn't like she didn't know him, and he'd always been kind. The fact that she hadn't recognized his voice seemed insane, now. The smoothness, the pause, calm way he spoke. It all screamed of the man she'd known.

"Excuse me, miss. Are you lost?" the receptionist asked when Ell entered.

"I'm here to see Dr. Asher."

"Do you have an appointment?"

"No." Ell froze, suddenly unsure what else to say. It was probably a bad idea to stand there and tell her that Ell had seen Fox at a BDSM club, then had lied during an explicit game, and now wanted to make up for it.

That felt like information she didn't want out and she was fairly sure Fox didn't want that either.

"Ell?" Fox's voice made Ell gulp even before she turned, before she saw him.

Still, she took a deep breath and faced him. Or, rather, she turned toward him but still didn't meet his gaze. Instead, she stared at his feet, at the nice black dress shoes he wore.

"It's fine, Sarah. Ell is a friend of mine. Come on back."

Ell followed him, clutching the cups of coffee, trying to reassure herself that she was safe, that it was a good idea for her to have come, even if she couldn't believe it.

Fox opened a door to what must have been his private office, since it wasn't set up for clients. It had a desk, a large shelving unit with books and a couch that had a blanket thrown over it as if he slept there often.

Then again, that wouldn't have surprised Ell. Fox was a hard worker, and he always came in, even when he wasn't on call.

"Sit down before you fall down," Fox said.

Ell followed his order without thinking, sinking down on the couch, just then realizing how shaky her legs felt.

"What are you doing here?" Fox asked.

Ell finally risked looking directly at Fox, his blue eyes so kind that it was almost painful. She held out a cup of coffee but said nothing.

Fox furrowed his eyebrows as he took the cup. "I don't understand."

"I lost our bet."

Fox paused, then let out a soft laugh before pulling his rolling office chair around, so he could sit just in front of where she was. "So, you came all the way here to admit you weren't entirely honest about your answers?"

Ell fidgeted in her spot. Just coming had been so difficult, but that was nothing compared to having to have an actual conversation about it all. "Yes."

"Why did you lie?"

She let out a slow breath, then met his gaze again, locked in by his patient expression. "Why wouldn't I lie? I mean, you put me on the spot there, and I was so sure I'd easily win, then became less and less sure."

"So? That doesn't explain why you would lie about it. I mean, you met us there, clearly we weren't about to judge you."

"Do we have to do this here?"

"No," Fox admitted. "But you were the one to lie, to cheat at our game and also the one who showed up here to apologize. You didn't do that because you just felt guilty."

"Of course, I did…"

He lifted an eyebrow.

"Then why do you think I came?" She had planned to ask it as a sarcastic question, as a defense mechanism. Instead, it came out like a plea for help, as if she needed him to untangle her head because she couldn't.

"I think you couldn't stop thinking about the things we said and coming to admit you lied was the safest way to talk to me again."

Ell dropped her gaze when he'd hit the nail on the head. That was exactly why she'd really come.

"Look at me," Fox said.

Ell followed the demand, unsure as they locked gazes, when she had to remember exactly what had been said the previous weekend.

"Better," Fox said. "Now, you came here. I knew you were probably lying in the game, but you used your safe word and we let you go. Safe word is a full stop. So, since you're here, you need to say what it is you're looking for."

Ell pulled in a deep breath, went about straightening the magazines on the side table. "I thought you were the nice one."

Fox chuckled. "I guess you made a mistake there, didn't you? Being nice is great, but not at the expense of what you need."

"You don't even know me, so why do you think you know what I need?"

"I don't, not yet. Still, you must think I can give you whatever that is or you wouldn't have come here under the guise of paying up for a bet."

Ell continued to stack the magazines, squaring them on the table. "I had time to think and realized that maybe I was interested in a few of the things you talked about."

"Good answer. Thank you for being honest with me."

A flush ran through Ell at the praise, at the way she reacted to it. She tucked her hair behind her ear, trying to find a way to deal with the anxiety running through her.

"I'm glad you came to see me," Fox said. "That took a lot of courage. The question is, what do you want from here? You could always return to Sanctuary with Dean, continue to learn and figure out what you might want, meet other people there."

"Is that your way of saying that night was all you're interested in?"

Fox leaned back in his chair, staring at Ell as if he could read each thought that crosser her mind. "Not at all. Again, you used your safe word. After that, I refuse to take the risk that I'm stepping over any boundaries with you. That means you're going to need to be upfront about exactly what you want."

"Are you never going to let that go?"

"It isn't about letting it go or about punishing you. Safe wording is a great thing, something you should do absolutely. It also means there needs to be conversations before anything like that occurs again, so I know I've done what I can to prevent putting you in a situation again where you need to use it again. I refuse to make the same mistake twice."

Which sounded good. That sounded like the exact right answer, like something Ell could hold onto during what felt like an extremely overwhelming moment.

"So you're not telling me no?"

Fox smiled, and it was breathtaking. Ell had no idea he could look like that. It was one thing to have seen him in his element at work, to watch how well he dealt with children, even frightened ones, and how knowledgeable and confident he was.

Now that she'd gotten a different feel for him, now that all that confidence was clothed in a different context, now that she saw him as someone who enjoyed dominating others, she couldn't help but shift beneath his gaze.

And that smile he'd given her spread. "No, Ell, I'm not telling you no. If I've forced you to be honest, it's only fair for me to offer you the same. Ever since that night, I've thought about you quite a bit. I was glad to see you today. So, you're saying that you think you're interested because it's us?"

"Well, you at least."

Fox lifted his eyebrow as if that statement surprised him. "And what do you want to do about that?"

"I guess…I'd like to come back to Sanctuary some time…"

Fox's smile came back, as if that were the best thing he'd heard. "Are you going to take coffee to Clint and Ethan too?"

"Do I have to?"

"You should."

Ell knew that was the answer, and, worse, he was right. If she'd apologized to Fox, she should do the same to Ethan and Clint. It was only fair, even if the two of them made her far more nervous.

Ell got to her feet. "Thank you for seeing me, and I'm sorry for showing up without notice. I'm sure you had patients…"

He waved off her concern. "I had a free minute, and you're worth shuffling things around for."

Why did that praise hit her the way it did? It made her feel warm inside, made her cheeks heat up. Even though a part of her wondered if he meant it, the rest grabbed onto the praise and held it tight.

"Well, thanks," she said.

"Next Friday night."

Ell turned to find Fox still seated and looking at her expectantly. "What?"

"What time do you want to meet there?"

"Oh." She thought back to her schedule, as if she had anything else going on on a Friday night. "Um, how about nine?"

"I'll make sure you're included on the guest list in case you don't come with Dean."

Ell nodded, totally unsure how exactly an exchange like this was supposed to end. Was she supposed to shake hands? Hug? She felt inept yet again when it came to dating.

"Oh, and, Ell?"

She turned back toward him once more, surprised by how quickly she responded to his demand.

Not just surprised, but a bit startled by it…

"Make sure you eat real food before you come and get to bed early the night before."

She frowned at the orders, at the way they both chafed and made her feel oddly taken care of.

Instead of acknowledging it, instead of saying she would or wouldn't, Ell simply dropped her gaze to her coffee and rushed out of the office.

She had a date at a sex club…

That wasn't something she thought she'd ever say.

* * * *

Well, well, well. What do we have here? Ethan couldn't hope to smother his smile while he watched Ell walk up, coffee in hand.

"You don't have to look so happy." Ell look absolutely put out as she held a cup to him.

"I can't help it. I don't often have a pretty girl bringing me coffee."

Ell narrowed her eyes before glancing around. "What are you doing here?"

"I thought a park was a great place for a date."

"This isn't a date. I'm just bringing you your winnings from the bet."

"In my world, a girl bold enough to bring a man a cup of coffee means a date." Ethan patted the bench beside him, glad he picked a spot with a great view of the mountains and enough shade to keep them cool.

Ell stared at the spot for a moment before shaking her head. It was strange, the way she almost seemed...wistful, as if she'd wanted to sit. So why didn't she?

Was she nervous about him? Did she want to have the chance to leave more quickly?

Ethan knew better than to ask, so he only filed that away to remember for later.

Ell shifted her weight from one foot to the other. "You don't look surprised I came."

"I wasn't—Fox gave me a heads-up. Why do you think I planted myself here when dispatch asked for my location?"

Ell didn't look all that impressed or won over by his gesture, but then again, women could be fickle.

It was one of the things Ethan liked about them. Women managed to always keep him on his toes in a world that too often felt boring. "So, your apology?"

"Excuse me?"

"Fox said you were apologizing for your absolutely betrayal with coffee."

"I don't have to apologize, do I? Isn't that a little much?"

"My mother always told me that wounds heal with time and sweet words, and I was pretty wounded."

Ell let out the longest sigh, the type that made Ethan wonder if he'd missed his calling as a brat.

"Fine, I'm sorry."

"Uh-huh, Ell, I think I'm owed a little more. Aren't you going to think long and hard about it? Maybe take a few times through to get it right? This isn't the sort of thing a girl should half-ass."

Ell pressed her lips together, and it made Ethan wonder if they were just as soft as they looked. Softer, he'd bet...

"This is why I didn't come see you first," Ell snapped.

"Keep going, if you want. It'll just add to that apology you're going to be working on."

Ell took a step backward. "Well, this seems like it was as complete waste of time. I just wanted to say I was sorry and pay up, but clearly, I shouldn't have bothered. You wouldn't take it seriously anyway."

She turned, giving him a nice look at her ass, which even in her cheap suit tempted him.

She really was something, wasn't she? Ethan had a pretty good idea that he wouldn't get tired of her, that she'd keep him on his toes with all that attitude of hers.

"Thank you for coming here," Ethan offered, meaning it. "And thanks for the coffee. It's a nice treat for the middle of a long day."

Her expression softened. Under all that bluster, she wasn't quite as much of a hard-ass as she pretended to be.

"I'm sorry you had a hard day," she said.

"You know how it is—it only takes one bad case to tank your whole day."

Ell nodded, and the shadows in her eyes said she really did. That kind of look sold that Ell didn't just deal with this day in and day out, disconnected from the horrors she saw, but that she understood them, she felt them.

On one side, Ethan didn't love that. He didn't want her hurting, and people who felt that way always hurt. *Look at Fox.*

On the other side, though, Ethan liked that she was the sort of woman with that kind of heart. He wasn't sure he'd have any interested in someone selfish, someone who didn't give a damn about others. No doubt, that was part of what drew him to her in the first place, the way she worked so hard for kids no one else seemed to give a damn about.

"That's the hard part of the job," she said, her voice soft. "It's seeing so many horrible things but still managing to get up the next day to do it again."

"That isn't the hard part," Ethan said. At her look, he gave her a smile he was sure wasn't entirely happy. "So many of us still get up and we keep doing it. We keep doing what we need to, keep at these jobs day in and day out."

"So what's the worst part?"

"How much it eats away at the rest of our lives. We devote every damned second, every bit of energy we have into our work because we think that if we take anything for ourselves, we're to blame for what happens."

Ell stared back, silently. Was she thinking about it? Ethan had seen how much she put into her work, noticed how damned tired she seemed so often. It didn't take much to see she was exactly that sort of person, to realize she was drowning as she gave away every bit of herself.

She swallowed, then a tiny shake of her head said she wasn't ready to accept it just yet. That was fine — people only accepted things when they were ready. "I should get going."

Ethan nodded, then held up the coffee. "Thanks for this. It was nice to see you again."

Ell nodded, and Ethan was again struck by just how sweet the woman was. She was tough, of course, and he'd seen that when she'd taken on prosecutors and cops alike. It was funny just how much she drew him in.

Still, Ell's words made it clear enough that she didn't want to talk about the club, about what had happened there. Ethan let it go, because pushing her would only get her to close up again.

"Well, I'll see you around," she said.

"You going to go give Clint some coffee?" Ethan asked.

Ell hesitated. "I don't think he cares if I apologize to him."

"No?"

"No," Ell said, her tone certain. "He doesn't ever seem that happy to see me, so I doubt he's waiting around for me to come clean."

Ethan could have told her how wrong she was. Clint could be difficult to understand, but he wasn't nearly as heartless as people first thought. Since that was the sort of thing Ell wouldn't believe, he kept it to himself. Instead, Ethan offered a smile. "Guess I'll see you around, then."

Ethan took a sip of his coffee as he watched her walk away, reminded again how damned much he liked her.

It wasn't smart, all things considered, but being smart never really stopped how a person felt.

Ell was sweet, determined and tough. She was sexy, but the sort where she didn't know it, didn't try to be it, and that was something that drew him in.

On the other hand, Ell also resisted what she really wanted, questioned it, and Ethan had been through that before.

He'd gotten his heart shredded by someone who had tried to fit into a mold they didn't really want. It was a losing bet, but that didn't stop the way Ethan's eyes seemed locked on the woman who walked away.

Looked like it was round two for his stupid choices...

Chapter Seven

"Come on, are you serious?" Donnie had his arms crossed and his eyes locked on the street outside rather than the building they'd parked in front of.

"Yes, I'm serious."

"This is a stupid idea." Donnie had refused to look at her ever since she'd told him where they were headed.

"I know you don't like this, but it's a good deal."

"How exactly is it a good deal? I make the right choice, I try to help someone, and look what happens."

Ell put the parking brake on, then turned toward Donnie. "You still broke into someone's house. You could have done time for this, but I got them to agree to community service."

Donnie grumbled, speaking so quietly it might have been to himself. "You know I'm going to end up getting my ass—*my butt*, kicked over this, right? Everyone's gonna think I'm a snitch, now."

"You only think that because you're focusing on the world you live in now. You won't always have to live there, though. You're going to keep growing up, and you're going to become an adult, and you'll have an entire life — an entire world at that point."

Donnie snorted, the sort of sound that was as far as he ever went when it came to disrespect with her. Still, that sound said everything. It said Donnie didn't believe her, that he saw no real future for himself.

All Ell could do was keep moving forward and hope that he realized the truth in time.

They left the car, and Donnie followed her, his hands tucked into his pockets, his head down. It had always broken her heart how he looked at everything with such wariness, as if sure something would jump out and attack him.

Then again, in his life, things often had.

"How can I help you?" asked a woman's voice that drew Ell's attention. She was polite, but her tone implied she was used to dealing with people she'd rather not.

"I'm Ell Hayden, and I have Donnie Denton who is going to be volunteering here."

The woman shifted paperwork on her desk, before finally reaching a page that seemed to have what she needed. She read over it, then nodded. "Right. He has one hundred hours of community service. He'll be working in our gangs division."

Ell hesitated for a moment. It seemed a bad choice to send Donnie there, where they worked on such dangerous cases. She wanted Donnie to get a feel for what else was out there, but the thought of him potentially ending up in danger made her stomach clench.

"It's fine." Donnie gave her a smile, one she was sure he forced.

Which woke her up. It wasn't fair to expect him to reassure her. She offered him a smile in return. "Right. You'll do great—I'm sure."

"I'll take the bus home, so you don't have to worry about picking me up."

"If you end up staying late, and the buses aren't running anymore, make sure you call me."

Donnie promised he would, though Ell knew better than to believe it. Once he'd headed back, past the reception area, following the direction the woman at the front desk had given him, Ell looked back at the woman.

"If he's here too late, is it possible to make sure someone calls me?"

"Are you his mother?"

Ell shook her head. "I'm his social worker. He lives in a bad area, and his grandmother can't drive. He tends to want to do things on his own, to not bother anyone, but I don't like him walking when it's dark."

The woman looked as if she'd refuse, but a man's voice broke into the conversation first. "I'll make sure someone gets him home."

Ell turned to find Clint behind her, looking larger than life and with the same unreadable expression he'd worn each time she'd spoken to him. His hazel eyes were intense, and it reminded her how differently he looked here than he had in that club.

And she cursed herself for her luck. What were the odds he'd just happen to be at the station when she showed up? That he'd be close enough to the front to see her?

"Thank you," Ell said, knowing better than to argue when he was doing her a favor.

Clint nodded toward the door that went farther into the station and lifted his eyebrow — a clear question on if she'd follow him, if they could talk.

A refusal perched on her tongue. She wanted to tell him no, to leave before she had to suffer through the embarrassment of an actual conversation, but nothing came out. With his eyebrow lifted as it was, she felt powerless to resist.

It left her nodding and following him into the station. They passed a few desks, passed officers she knew, that she'd worked with. It made her cheeks heat.

Ell knew what everyone saw when they looked at her. She was difficult, stubborn and used to things going a certain way. People looked at her like a hardass, like an annoyance. She'd accepted that's who she was, embraced it.

Except... Clint had managed to get a view of her few others had, and the idea that that part of her could shift over, could become part of this world made her lightheaded.

Clint held open a door to conference room, then shut it when she entered.

He stared at her, not moving away from the door, and Ell had no idea how to deal with that.

Ell looked like she might just fall over. It was strange to realize this was the same woman who'd dressed him down more than a few times in the past, who hadn't wilted no matter what was thrown at her.

So why exactly did she stare at him as if he were the big bad wolf?

"I heard you went to see Fox and Ethan."

She dragged her tongue along her bottom lip, an action that caught his attention. "I just wanted to apologize for running out like I did."

And she'd wanted to ask Fox about meeting her again, about seeing how much farther she wanted to take things. Of course, she didn't say that to him.

People didn't tend to open up to Clint, something he was used to. Then again, if it was so commonplace, why did it bother him this time?

"I kept figuring I'd see you, but you never showed up to talk to me."

"I didn't think you cared if I did or not."

"Why is that?"

She shrugged, then lowered herself into one of the two chairs in the room. "You never seem all that happy to see me."

Clint pressed his lips together. While he was used to that reaction, it still bothered him. "I'm a direct person, Ell. If I have something to say, I say it, and I mean exactly what I say. If I didn't want to see you, I'd tell you that outright."

She furrowed her eyebrows as if that didn't make sense to her. Then again, that was rare in most people. He'd found people exceedingly hard to understand, all too willing to hide what they really wanted or thought beneath miles of niceties and white lies. They dug into each little word, each tone of voice, sure it meant something other than it did.

Clint was simple. He said what he meant, and he meant what he said. Nothing more and nothing less.

"Well, I'm sorry about what happened. I admitted that I lied that night, that I was embarrassed." She tapped her finger on her knee.

It made Clint watch, silent, drawn in by the way she moved. She'd always calmed him in an odd way, something he couldn't ever quite put his finger on. It was as if she wasn't quite so loud as the rest of the world, so chaotic. Perhaps that's why it bothered him so much that she'd chosen not to speak to him, unlike his two friends.

"People often bend the truth when they don't like it."

Ell turned her gaze toward the door, her eyebrows pinched together.

"Something bothering you?"

She let out a long breath. "Donnie is doing community service here and they assigned him to the gangs division."

"That's probably a good place for him."

"It's a dangerous department, isn't it?"

Clint nodded and crossed his arms. "It can be, but they don't put children who are volunteering in the middle of shootouts."

Ell offered him a glare that said she didn't appreciate the statement. "I know that. I just think he would have been better working in a less dangerous department."

"I've worked here a long time, Ell, and whether or not you like what we do some of the time, I've seen my share of kids like Donnie. He's headed down a path that leads nowhere good, and the more someone can shake some sense into him, the better."

Ell dropped her gaze, as if considering Clint's words. When she spoke again, her voice was low, as if testing if she believed what he said. "So you're saying that him being in the gangs division might shake him more?"

"Would seeing people getting tickets for speeding make him think about his future much?"

"Instead, he'll see what happens to people who are in the life he's headed toward?"

Clint nodded. "That's right. That's why when I saw his application come across my desk, I recommended him to the gangs division."

"You did that?" Ell lifted her gaze to Clint's, just in time for him to drop his. When he didn't respond, she pressed. "Why?"

"Because I knew he was important to you. I'm not as heartless as people think."

She pressed her lips into a thin line. "I never said you were heartless. I said you didn't seem to like me, that you're hard to read."

Clint kept his arms crossed so he stayed where he was, to resist the urge to touch her hair, to see if it was just as soft as he expected. "I get that a lot. Like I said, though, I'm upfront about what I think and feel, and I'm glad I got to see you, even if you didn't come wanting to see me."

Ell's cheeks reddened, but Clint wasn't sure if that was due to embarrassment or excitement. It was strange how often the two things were similar, how they mirrored one another. Clint had seen that so often in women, the way they could want something so badly and yet feel such shame from it.

He'd never quite understood it, but understanding wasn't needed for him to be able to read it.

"Well, I should get going," Ell said as she rose from her seat.

Clint wanted to talk to her longer, to enjoy the way she eased him, to ask if she would really be there that weekend as Fox had said.

However, they'd made progress, and he didn't want her to feel trapped. "Sure," Clint offered instead. "I'd like if you stopped in again some time."

Ell pulled her shoulders back, as if the motion made her feel more confident. She said she might, but the tone gave Clint little hope that she meant it. After she left, he sat in one of the chairs.

Why couldn't he be better at this? Ethan had a humor that drew people in so easily, and Fox could disarm anyone with a few words. Why was it that Clint couldn't seem to learn those skills? Even when he could read a person, even if he knew what they were thinking or feeling, being able to connect had always been an issue for him.

Yet, he wasn't sure it had ever bothered him as much as it did right then.

A soft knock had him frowning and calling for the person to come in.

Ell walked into the office, her gaze down and her cheeks a bright red. It took him off guard for a moment, the way she looked so damned adorable right then. He wanted to wrap his arms around her and pull her into his lap, to kiss the flushed skin on her face.

She held out a cup of coffee for him, but she said nothing.

Right…the bet.

Clint reached out, and when he took the cup, he pressed his hand over the outside of hers before she could yank away. "Thank you, Ell."

She nodded, pausing for a moment almost as if she enjoyed the contact. After a heartbeat, she pulled back and all but ran from the small room.

Clint looked down at the cup, at the peace offering, and an unfamiliar tightness occurred in his chest. Then, a smile tugged at his lips at the sweetness of the action, at the unusual apology from her.

The weekend really was looking up...

* * * *

I can't believe I'm here again...

Ell wondered what the hell she'd been thinking as she sat at a table in the main area of Sanctuary, a hot chocolate in her hands since she couldn't seem to warm herself up. It wasn't cold in the club, yet goosebumps on her arms refused to go away and a tremble ran through her, as if her body thought it needed to shake to keep warm.

It's just nerves. Knowing that didn't stop any of it from happening, though.

Ell had considered coming with Dean again, but had chickened out of telling him that she planned on returning. She'd worried she might run into him, but so far, he hadn't shown.

Whether that was better or worse, she wasn't sure. He would have given her a sense of security, of backup, but she also couldn't stand the idea that he might have seen some other side of her.

Ell was who she was, and it wasn't the sort of woman to come to a place like this. Dean may have seen her at her worst, but that didn't mean she wanted to advertise it.

"Is Fox here yet?" A woman's voice made Ell frown as she picked up the familiar name. Just behind her was another table where two women sat, dressed in little more than lingerie and looking relaxed in a way Ell always envied.

She felt like she was always pulling at her clothing, always checking to make sure things were in their place. She'd never managed to look so at ease, especially when dressed like *that*.

In fact, Ell had gone with what seemed downright frumpy compared to everyone else there. She wore what she normally wore to work — a pair of well-fitted gray slacks and a button-up shirt. Peering around, Ell wondered if she hadn't made a misstep.

Was Fox going to take one look at her and rethink tonight? Would he realize that there were far better-looking women around, ones who were wild and crazy and far more fun?

"I haven't seen him yet, but he usually gets here after Clint and Ethan."

She frowned. All three of them? She knew they were friends, but were they always there together?

Had she set up a date with all three of them on accident?

The idea made her cheeks heat again and forced her to admit she knew so little about them, about this world. In her world, a date was two people, not four…

"Have you ever played with them?" the second woman asked.

I shouldn't keep listening. She knew it, knew it was wrong to eavesdrop on such a personal conversation, but she couldn't help it. She didn't like going into anything without all the information she needed. She'd spent nearly every night since planning to meet Fox here researching everything she could about BDSM.

It made her realize just how many things they hadn't asked in their game, and how quickly they'd have scared her off if they had.

Still, that lack of knowledge left her listening in on the women, wanting some sort of information to help her know what to do, what to expect.

"A few times," the first woman answered, no shame in her voice, as if admitted to having sex with them was no big deal.

This really was a world Ell didn't understand.

"They're sweet," the woman said. "And they know their way around a woman's body, no doubt. You know how fake Doms are, the ones who think it's all about getting whatever they want, who don't have a clue what they're doing? Yeah, that isn't those three."

The second woman laughed as if they both understood the point. "Yeah, but the whole Daddy thing? You don't find that *weird*?"

Daddy thing? Ell's eyes widened at that while she tried to put together what exactly the women meant.

"Maybe a little, but what isn't weird here? Look, they got me off *five* times that night. I'll call a man whatever he wants, including Daddy, if he can do that."

"So why didn't you ever play again?"

"They're a bit intense for me. I'm casual—I like to play here, maybe a scene here or there at night, but that's it. Those three were looking for twenty-four-seven and that's not my thing. They could almost convince me it was worth it, though…"

They giggled together, and it broke Ell's confidence. She'd been ready to discuss things with Fox, to consider that she might be interested in something, but this was *much* too far for her.

She wasn't into calling some man Daddy, into having someone take over her life. The last thing Ell wanted was something so *intense*, using the word the women had said.

She rose from the table, realizing what a horrible idea this had been. She'd jumped into it without looking, without knowing all the facts, and look what happened. This was why Ell liked her life regulated, why she liked her rut.

In her old rut she didn't have to run out of sex clubs to avoid men who liked to be called Daddy.

She rushed toward the front desk, ready to remove the cuffs she'd gotten from the receptionist and leave, to never look back, to go the whole rest of her life without ever thinking about this place again.

At least, that was her plan until she found Ethan walking in, standing between her and freedom, thus stopping her escape.

"You okay?" he asked, his tone full of worry.

"Something came up and I need to get going," she said softly, refusing to look up.

A finger tapped her chin, and before she knew it, she was staring up into Ethan's green eyes. "What's going on in your head that has you running out of here with a lie like that?" The way he called her out made her fidget.

Usually, people let her get away with polite lies like that, where everyone knew the truth but let a falsehood stand to ease feelings. That wasn't Ethan, apparently.

Ell wet her bottom lip with her tongue since they suddenly felt dry. "I just realized this was a mistake," she admitted.

"You realized that in the last five minutes? What exactly happened that made you realize that?"

Ell opened her mouth, but nothing came out. It was because of his intense gaze, because of all the people around, the loud music, the movement. It all overwhelmed her and made it hard to focus and harder to put into words what she wanted to say.

Ethan peered over his shoulder, which let Ell see past him. Clint and Fox both stood there, answering one question for her. *Yeah, they all seem to be a package deal…*

"Why don't we go to a quiet private room, hmm? You might be more comfortable to discuss things there," Fox offered.

"What if I don't want to go to a private room with you?" Ell asked quietly.

Fox didn't laugh at her, didn't make her feel bad for the question. "Just like the last time, you can leave when you'd like. You came here for a reason, though, asked us to meet you here for a reason. Do you really want to run out without even explaining your change of heart?"

Yes. No? Ell wasn't sure, and that frustrated her worse than they did.

"Are you afraid of us?" Clint asked.

Again, her answer of yes and no hit her. She had to sort through it. She wasn't afraid that they'd hurt her, or afraid to be alone with them. Instead, her fear was in the unknown, in how terrifying her lack of control was to her. That wasn't being afraid of *them,* so she shook her head.

Clint nodded, as if the answer pleased him. It was hard to read him, but she felt like she she'd started to get glimpses of the real him, of what he meant. "Good. So if you're not afraid, and you know you're safe, why not at least talk to us like you'd planned? You might be surprised how much getting your thoughts out of your head can help you sort through them."

Ell wanted to say no, but the word wouldn't come. She thought about going back to her house and wondering about this, about what she might have missed out on.

She'd come here to learn more, to understand this. She couldn't back out now…

Ell met Fox's gaze. "Okay, let's talk." She just wished her words didn't sound as terrified as she felt.

Chapter Eight

The private room made Ell's anxiety soar, especially because the room felt even smaller with the three men in it. They didn't crowd her, didn't touch her, yet it seemed each pass of their gaze over her was a caress she didn't know how to deal with.

"You look confused," Fox said as Ell stared around the room.

"This isn't what I was expecting from a private room," she admitted softly.

"Oh? You were thinking it would be a big bed with tie-downs, I'm guessing?" Ethan said, a laugh to his tone.

Well…yeah.

Instead of letting Ethan make fun of her anymore, Fox broke in. "The private rooms are all set up differently. There are some that have beds, others are set up for specific types of scenes, with offices or medical equipment or dungeons. This is a room that's set up for general use, for people to talk."

Ell turned her gaze to the coffee table between the couches, where metal loops hooked to the frame, then to the ceiling where hook sat.

Ethan let out another of his chuckles. "Well, I mean, it *can* be used for more than just talking. He meant it's supposed to be casual and relaxing."

*This doesn't feel relaxing...*Ell took a seat on the far end of the U-shaped sectional couch that surrounded the coffee table in the center. When the men sat, they gave her room, didn't sit right next to her. It almost made her feel guilty for her nerves and fears.

Guilt didn't change how she felt, though.

"So, Ell, do you want to explain what sent you running? Because you had days to consider whether to meet us here, and you still came, yet something scared you off once you arrived." Fox asked, then sat back on the couch, waiting as if he didn't care just how long it took her to answer.

In fact, none of them pressed, none of them showed any signs of annoyance at all when the question was met with a long silence as she worked to put her thoughts together.

Instead of all the well-crafted things she could have said, Ell opened her mouth and blurted out the truth. "I overheard some women talking about you three, and they said you liked them to call you Daddy." As soon as she said that, when they didn't react, the rest came pouring out like a tidal wave she couldn't hold back. "And they said you were too intense, that you wanted to control them twenty-four-seven, and that you three always share women. I wasn't expecting any of that, and I was sitting there, and I realized I was in way over my head." By the time Ell finished, she gasped in a breath because she'd spoken so fast, she hadn't even inhaled during her tirade.

She kept her gaze locked on the table instead of any of them, not sure she wanted to see their reactions.

Finally, a soft, familiar chuckle from Ethan eased some of her fears. His voice was gentle when he spoke. "Well, I can see why that might send you running. First lesson, though, is not to hold all that in your head. Instead of hearing rumors and running away, you should have spoken to us, and we could have gone through it all together. There's no reason for you to shoulder all those worries on your own."

The statement made no sense to Ell. They were her problems—of course she needed to shoulder them on her own...

"Are you telling me that stuff isn't true?"

"No, I'm not saying that at all." With that, Ethan crushed that tiny bit of hope Ell had felt when he'd laughed at her statement. She'd still thought perhaps the men would explain that she was confused, that it wasn't right at all, that she'd misheard or misunderstood what those women had said.

"So it is true?"

"Mostly, yeah. I thought you knew we tended to take women together, since you spoke to us together the first night."

"No. I just thought you were friends. I didn't realize you always came as a package."

Fox shook his head. "I'm sorry for the confusion on that. While we occasionally play with women here at the club on our own, it's rare." He held his hand up before she could speak. "And no, we wouldn't do that this time. To be entirely honest, Ell, all three of us are interested in you. If you're not okay with that, it's fine, but that's the only way anything happens. It would cause difficulties between us if only one of us were to be with you."

Ell let her shoulders drop as her hope fled. Though, at the same time, she couldn't deny a certain tingle inside her at the thought of all three of them... While Fox might have been the easiest to talk to, at least at first, Ell had to admit that she'd rather enjoyed her small talks with Ethan and even Clint.

Maybe they aren't so bad.

Though, that didn't solve the *rest* of what she'd heard. "And the other parts?"

"If it's that hard to say out loud, I have a feeling this isn't going to work," Ethan said, his voice having lost some of that humor he usually had. Was he disappointed?

"I'm not trying to shame you or anything. I just don't know if I'm a good fit with what it sounded like you were wanting."

"And why do you say that? Have you asked us what we want?" Leave it to Clint to be right to the point.

"No but..."

"Then don't make assumptions before you've even asked."

Ell reminded herself that she'd already let these men see her in a way others hadn't. What was the risk in just coming right out and asking?

Because if they admit they want something I don't, I'm afraid of saying goodbye...

Even still, she pulled in a deep breath, sat up straight, and risked looking right at the men. "What is it you want?"

The question seemed to please them, even if it was harder to read on Clint's face. Fox was the one to answer, though. "The women you overheard weren't wrong. We don't tend to be casual in our interactions. There isn't anything wrong with people who are only interested in a bit of bondage here at the club, or those who play rough a few nights a month. That just hasn't ever been anything we're interested in."

"I don't know what that means," Ell admitted, hating how little she felt like she knew.

"Like anything, there are degrees, there are different levels. We prefer a higher level of interaction."

Frustration nipped at Ell until she snapped out her next statements. "You laugh at me for being vague, but you're doing it, too! Why don't you come right out and say what you want, what your ideal situation looks like."

No one spoke for a moment, but Ethan's laugh broke some of the tension. He offered a smile, as if charmed by her outburst. "You want to understand it plainly? Sure. Ideal situation for me is a submissive who trusts us entirely. We'd help her with her morning plans, schedule her day, make sure she eats properly, drinks enough water, sleeps enough. She'd have expectations of things to do, rules for behavior and punishments when she didn't follow through. I'm not interested in someone who plays for a few hours now and then—I want someone who submits to me entirely."

That made Ell's heart speed, as if a spider were crawling across the floor toward her, one she couldn't escape. Still, she swallowed hard and tried to center herself. "That sounds like abuse," she admitted. "It sounds like what every controlling man wants."

Ethan dropped his gaze. Had she hit a sore spot?

Fox picked up the conversation. "It's abuse when only one person wants that. Just like rape isn't sex because of a lack of consent, a Dom/sub dynamic is different from abuse because both people consent and can stop or leave at any time. The part Ethan didn't say is that we want a woman who *wants* that sort of dynamic, that lifestyle."

Do I?

The question hung between them, something unsaid, something Ell couldn't wrap her head around. The thought of someone else taking over her life, of her listening to anyone else, created a panic inside her that made her want to run.

And yet...a tiny part of her couldn't entirely shake it. She wondered...*what if?* What if Ell found some sort of peace that had escaped her thus far?

She remembered Dean asking why she kept doing what wasn't working, why she didn't risk something since she wasn't happy where she was.

She was comfortable, but maybe comfortable was a far cry from happy.

Ell owed the men the truth, though. "I don't know if I can be that person."

"Of course you don't," Clint said. "You've never tried, never experienced any of it. How could you know what you want if you've never gotten the chance to figure it out?"

"That feels like an easy way to get a woman to do what you want."

Again, that same expression crossed Ethan's face. She wanted to ask what was wrong, wanted to find out what he thought about that made him grimace like that, but she kept the question in. It felt too person, like something she wasn't entitled to.

Fox spoke, his voice soft and careful. "We aren't the sort to trick anyone into anything they don't want.

You've reached out to us, you wanted to meet here. Clearly, you're curious at least. Just like last time, if you change your mind, if you decide this isn't for you, you can leave at any time. So, Ell, what is it you want to do?"

She pressed her lips together, thinking about her perfectly organized house. She considered the way her coffee mugs were all placed the exact same way, with the handle pointed to the right and how the countertops were spotless. The way her home was both her sanctuary and this unruly thing that she felt chained to warred inside her, the way the things she did to calm herself sometimes only served to create chaos in her head.

She'd spent years stuck and unable to move forward.

What if one night could change that all? What if giving into these three men could be the thing she'd needed but couldn't ever get?

"Yes," she said softly.

"Yes what?" Fox pressed.

She closed her hands into fists to try to stop the trembling. "I'm willing to submit to you three, at least for tonight."

Even as she said it, as her heart sped more, as a heat rushed through her at her words, Ell couldn't help but worry.

She wasn't sure if she was afraid of hating it or liking it. They both seemed equally dangerous...

Something about watching Ell excited Fox in a way he hadn't experienced in a long time. Maybe it was the unknown, or the fact that someone he'd thought wasn't a possibility for him was suddenly offering herself up.

Fox had told himself that Ell wouldn't ever happen. Even if he'd flirted with the idea, at least in his head, he'd accepted that some things just weren't going to happen.

And yet here he was, with Ell sitting there, her cheeks red and her gaze on the floor. She looked perfect—so much more than he'd even expected. She was dressed in a way that made him smile, all comfort and ease rather than seduction.

It fit her, though. She wasn't the sort of woman who would choose to be uncomfortable just because she thought it looked nice, and Fox understood that. How often in his career had he dealt with sprained ankles when the only reason had been impractical shoes?

Ell shifted in her seat, as if she couldn't get comfortable.

She probably couldn't. One of the advantages of being the Dom was having a clearer idea of what exactly would happen. No doubt Ell was sitting there, stewing over all the things they could want from her, all the things that could happen, how she might feel about them all.

No doubt, giving themselves over to any person required an amount of trust and courage Fox wasn't sure he possessed.

"You look tired," Fox said, noting the dark circles beneath her eyes.

"I thought you were the nice one."

Fox offered her a smile. "I am—sometimes. You just seem like you're not sleeping well."

When he didn't continue, Ell gave in. "I guess I've had some trouble falling asleep."

"Why not?"

She didn't answer, but that was enough for Fox to make a good guess.

"Were you nervous about tonight?"

Ell nodded, then paused. "Yes, but it wasn't that I just wasn't sleeping. I was researching."

"Researching what?"

She gestured around her. "All of this. I don't like to go into anything blind, not when there's no reason to. I wanted to understand a little more before I showed up."

That made Fox grin wider at the idea of Ell sitting in front of a computer, poring over websites as she tried to anticipate anything, tried to organize it all so it made sense in her head.

The more time he spent around her, the more he spotted her anxiety, the more he realized just how deeply it ran.

"And what did you find out with your research?" Ethan asked, his smirk saying he enjoyed the conversation just as much as Fox did.

"I found out that there were a lot of things you all didn't mention…"

Clint snorted. "If we'd gone over every kink, not only would we have been sitting there all night, but you probably would have taken off running before we got through a handful."

Ell looked as if she might argue but shrugged instead. "You're probably right. There were a lot of things that were too…far."

Fox chuckled at the very polite phrasing. Then again, there was no doubt there were some strange things people were into, things not at all to his taste, and he said that as someone experienced in the lifestyle.

He could imagine the way someone like Ell reacted, someone with no knowledge.

"Well, don't worry so much. We aren't going to try anything weird," Ethan said, though he paired that with a grin. "Well, not at first, at least."

Which made Fox huff out a soft laugh. Ethan always did enjoy pushing limits, liked to watch everyone squirm but especially submissives.

Fox hadn't really ever understood that desire, but there was no doubt women tended to enjoy it just as much as Ethan did.

"I don't know what's supposed to happen," Ell admitted softly. "I researched, I tried to get ready, but I don't know what I'm supposed to do."

That did pull at Fox's heart, though. It was in the lost way she asked, in the way fear played through those words. The girl did have some hang-ups, didn't she? "Does that scare you?" Fox asked even if the answer was obvious.

"I prefer knowing what's going to happen, to prepare for it."

"Because that feels safer. It means you don't have to trust anyone. It means you keep your control of the situation. The issue is that what you're asking for is the opposite of that. You came here because you want to let go, at least for a little while."

"I know that, but it doesn't make it any easier to do."

Fox tapped his foot for a moment, studying Ell as she sat there. Finally, he nodded. "Fair enough. For tonight, would it make you feel better to know general limits?"

She breathed out slowly, then nodded while offering Fox a gracious look. It made him want to pull more of those looks from her.

"You're too nice," Ethan said under his breath.

He knew the reality. If they did it this way tonight, she might just learn she *could* trust them, that anything she had to hold they could carry for her with ease. Tonight would be about showing her she was safe, that she could let her guard down, that they'd do exactly what they said they would.

"First, do you recall the safe word?"

"Red."

"Good girl," Fox said without thinking about it, using the praise as if it were natural. He tried to ignore the way he enjoyed saying it. "For tonight we won't use any bindings, no toys, no punishments, no real pain."

"Real pain?" Boy, did her voice get nervous, there.

"Meaning nothing that even leaves a mark."

She let out a soft breath, as if that reassured her but didn't full alleviate her worries.

"Am I supposed to call you Daddy?"

So much for nerves... If that wasn't the tone of a brat trying to tease, Fox would have been shocked. It seemed Ell had a bit more playfulness than one might expect at first.

Ethan leaned in, catching her chin so her gaze met his. "If you want to, I wouldn't stop you."

Red covered her cheeks, and the way her tongue darted out to touch her bottom lip said she was drawn into Ethan's words even if she'd tried to mock them at first.

Which of course made Ethan grin. "The way these things work, Ell, is that trust has to be built up. We've just met, at least like this, so I'm not going to demand you call us anything—we haven't earned it yet. Just be respectful and we'll be good. If you felt so inclined to call us something, though, you won't hear a complaint from any of us."

The way Ell leaned slightly closer to Ethan was a thing of beauty. It was unconscious, as if she yearned for something from him that even she didn't quite understand.

The way Fox reacted to her made him uneasy. Hell, not just him. Ethan seemed entirely smitten and even Clint had mentioned her numerous times, something odd from the normally quiet man.

However, Fox had learned that in life, a person needed to take all the happiness they could get because it never lasted long enough. Doubting things, questioning them, it only stole some of the happiness and joy a person could find.

Which meant he had no intention of questioning why Ell was different, why he felt this pull. No doubt something would happen to make this a very temporary affair, in which case, why ruin it prematurely by overthinking?

Ethan leaned in and kissed her, and the moan she let out went straight to Fox's dick. It was the sound a woman made when she was surprised, when she finally got a taste of something she'd been missing. It also said tonight would be more than a little fun.

They didn't need all those things they'd mentioned, the toys and the ropes and all of that. Those things were fun, sure, but Fox was certain the little brunette could keep their attention all on her own. Five minutes into touching her and Fox was already losing his mind...

Ethan groaned at the slightly sweet taste that clung to Ell's lips. Shirley Temple? The grenadine rested on her breath and her lips tasted of maraschino cherries.

It was funny, since Ell on her own could seem so cold, yet this taste of her felt more honest. He'd seen it in the way she looked after the kids who were her clients, in the sweetness when she spoke to them. She might treat the rest of the world as an enemy, but Ell had far more sweetness inside her than most people would expect.

She deepened the kiss herself just as she gripped the front of his shirt. *So responsive...* Ethan didn't mind aggressive women, ones who needed his touch and didn't mind him knowing it.

In fact, he rather enjoyed it, especially when they were made aware of it.

He undid the buttons of her shirt one at a time, speaking between the kisses, his voice low and teasing. "You're desperate, aren't you? I like the way you moan, the sounds you're making. You want this bad, don't you?"

She nodded as she scraped her teeth over his bottom lip, then gasped when he touched her side directly, her shirt gaped open in the front.

Her skin was beyond soft, though goosebumps covered it. It wasn't cold in the room, which meant they were most likely from nerves, from excitement, from all the things running through her body that she didn't know how to control or deal with.

He stroked up her side, over her ribs, enjoyed the way she arched into the touch. When he found the simple cotton of her bra, his smile widened.

Ell wasn't the sort of girl to wear lace and satin, and why exactly did that excite him so much?

He brushed his thumb over her nipple, pleased to find it hardened already, as if begging for his attention.

Instead of focusing there, he kept going up until he set his hand behind her neck, tugging her closer, feeling her body pressed against his. It was a moment of control, of restraint, just enough to test how she liked it.

And *boy* did she like it... Ell let out another little gasp, followed by a roll of her hips he had no doubt hadn't been intended.

But Ethan soaked it up, the fun of the game, of discovering what she liked, what she reacted to. It was the best sort of puzzle, one he wanted to lose himself in for hours. He wanted to hunt down every kink of hers, to uncover what she loved, what she hated and what she was too embarrassed to admit she wanted.

Ethan broke the kiss, met with the lust-drunk eyes of Ell, the girl having moved to that point where her brain had shut off, where she wasn't thinking or doubting or questioning a damned thing. *That* was where he wanted her.

"You're pretty when you're needy," he whispered, rewarded with her eyebrows furrowing as if she couldn't keep up with what he meant.

Adorable.

Someone caught her chin, turning her face to the side. *Fox.* The man took a kiss of his own, and Ethan stepped back to give him room. It was possessive, which always amused Ethan. Everyone expected Fox to be the sweet one, but he had a dark streak all his own. He was demanding, territorial, and expected others to listen to him.

He showed it with his actions, with the way he made her tilt her head so he could deepen the kiss, so he could show her exactly how much he wanted her.

And Ell responded as she had to everything else — like a dream.

Ethan undid the buttons of his own shirt, then shrugged it off and tossed it to the floor.

Clint shook his head and picked the item up — along with Ell's — and folded the clothes before setting them on the table by the door. The slight glare made Ethan smile. Clint was particular about where things went, and instead of being annoyed with it, Ethan had learned to just let the man do as he pleased.

Ethan came over behind Ell, then reached around her to undo the button of her slacks. If she hadn't been kissing Fox, she might have noticed, might have been concerned. It seemed Fox kept all her attention, because she didn't react at all, at least not until Ethan slid the fabric down her legs. It seemed *that* was enough for her to notice.

Not that Ethan cared. In fact, he preferred the way she broke the kiss and swung her head around to where he knelt behind her, the way her gaze was wide. An unguarded woman was a sexy thing.

He didn't apologize or explain, only offering her a smirk before pressing a kiss to the line of her simple cotton underwear right over her left ass cheek. After that — his sign that he wasn't going anywhere — he grasped her ankle and tapped her knee. She shifted her weight to the other foot so he could lift that leg and remove her slacks. He repeated the action on the other side as well, leaving her there in nothing but her bra and panties.

They were basic black cotton, yet his cock ached at the sight. It made her look almost innocent, like this creature who didn't realize exactly how dangerous the world was. It was a time when he had to wonder what the hell was wrong with him, why that excited him, but he pushed it away before he had to consider it.

What did it matter why he was into it? Might as well enjoy it…

Ethan pressed a kiss to the other side of her ass before he stood, making sure to remain close enough that he pressed against her back, that she could feel exactly how much he wanted this. Even though they didn't plan on anything crazy, even if it was only a few steps beyond vanilla, Ethan's body hummed in excitement for any chance to touch her.

He was pretty sure she could have slapped him across the face and put on a strap-on and he'd have agreed happily if it meant having more of her.

Which was pathetic…

Ell leaned back against him, not the slightest hesitation in her actions. She didn't hold anything back, didn't fight him. He'd been so sure she'd do both, that the closed-off woman would have done anything she could have to distance herself from them, from the risks.

However, she didn't. It was as if each touch unlocked something inside her she couldn't hope to fight.

Ethan ran his hands up her front to cup her breasts through her bra. He thumbed the hard tips as he ground against her, then closed his fingers to a pinch.

She didn't just gasp—she *yelped*. It put him on the edge already, made him worry he wouldn't last long enough to take her, not when she made beautiful sounds like that.

"See? A little pain isn't so bad," Ethan whispered into her ear. "I can't wait until we have time to see exactly how much you like, where that limit is."

She shivered, whimpering as he didn't let go of the hold, and he tugged softly at her nipples, stimulating them as she all but melted for him.

Fox tapped once on the tip of her nose, the action forcing her to open her eyes. "You said you'd submit to us, but I want you to be more clear than that. For tonight, I need to know your limits. Giving oral sex? Receiving? Intercourse? Anal?"

Ell seemed almost drugged as she answered with quick nods, all except for anal which had a certain rejection. Not that it shocked him. That was the sort of thing that needed more trust, more working into. Too many fuckwit men had chased women off the idea when they'd given it a try without enough knowledge or patience.

It didn't disappoint Ethan, either, since he chose to chalk that up to something they'd get to ease her into later—he refused to think there wouldn't be a later.

"What a good girl," Fox told her, the words drawing another of those delicious shivers from her. "I know it's scary to have these conversations, and most people don't do it. Normally, people have sex and never seem to say a word about what they want, what they don't. It's funny that BDSM is seen as dangerous and controlling when it's all about communication, when people who participate talk more openly than any vanilla sex I've ever seen. See, we need to know what you want, what you don't, or none of this works. So we'll ask you questions, and I expect you to be honest and open with us. Do you understand?"

"Yes, Sir." The title fell from her lips so naturally, and the tightening of the muscles in her back said even she hadn't meant to say it.

Which made it all the sexier, the way she responded to them, the way she slid into that role despite her nerves.

Fox smiled, then ran his thumb along her bottom lip. "You are full of surprises, aren't you?"

She didn't respond—unless something was a direct question, Ethan doubted she could have formed much of a sentence.

Which was exactly how he liked her.

Ethan released her breasts so he could slide his fingers along the band and to the hooks in the back. He undid it, then slid off the fabric. It let him cup her breasts again, to feel the weight of them, the warmth. She felt larger than he'd expected, but that was probably because she didn't wear push-up or padded bras. It was a hell of a nice surprise to find they filled his palms so well, and he was disappointed for a moment to be behind her, where he couldn't get a good look.

He wanted to swirl his tongue along the edges of her areolas, to discover the exact color of her nipples, to tease every little bump.

Of course, that was one of Ethan's biggest problems—he tended to go all in. He wanted everything and he wanted it all now. He lacked patience, something his friends always harped on him about.

Life was a banquet, though, and he'd learned time was shorter than anyone ever expected. It meant he wanted to experience it all now, and at the moment? All meant Ell's bare, hot body.

He pressed his lips to her shoulder, then sucked hard at the spot, wanting to leave a slight mark, as if proof that he'd been there.

The sting on Ell's shoulder made her arch her back, but it didn't hurt, not exactly. Instead, it was as if Ethan managed to breathe life into this raging desire inside her. It heightened sensation, made her more aware of each touch from the men.

Especially Ethan's large hands on her breasts, and his warm skin against her back. She was drowning, but she couldn't fight it, didn't even want to.

She thought for a moment about the sex she'd had before, about how unsatisfying it always was, about why it had been so long since she'd tried. She'd had that period, as a teenager, when she'd thought if she slept with enough men, one of them would want her. One of them would make her world a better place.

She'd craved being wanted and had done a lot of things she was ashamed of to try to get it, and none of those times had ever made her feel like this.

Even if she'd wanted to resist anything, she wasn't sure she could. Ethan, Fox and Clint seemed to have a guide to her, as if they'd studied up and knew exactly what she wanted, what she needed, and had no issue delivering it all.

A brush of warmth against her lower stomach was all the warning she got before Fox slid his hand down her front and into her panties. His fingers danced along her slit, not rough, not quick, not as if in any sort of hurry. Instead, it felt like an exploration, like Fox was trying to memorize her.

When had any man done that? If they touched her much before the main event, it was always quick, as if they thought they got a medal for the mere half-assed attempt.

That was nothing like what Fox did, and even if he didn't focus on her clit, even if he didn't press into her, it wound her body up all the same until she was almost shaking.

"You're so damned pretty," Ethan whispered, his smooth voice teasing her ear.

And again, a moment of shame hit her. Why had she worn what she had? No doubt these men had been with plenty of women who wore nicer things, who knew what they were doing.

The doubts snuck up on Ell, surprised her. She'd never doubted herself much before, had always known what she wanted and how to go after it.

"What's happening in your head?" Fox asked her.

She went to say nothing, but Fox tapped his thumb against her chin as if warning her about not lying. It made her pause, even as her body was in havoc, to try to answer. "I just wish I wore something nicer," she admitted.

Fox tilted his head, as if confused by her statement. It made her think back, made her wonder if she'd said what she'd meant to, if it had come out wrong.

Except, as quickly as that happened, Fox smiled again. He almost looked charmed. "Trust me, Ell, I have no complaints about what you wore. For one, it all comes off anyway. For two, if you came here in fuck-me-heels and lingerie that costs in the triple digits, I would have wondered what exactly you were up to."

"But other women —"

"Aren't my concern. Were you wearing other sorts of clothing when we've seen you before? No? Then why would you think we'd want something different now?"

The words made sense, and even if Ell struggled to believe them, she let them stand for the moment. She'd already committed herself to coming here, to doing this, so why worry about something she couldn't change?

He tilted his head, then shook it as if she were difficult. "You're going to take a lot of work, aren't you? Good thing I don't mind that." He brushed his lips once more against hers before pulling away, taking his hand from her panties, Ethan doing the same.

It left her standing there in just her panties and all too aware of the fact. She felt on display and couldn't help but wrap her arm around her chest.

Clint snorted, making her twist to find him standing there, having stripped down.

And that derailed any shame she felt. Clint naked was enough to stop her in her tracks. He reminded her of a bodybuilder, with his wide shoulders, his defined muscles. He was large, seeming even larger and more intimidating than he had before. His hazel eyes were as intense as ever, and his shaved head added to the slightly scare aura he gave off.

Of course, that could have also been due to his cock. Her gaze locked there, something she might have been embarrassed by any other time, but right then? She couldn't help it.

It had been *years* since she'd had sex, and she suddenly wondered if her lack of recent action made him seem larger or if he just was far above average. Even as excitement roared inside her, it was tempered by worries.

"Nervous?" Clint asked.

It made her lift her gaze, but he only let out another huff, as if she amused him, before he crooked his finger to beckon her forward.

And Ell went, no thoughts in her head, no questions. It was as if he called and she obeyed, as if she couldn't not do it. It terrified her, but she still couldn't help it.

When she reached him, he leaned in, but instead of the kiss she expected, he pressed his lips to the front of her throat. He scraped his teeth down her neck, then wrapped his fingers in the waist of her panties. He slid them down, and she set a hand on his shoulder for balance when he knelt to remove them entirely.

"I want you to go sit on the couch for me." He didn't ask her, didn't see if she wanted to, didn't even wait to see if she would. He rose and turned his back on her, taking her underwear to where he'd already folded and placed the rest of their clothes.

It gave her a look at his ass, and she bit down on her bottom lip to hold in any sound. She'd never been a woman who cared about a man's ass, but maybe she'd just never seen one that looked like *that* before.

Except, before he turned back toward her, he cleared his throat. *Right. The couch...*

Ell hurried over, not wanting to find out what he might do if she didn't listen. They'd said no punishments, but even the thought of disappointment on his face made her rush to avoid it.

When she sat, doubts crept in. What did they want? Did he want her to try to look sexy? To pose? Her head swirled when she suddenly felt out of control, when she tried to recall what the things she'd read had said about protocol.

Clint turned finally, and the curl of his lips said whatever she'd done had been good enough for him.

"I've told you before—stop worrying so much. If I want something, I'll make it clear. You won't ever get in trouble for something you didn't understand."

Right, he had said that, hadn't he? And Clint had proven that to be true so far, that he was direct and upfront with what he wanted and what he didn't. It was strange, to think of people as being honest, but Ell tried to accept that he was—at least she could accept it tonight.

"Ethan isn't wrong," Clint said, his tone the same matter-of-fact one he used for everything. "You are pretty."

Ell almost smiled, at least until Clint kept talking.

"Spread your legs, Ell."

That seemed too far. She froze, the thought of baring herself to their gazes feeling like leaping off a cliff with no parachute. Sex was one thing, but *this*?

Clint lifted a dark eyebrow, his gaze on her lap. "I believe I gave you an order, Ell. Is there a reason you can't do it?"

"It's embarrassing?"

"Why?"

"Because no one has looked at me like that."

"And?"

She opened her mouth, but nothing came out. She shifted on the couch, acutely aware of the fact she was entirely naked, that Clint was as well.

"We are about to see you much closer, aren't we? To touch you? So why is it that it bothers you here and now?"

Ell let out a sound of pure frustration. She had no doubt the men knew exactly why it was uncomfortable even if they played dumb. No doubt it was so she had to say it, because they were hoping that after having to explain it, she'd realize how stupid it was. "Do you just get off on making women do things they don't want to do?" she snapped, then slapped her hand over her mouth the moment the words escaped.

She was pretty sure that didn't fall into the 'be respectful' thing they'd said.

No one spoke for one long minute, and Ell felt like she had when she'd been a kid and an adult had asked her a question, then waited until she cracked from the pressure of silence.

And just like back then, Ell snapped first. "I'm sorry," she whispered.

"It's fine," Fox assured her, his tone kind. "Don't get us wrong—we are well aware that we sometimes ask things that are hard. If you have a problem with anything, you can tell us, and we'll discuss it. That's what we're doing right now—discussing why you have an issue so we can see if something needs to be done differently. If you can't explain it, though, then I doubt even you fully understand your own actions."

Which felt far too true... How often did Ell do things and later wonder just why the hell she'd done it?

So she gave in and spoke while keeping her eyes down. "When you look at me, I worry about how I look, about what you think, about if I should be doing something differently."

The three surrounded her, and since she sat while they stood, they towered over her, highlighting the differences between then.

It was Ethan who spoke next. "I have an idea." He turned around and went to a small closet at the far wall, and when he turned back around, he held a piece of black fabric. When he came back toward her, Ell shifted away as if the thing he held might bite her.

He let out a laugh. "Relax. It's just a blindfold."

"Why do I need a blindfold? My issue was *you* seeing me, not the other way around."

"No, your problem is *you* seeing us see you. There's a difference. With this on, you won't spend your time trying to read our expressions, doubting how you look, nothing. You can just feel us, just listen. Is that okay?"

Ell wanted to say no, but the truth was that she had no specific hang-ups about being blindfolded. If she'd been bound as well, or gagged, that might have been different, but just not being able to see didn't strike her as a real problem.

So Ell nodded, and Ethan whispered, "Brave girl," as he tied the cloth around her head, stealing her vision.

Which made everything else instantly more alive. It was as if by removing her sight, Ell could feel each breeze over her bare skin, could hear the pounding of her heart, could smell the cedar from Ethan's soap.

And when Ethan ran his fingers over her breast, she pulled in a stuttering, gasping breath.

"Now, Ell," Clint said. "Spread your legs for me."

Ell moved slowly, but she parted her legs just as he'd ordered. The men were right, it was *far* easier without having to see them, without trying to stare at them and decipher what they thought, what they wanted, whether they liked what she did or not.

"You're such a good girl," Ethan whispered, still toying with her breasts, teasing her sensitive nipples. "You listen so well, you know that? I even like that little tremble that's going through you. You're worried for nothing, though. Your pussy is just as sexy as every other part of you. Maybe I'll put you in front of a mirror, make you spread these legs so I can explain just how much I like seeing your cunt. I'll play with it for just as long as I want, make you watch while I do all sorts of twisted things to it, and by the end? You won't be so shy anymore."

Ell cried out from the words alone, as if they were another set of hands.

But it was nothing compared to the warm air that brushed her clit. Then something hot and wet stroked up her slit, and she damned well knew it could only be one thing.

A tongue.

She didn't know whose it was, not at first. Ethan was still beside her, meaning it was either Clint or Fox. She guessed Fox, as Clint didn't seem like the type to enjoy this sort of thing.

"How does that feel?" Ethan asked. It was strange, how she'd written him off as funny before, as someone who took nothing seriously, whose voice alone could make her roll her eyes. Now, however, his voice was hot. It was promising and erotic and seared through her. His every word drove her need higher. "You're twitching like you haven't gotten this sort of attention in a long time. Just how long has it been?"

"Since what?" she managed.

"So long that you have to ask what I mean?" His laugh made her cheeks heat, even as the tongue lapped at her drenched cunt. "Let's go easy. How long has it been since you've had sex?"

She struggled to make her brain work, to do the math. Even still, she wasn't sure, her answer more of a question. "Nine years?"

"Well, that's just criminal. A cunt this lovely shouldn't go nearly that long without attention. At least it explains why you're so needy, doesn't it?"

Needy. The word did what so much of his did—excited her. It was like he'd reached inside her and woken parts that had slept for years, maybe forever.

"Do you like not knowing who it is that's eating you out?"

She shook her head.

"No? Well, I have to admit, that makes me want to tie you down sometime on all fours, blindfolded, and the three of us will fuck you to our hearts' content. You won't have a clue who is taking what—we'll stay silent, and you'll just have to wonder while we use every last hole on your sweet little body."

Her reaction to his words shocked the hell out of her. Ell came—*hard.* She hadn't expected it, hadn't felt that slow building, that frustrating need she knew from her previous experiences. She was used to an orgasm being something almost mythical that took time, effort and a sacrifice to the gods to achieve.

So how had Ethan gotten her to come so easily? With his words? With the ideas he'd placed into her mind? Whoever was licking her hadn't even focused on her clit, hadn't seemed to be trying to get her off, yet they'd managed it.

She twisted as the intense pleasure ransacked her, as it rushed through her and took over. By the time it lessened, when she whined at the way the man between her thighs wouldn't *stop* licking her, Ethan's warm breath was still at her ear.

"You're so sensitive—fuck, I like that. I mean, maybe we'll teach you to control it, make you resist, but hell, maybe not. I might just enjoy sending you over that edge so many times, you're crying and worn out and so sensitive it's almost painful to keep touching you."

She shook her head, wanting to deny that, to tell them no, but like everything else he said, it painted a far different picture in her head. He made her crave it, made her want to experience exactly what he said. How he managed to do that, she had no idea.

His laugh called her a liar.

The lips at her cunt pulled away, then large hands slid along her inner thighs. "You taste like sugar."

Clint? Ell had been so sure it was Fox that she shivered at the idea of Clint there, of that single-minded focus he had being devoted to pleasuring her. It was almost enough to make her worry she might fall over that edge again, when she thought about his large body kneeling in front of the couch, his tongue teasing her the way he had.

"I'd love to fuck you tonight," Clint said, his breath spilling over her drenched and sensitive cunt as he spoke. "But since it's been so long for you, I think we'll wait before I make you take my cock. I will make you, though, and your pussy will stretch so well around me, won't it? You'll take me like a good girl?"

She nodded. Even as the logical part of her brain said hell no, as it tried to do math to figure out if it was even possible, she nodded because something about the way he said 'good girl' called to her, made her want to live up to his expectations, wanted him to look at her with pride.

He pressed a kiss to her thigh before groaning softly, his body heat leaving her.

"Looks like I'm the lucky one," Ethan said with a chuckle.

Ell had no idea what he meant until the world moved around her, the blindfold meaning she wasn't even close to expecting it when Ethan grasped her hips and tugged her into his lap.

And also discovered that he'd stripped down to nothing, his heated skin pressing directly against hers, his cock trapped between their bodies. Ell moved, fears about being too heavy, about everything else hitting her.

Ethan didn't give her any space, though. Instead, he wrapped an arm around her to keep her tight against him. "Easy, baby girl. You're fine."

"I'm too heavy."

He chuckled. "You aren't even close to too heavy, and the more you squirm, the harder you make me want to fuck you, so you might want to decide if it's worth it."

That made her still. It was a threat that did its job, because Ell was nervous enough about having sex with them without adding in the predatory way he said *harder*.

"Good job. Now, since it's been a while, and you can't see, I'll let you know so you can relax. I'm wearing a condom, and as members here, we get tested every three months. I know you were tested as well, since you have to be to attend as a guest."

The reminder of the realities were like cold water on Ell, turning a fantasy into the harsh truth. Still, it also let her breathe, reminded her that they were all being responsible.

It was a good thing the men were, at least, because Ell had a feeling they'd drugged her to the point that she wouldn't have asked such things. She was too out of control, too deep into the demands of her body to think about safety.

Someone grasped Ell's arms, making her jump—would she ever grow used to there being so many people around her? — and helped her rise slightly. She wasn't sure why, until a hand on her hip pulled her back and Ethan's cock pressed to the opening of her cunt.

Ell tensed. How many times had men slammed home at this point? How many times had they ignored whether or not she was ready and just taken what they wanted? Even as turned on as Ell was, fear prickled at her, made her prepare herself for the inevitable sharp pain.

Except...that didn't happen.

Ethan's thumb rubbed at her hip, calming her.

"Relax," Fox whispered from in front of her, telling her who had a hold of her arms. "Don't worry — he'll go slow."

The fact they could read her so well both bothered and reassured her. Ell exhaled, then let her head fall forward, her forehead resting against Fox's chest. It was a surrender, a decision to trust them for now.

The pressure against her cunt increased, even with how wet she was, until finally the first inch of Ethan's cock sank into her.

She squirmed at the strange feeling, at the fullness it had been so long since she'd experienced. Her body went wild, as if her first orgasm hadn't come close to sating her, as if it had just gotten her more excited, more desperate.

"Fuck," Ethan groaned. "She's like a fucking vise. Forget lasting long, I'll be lucky to make it inside her entirely."

That shouldn't have pleased her, but it did... Hearing Ethan praise her, hearing him say he wanted her, that he felt good, it tugged at her. It also let her relax further, and the next tug of his hands let her slide farther down his cock.

She whined softly, but it didn't take long until her body pressed against his, until he'd filled her with every inch of his hard cock.

Fox released her arms, then shifted to her side. He dragged his fingers over her cheek, and even though she couldn't see, she could feel his gaze on her.

Impossibly large hands cupped her breasts, roughness in the palms scratching against her heated skin. "You have tits I haven't been able to stop thinking about," Clint admitted. "Since you aren't ready to take my cock, I'm going to fuck between them like I've fantasized about."

Ell nodded as if it were a question.

"Hold them together for me, would you?"

An hour before, Ell would have hesitated. She'd have considered what it would look like, would have hated having to participate. However, when Clint gave her an order like that, the simple way he did so, it drew her in. It made her feel safe, made her feel as if Clint had it handled. She didn't have to doubt anything, question anything because she trusted Clint to tell her the truth.

So Ell replaced Clint's hands, cupping her own breasts and pressing them together to create a valley of tight cleavage there.

"You look pretty like that," Ethan said into her ear, his voice broken by panting. "Might have to put you on your knees someday, have you press your tits together like that and keep your mouth open. Hell, that'd be a sight to come home to, to get to use your pretty mouth, then come on your face, on your tits."

Ethan didn't give her time to wonder about his words, since he reached out and slid his fingers over her clit. He lifted his hips, but since she couldn't really ride him, not with the others so close, he only ground into her deeper.

Still, it gave her everything she wanted, and the breathless way he spoke said it worked for him, too.

"Loosen for a minute," Clint ordered, then something hot, wet and hard pressed between her breasts. "Good. Tight again." When she did so, Clint thrust slowly, gliding against her so well she had to assume he'd used lube. "Now, I want you to play with your nipples while I do this. *Harder.* I saw how you reacted to Ethan pinching you, so I know what you want. There you go, little one."

The way he drawled out 'little one' made her cunt tighten even more than the torment of her nipples did. Why did they have to know what she wanted? Why did they have to push her past what she thought she wanted? It was as if they got off by taking her to a place she feared, as if they weren't content with her comfort but had to shove her outside of that rut she'd made for herself.

And she drowned in that happily, especially because she was pretty sure that was exactly why she'd come, why she'd met with them. She'd spent years in that safety, and she knew she'd never leave it on her own.

A hand on her chin turned her face toward where Fox was. Something ran across her bottom lip in a tease that had her parting. Fox didn't ask her if she wanted to give him a blow job—though they'd already asked if she was okay with it at the start—and somehow that excited her more. Instead, he pressed the blunt head of his cock against her lips, forcing her to part them more, to open for him.

The heat of his cock was almost as wonderful at his masculine taste. He slid his fingers into her hair, making her tilt her head. "Open your mouth wider, princess."

Princess? The name would have set her off any other time, yet when Fox said it, it held such affection that it melted any resolve she had.

She opened her mouth, obeying him even if it felt strange. She was used to men who demanded she suck hard, who wanted her to tighten her lips around them. Keeping her mouth open and almost lax felt odd, and she ignored the depraved way she must look.

Fox slid his cock against her tongue, then used his grip in her hair to turn her head, to press against the inside of her cheek. He seemed to be playing with her, using her mouth like a toy for his own amusement. His grip in her hair was tight, leaving a sting in her scalp, as if a reminder he was in control.

It all overwhelmed her senses.

Ethan's cock deep inside her cunt, his fingers tormenting her clit in a way that kept making her tighten around him, as she dangled on the edge of another orgasm. The way Clint thrust between her breasts, and how she pinched and tugged at her own nipples, just as he'd told her to. Then there was Fox, who used her mouth as he pleased, who had her there with her mouth open in the lewdest way, as he used her like a plaything he couldn't get enough of.

Ell had *never* felt like this before, never felt so wanted, so desired, so taken over. She was completely out of control, but the world wasn't falling down around her. Even when she let go, when she just tried to be present in the moment, all the things she feared didn't come to pass.

Ethan stroked harder against her clit. "I'm going to come, baby girl," he whispered like a threat. "Fox and Clint seem pretty close, as well. Who can blame us, though, when we have such a sweet, sexy thing to play with? So, you need to be a good girl and take our cum. After that, we'll take good care of you and get you off again, too."

Ell nodded, broken by his words, by their touches. Yes, whatever they wanted, *yes.*

His chuckle was strained, but he closed his fingers around her clit in a tight pinch.

"Tighter on your nipples," Clint said, his voice rough, his thrusts erratic. "You can do better than that."

Ell tightened her fingers, wetness tracking down her cheeks as it all was too much. Still, when she obeyed when the pain from her nipples scorched through her, she teetered there on the edge.

"Fuck, yes, take it," Ethan said so softly, she almost didn't hear as he raised his hips especially hard, yanking her against him as if he worried he hadn't gotten deep enough.

Clint pulled back, then something hot landed on her breasts, on her hands, on her nipples that she still pinched and twisted. It branded her, like a claim, and even if she couldn't see it, she knew his cum covered her breasts.

Lastly, Fox pulled from her lips. "Keep your mouth open for me."

Ell did as he demanded, ignoring how it had to look. A sound that seemed far too feral for the reserved and civilized doctor filled the space just before his cum landed on her tongue. She didn't move, even when he traced her bottom lip with the head of his cock, when he left more of his cum there.

Light hit her as Fox tugged off her blindfold, as she blinked and was forced to look into his eyes, her mouth still open, his cum coating her tongue.

"Swallow," he said, a light in his blue eyes, a contagious excitement there.

Ell closer her mouth and did so, then licked her lip clean afterward, wanting every drop.

"You're such a messy girl," Ethan whispered to her. "Look down at yourself."

Ell peered down her body to find streaks of Clint's thick cum on her, her fingers still tight around her abused nipples, and her legs spread lewdly. It meant Clint and Fox could see how Ethan's cock filled her, the way her pussy was wrapped around him.

Heat overtook her.

Ethan didn't seem done, though. He kept speaking, his voice so quiet that it was like a filthy secret. "Covered in cum, in sweat. What a perfect, filthy little girl."

She never would have expected to like that kind of talk, especially with how nervous she'd been about how she looked, about what they wanted. Why was it then that when he spoke, when he humiliated her in a way that held so much affection, she wanted nothing more than to purr?

He kept his fingers tight around her clit, not stroking, keeping her right on that edge of release. "You are *our* filthy baby girl, though, aren't you? Our little fuck toy?" He nipped at her earlobe, making her arch her back. "Now you're going to come once more for us, and you don't get to hide from it, from *us*. You're going to get off right here, while we watch, with Clint's cum dripping down your front."

He didn't give her a chance to argue, didn't ask her.

"I'm going to let go of your clit and the blood will rush back in and, trust me, that'll be enough."

Ell almost doubted him—a stupid thing since he'd proven himself right each time so far—but when he released her clit, the moment of relief was short-lived.

It *ached* a split second after he let go, and Clint moved her hand from her left breast. The same burning happened there, but that wasn't what really got her.

As soon at that pain hit her, Clint leaned in and closed her teeth around her nipple. He bit down, but she wasn't sure if it was hard or if it was just how sensitive she was after she'd pinched for so long. Ethan similarly pressed two fingers directly against her clit and ground hard, not letting her squirm to escape the pressure.

Ell let out a sound that was almost a scream, something so unlike her, as she collapsed into the pleasure that swamped her. It pulled her under, made her gasp and worry she was dying.

Everything around her dimmed, as if her brain shut off, as if everything else faded away. In fact, when she blinked, when she dragged in a breath and came back to herself, everything had changed.

She wasn't in Ethan's lap anymore, and she wasn't naked. She was curled up on the couch, a blanket wrapped around her, with her head in Fox's lap. He slid his hands through her hair in a gentle touch.

"She's something else," Ethan said softly.

She felt half-asleep, in a state where she heard them but couldn't make sense of their words.

"Yeah, she is," Fox acknowledged. "But I doubt she's long-term."

"She might be," Clint said. "She just needs to figure that out."

"We've done that before," Ethan said, bitterness filling his tone. "There's no reason to think she actually wants to do this. Don't count your chickens till they hatch."

Fox sighed, his fingers pausing for a moment. "Maybe," he admitted.

That was the last thing Ell caught before sleep took her, before she gave in and cuddled against Fox.

Chapter Nine

Ell stared at her phone but didn't reach for it. It had been the sixth time in the past hour she'd done that, like a ritual she couldn't avoid, but still she left it untouched.

The reason was clear enough.

Clint, Ethan and Fox had put their numbers into her phone before she'd left Sanctuary that night and had made it clear they wanted to hear from her.

And…she had texted back and forth with them the day after her night with them. The very next morning, when she'd woken sore and happy in a way that was unnerving, Ell had rolled over to find a text from Fox waiting for her.

Take one ibuprofen and drink plenty of water today. Make sure to relax and go to bed early. Call me if you need anything.

The message had taken her off guard, the tone of it, the fact anyone gave a damn what she did. It had been a long time since anyone cared enough to tell her to do anything. Even as a child, she'd been mostly on her own. No one worried if she'd eaten, if she'd drank water, if she'd hurt.

That wasn't the only message she'd gotten, though. Ethan had messaged her to say he couldn't get the sight of her out of his head, and Clint had messaged to ask if she needed anything.

Ell had, of course, declined. Not only did she not need anything, but she didn't want to see them.

Not yet, at least.

She needed to figure out what had happened exactly, needed to work through her feelings about it. It had felt so simple in the darkness, when they had touched her, but now?

Now it felt monumentally more complicated.

Ell tried to focus on organizing her hallway closet. Pulling everything out and sorting it always made her feel better, as if controlling the chaos in her home made her able to deal with it in her life.

It didn't help, though. Even as she put right every little item that had gotten misplaced, she didn't feel any more comfortable, any surer of how to proceed, how to react.

Something inside her had enjoyed what they'd done, and that part of her craved more, but that didn't stop Ell from wondering if she should put all of herself into it. She'd learned trusting people lead to only pain.

An odd sound caught Ell's attention, made her frown and turn. She had the day off, and she didn't expect anyone.

Dean often showed up without notice, the only person who could get away with that. He also might have heard that she'd gone to Sanctuary and come over to interrogate her.

Ell closed the cabinet and walked toward the front door, ready to scold Dean for not calling first.

Except, when she walked into the room, it wasn't Dean in her living room.

Two men she didn't recognize stood there instead. She didn't *need* to know who they were to know they were up to no good, though. Ell had grown up in terrible areas, and she knew how to spot a person who planned to cause trouble.

As if them breaking into her home didn't tell her that already.

"You need to leave," Ell said, using the tone she always used to delinquent kids. These weren't kids, of course—they were full-grown adults. Still, that no-nonsense tone often worked wonders on everyone.

The men turned, and no surprise crossed their faces. Clearly, they hadn't broken in expecting the place to be empty. They'd known she was there, had entered knowing they'd find her there.

Which was more terrifying than anything else.

And…Ell had left her phone in the hallway where she'd been working.

"Well, aren't you a pretty girl?"

Ell kept her shoulders back and her chin lifted. *Show no fear.* Predators pounced on any sign of weakness. "I don't know what you're after, but you need to go—now. I don't have jewelry and I don't keep money in the house. If you broke in looking for something, you're going to leave disappointed."

Ell backed away, but too soon, she ran into the kitchen bar and had nowhere else to go.

When he cornered her, the man reached up and caught Ell's face. His eyes looked impossibly bright, the amber almost glowing, reminding her of how a cat's eyes shone in the darkness. His smirk made her want to tremble, but she refused to show fear. "You said you don't have anything, but I doubt that. Everyone has something."

Ell tried to shake her head, but it made his fingers on her cheeks dig in. "I'm a social worker. I don't make very much, and I don't keep nice things around. I have a laptop below the television—that's the most expensive thing I own."

She wasn't holding out, either. Ell had learned as a child that things could be stolen. They were worthless, transitory. It was stupid to spend large amounts of money on items, especially because she'd seen how fast people could lose everything. So she lived on very little, saved the majority of what she made and invested it for when she might not have so much.

Her car and her laptop were the most expensive things to her name, and these men could have either of them if they just left.

Though, the way the man peered at her laptop made her heart sink. He didn't have the expression of a man who was planning on leaving anytime soon. "That isn't much, you know. A lot of risk for not much reward."

Ell swallowed hard, then met his gaze head-on. She reminded herself to be strong, to be confident. She'd faced down worst men in her life. "The risk for breaking and entering isn't much. The punishment if you hurt me is *far* greater."

"That's if anyone finds you afterward. I can promise that if I want you to disappear, you will."

Ell pulled her hands into fists, wishing she'd listened to Dean when he'd wanted her to keep mace in every room of her house. She'd rolled her eyes and called him paranoid, but look where she was now...

Of course, when Dean found out—if he found out— he wouldn't be laughing. While she trusted her friend, she'd seen his scary side a time or two in the past, and it wasn't something she liked witnessing.

"I told you, I'm a social worker. I work with the police all the time. If something happens to me, they won't just let it go." That might have been a lie, seeing as she'd caused more than her share of trouble for the cops, but if it got them out of there, she'd take it.

The man let out a laugh, his breath sour from stale beer, even that early in the morning. "You sure talk a lot of shit, you know that? You should learn to be a good girl and keep your trap shut."

Again, his use of *good girl* didn't give her any tingles, didn't make her want to listen.

Ell pulled in one more deep breath, trying to steel her voice. "You need to leave right this minute. I've told you you can take my laptop and the keys to my car are hanging by the door along with my purse. There are a few bucks inside. That's everything I have."

He sneered, squeezing his fingers on her until it hurt. "You think we can be bought off so easily? That we don't know exactly what we're here for?" He dropped his gaze meaningfully down her front, and her stomach rebelled in response.

It also broke Ell's leash on her 'calm and collected' thing she'd been going for. She lifted her knee into the man's groin, moving fast and with nothing to warn him. She made contact—even that made her shudder, wanting to go nowhere near his goods.

He crumpled forward, reminding her that even the toughest of men couldn't handle a shot there. Ell twisted, trying to take off toward her back door, since the other two stood between her and the front. She could hop the back fence of her duplex and run.

Something caught the back of her shirt, tearing it and yanking her off her feet. She hit the floor hard, her cheek smacking against the tile and knocking the breath from her.

"You bitch," the man snarled. He got on top of her, trying to roll her to her back and pin her.

Ell fought, squirming, throwing her weight, tossing her head backward and hoping for contact. Growing up in foster care, thrown from bad place to bad place, had taught her that when she needed to fight, she needed to go all in. Sometimes that was all that stood between surviving and ending up another statistic.

She twisted to toss the man off, but she knew the back door wasn't possible. They were too close—she'd never get it open in time.

The stun gun Dean had bought her when she moved in hung on a hook by the back door. She'd much rather run than fight, but running seemed out of the question.

Ell flung herself forward, desperate to reach the small weapon. Just as had happened the last time, she didn't make it far.

A hand caught her ankle, and she hit the ground again as he pulled her backward. She let out a scream. She didn't know if any of her neighbors were home, but it seemed her only chance.

The slap of skin on skin came a heartbeat before pain exploded through her cheek. It shocked her, the way it seemed to short her brain out for a minute, the way it dazed and silenced her.

He managed to roll Ell over, to pin her hands beside her head. He stared down at her, panting hard, far too much excitement in his face as if that had all been foreplay. "You're fucking trouble, ain't you? Bet I'd have a good time taming you, though, bringing you to heel."

The idea made her stomach churn, made her swallow to keep from throwing up.

"We need to hurry up," the man who hadn't spoken yet said from the back. It seemed obvious he was in charge, especially with how the one on top of Ell turned at the sound of his voice.

"We got time, don't we?"

The man by the door shook his head. "Someone might have heard her scream."

With the man turned the other way, his grip had loosened. Even with her head clouded, her thoughts sluggish, she knew it was her only shot. She lifted her hips to knock him off balance, and when he came forward, she swung her head up.

She aimed for his nose. A crunch said she'd hit her mark, and something warm and wet dripped onto her face.

Even still, he rolled off, cradling his nose, so she reached for the stun gun at the back door. She held it out in front of her. It wasn't much against these men, but it was *something*.

"Get out," she repeated, her voice low and sounding far more dangerous than she'd ever heard it before.

The man who was bleeding stared at her, flames dancing in his eyes, blood streaming from between his fingers. He got up and looked ready for another round, the stun gun be damned.

Except that man from the back spoke up once again. "That's enough. Let's go while we still can."

The man who was bleeding narrowed his eyes. "This isn't over." He didn't wait for anything else from Ell before he left, following the other man, a trail of blood on the floor.

They left the front door open, and Ell collapsed to the tile, shaking spreading through her whole body, too afraid to move despite knowing she needed to.

And for one terrifying, pathetic second, all she wanted was to feel Fox stroking his fingers through her hair again...

* * * *

Ethan grinned as Clint narrowed his eyes at the poor joke Ethan had made.

Well, Ethan didn't think it was a poor joke—he felt all of his were great. It wasn't his fault is others didn't appreciate them.

"You seem more annoyed with me than usual," Ethan pointed out.

Clint let out a huff before pouring himself a cup of coffee in the break room of the police station. "Maybe you're just more annoying than usual."

"Maybe," Ethan admitted. "But I have a feeling it's more than that."

Clint added a sugar cube to his cup. "We haven't set up another time to see Ell. What if she's backing away?"

Oh, that.

Ethan couldn't exactly blame Clint for being on edge over it. Ethan had spent plenty of time the last few days thinking about that girl. Her text messages had dwindled so that she hadn't responded for the past two days.

Of course, he knew that wasn't uncommon. She'd had a good time, hadn't run off afterward. In fact, she'd slept there in Fox's lap for *hours* before finally waking up and letting them help her get dressed.

Ethan had wanted to drive her home, had offered and said Clint could pick him up from her house so her car made it there as well, but she'd refused.

It probably felt like too much to have them that close, to have them at her house. Ethan could understand that. The reality was that sex—especially when it involved power exchanges—could make people feel as if they were closer than they were, as if they were farther along in a relationship. It fostered feelings of intimacy that normally took much longer to build. That could be overwhelming.

Still, just like Clint, Ethan wanted something planned. He wanted to know they'd see her soon, that they had something on the books. It would help him relax, help him know that she wasn't ghosting them.

However, pushing her wasn't fair, either. He had to give her the space to make her own choice.

He knew damn well what pushing led to, and it wasn't anything he wanted a repeat of.

"The break-in on Campus Road," a uniformed officer said as he walked into the breakroom, speaking to another office. "She got damned lucky."

"Did you see how much blood was on the floor? She's a tough one, all right."

An uneasy feeling pulled at Ethan's chest. While he was proud when someone fought back, he always hated that they had to be.

He turned his head toward the new men and gestured at the coffee pot in question.

The office nodded. "Yeah, thanks, I could use a cup. Spent the last couple hours on a breaking and enter. Two burglars attacked some woman in her duplex."

Ethan poured two cups and handed them over to the officers. "She's okay, though?"

"Roughed up a bit, but she's breathing, which is pretty good from what could have happened. From her story, she kneed one in the jewels before she headbutted him and probably broke his nose. I walked into her place to find her with a stun gun in her hand, a lot of blood on her face and the look of a woman who is done with men's shit."

Ethan let out a soft laugh. Yeah, in his experience women had a hell of a lot more strength than people gave them credit for. He'd seen girls pulls themselves out of hell, had watched them take down others who were bigger and stronger to protect their kids or themselves. "Atta' girl," he said.

The officer took a seat at the table, looking exhausted. Then again, police work did a number on people. It wasn't easy to see the worst of the worst, to know what people were capable of, and to keep going, keep fighting. It was why so many burned out eventually, why they found themselves too overwhelmed to do it anymore.

"She at the hospital?" Clint asked.

The officer shook his head. "No. She went, but got cleared quickly. Some bruising and a sprained ankle, but it sounds like she came out of it a lot better than the men she tangled with. Gotta say, I'm not so shocked now that she defends her kids like a tiger."

"Kids?" Clint frowned as if trying to keep up.

"She's a social worker. Sounds like she's given us more than a few headaches."

Panic gripped Ethan's chest. The man couldn't mean...

Clint spoke up first. "Ell?"

The officer frowned. "You know her?"

Ethan didn't bother to answer, already halfway to the door, his phone in his hand to dial Fox's phone. Ell could have all the damned time she wanted to figure out what she thought about them, about what they were doing, about what she wanted.

None of that had anything to do with the fact that Ethan was going to go to her house, he was going to check on her, and if she didn't like that?

Too fucking bad.

* * * *

The time between Fox knocking on Ell's door and a hesitant, 'who is it?' coming through stretched out forever.

Still, just hearing her voice — even if it was terrified — helped him grapple with his temper.

"It's Fox," he responded.

Silence met him. He could almost picture her on the other side of the door, trying to work out whether or not she wanted to open it, whether or not she wanted to let him in.

Especially after what had happened.

Ethan had called him, since Fox could arrive at her place quicker than the other two. Ethan and Clint first wanted to review the files from the other officers, which left Fox as the one to go see her first.

He could have called or texted, but he knew she'd just lie. Hell, she might have taken off just so she didn't have to see him.

"I wanted to check on you," Fox said.

Another long minute, then the click of locks said she'd given in. When she opened the door, he found the inside of the duplex dark, the lights off and the curtains drawn.

Fox walked in, and Ell quickly shut the door again, locking the handle, the deadbolt, and a chain lock at the top. He couldn't see much of anything, not while his eyes adjusted slowly.

"How did you find out?" Ell asked as she moved away but didn't turn her back on him.

Afraid?

The idea tore at him, especially because while nerves sometimes got the best of her, she'd never been afraid before.

"An officer at the station was talking about it and Ethan overheard."

"Oh," she said softly, her words slurred.

Had she hit her head and they hadn't treated her properly? "Are you dizzy?" He slid into doctor mode, needing to diagnose the problem, to try to fix it.

"What?" Ell walked slowly, wavering slightly. "Oh, no. I mean, yes, I am, but it's the pain pills they gave me."

He let out a breath in relief. "Oxycontin?" he asked.

"Yep. I don't normally take it, but the nurse said it would help."

"And did it?"

He could make out her silhouette, and her small shoulders lifted in a shrug. "I guess so. My head doesn't hurt, and my ankle feels better. Tight, but it's not throbbing anymore."

It was then he noticed her gait was off, that she limped, babying her left leg. That was the bad part of painkillers — they helped make patients more comfortable, but they also made them think they were better off than they were. People on painkillers tended to overdo it.

"Come on, Ell, get off your feet. Clearly you injured your ankle."

"They did an X-ray — it isn't broken."

"So? A sprain can be more painful and take longer to heal."

Ell sat on the couch, but Fox got the feeling it was because her legs wouldn't hold her than because he'd told her to. She leaned forward and wrapped her arms around herself as if to hold herself together.

Fox went to the spot beside her and turned on the lamp without asking. She'd only complain, and he needed a better look at her.

Though, the moment he did it, he regretted the choice.

A bruise covered Ell's cheek, and on her forehead sat a circle of dark blue along with swelling. While he'd seen plenty of injuries in his line of work, somehow seeing them on Ell affected him in a way few things did.

"*Princess*," he said softly.

Ell turned her face away, dropping her gaze to the floor. She wanted to hide, did she?

He let her as he sat on the ottoman in front of her. "Let me see your leg." When she didn't move, he caught her calf and lifted it to set her foot in his lap. She had no shoe on, thankfully. Removing a shoe when someone's ankle was swollen was a painful process he had no desire to perform.

He peered at her ankle after shifting her pajama pants up. Sure enough, it was swollen and warm to the touch, telling him she probably wasn't taking care of it properly.

"You're going to need to stay off this for at least a few days. By that, I mean keep it elevated and stay lying flat."

She didn't respond, and when he risked a look at her face, he had a feeling she was miles away. Reliving the attack?

Fox wished he could take that away from her, that he could carry it for her.

"Why didn't you call us?" he asked instead.

She swallowed hard. "I didn't know what to say."

"You only had to say 'help,' and we would have been here right away. Hell, if you went to the hospital, you could have just asked for me there."

She blinked slowly. Was she trying to keep tears in? "I can't stay here," she said instead of acknowledging what he'd said.

"I know it might not feel safe after what happened—"

She shook her head. "It was personal. I don't know why, and I don't care what the police officer said. The men who broke in weren't there to steal things. They were here looking for me."

Fox pressed his lips together, an uncommon rush of anger through him. He schooled his tone before answering. "Why do you think that?"

"They weren't surprised when I walked in—I think they knew I was here. When I offered my laptop and car, they weren't interested. They didn't seem like they wanted to steal anything."

"What would they want from you? Did you recognize them?"

Ell shook her head. "No. I don't think I've seen them before. Maybe it was a family member of one of the kids I've helped? I get threats sometimes when court doesn't go the way they want. Or, maybe it was random, like they saw me and decided to break in to—" She stopped speaking, and that was when she seemed to shatter. A tremble ran through her until even her foot in Fox's lap shook.

"It's okay," Fox assured her. "You're safe now. Take a deep breath. Better. Who are you here with?"

She frowned, then answered with a whisper. "Fox."

"That's right. And have I ever let anything happen to you?"

She shook her head.

"Good girl. So, I won't let anything happen now, either. Have you eaten anything? Did you drink anything?"

When she again answered with a shake of her head, Fox sighed. He knew very well how rarely patients took care of themselves, and it was another example of why she couldn't stay there alone.

"Where am I supposed to go?" she asked, yet again ignoring his questions and changing the subject. "I liked this place, but I can't stay here anymore. Maybe I'll stay with Dean for a few days, at least until I can find a new place and get my things moved."

Hell no. It surprised Fox just how quickly his mind threw that idea out. She might be friends with Dean, but the idea of letting her go anywhere else in her vulnerable state made his entire brain rebel.

He wanted her where he could keep an eye on her, where they knew she was safe.

"He doesn't need to be taking care of me again, though," she whispered.

The girl did have trouble accepting help, didn't she?

"Stop worrying," Fox told her. "I'm going to pack you a bag with the items you need, then you're coming with me."

That seemed to wake her up. "I can't stay with you."

"Why not?"

"I barely know you."

He lifted his eyebrow as if calling her out on that statement. After everything they'd done, she knew him at least a little. Still, he tried to keep his tone gentle. "I'm not moving you into my place—not exactly. Clint, Ethan and I bought a small apartment complex a while back. There are four apartments on the top floor, so there's one empty already. I want you to take that one."

Ell furrowed her eyebrows as if trying to work through a very complex issue. Fox blamed that on her meds, since she was typically much sharper than that.

"How much is the rent?"

"We can work that out later."

She shook her head. "I don't need a handout. I can take care of myself." The way she spoke said that was a sticking point for her, and it was yet another glimpse into the woman she was, into the fears she held. She really didn't like help, did she?

"And I never said it was a handout. The place sits empty, fully furnished, so we aren't out anything. We'll go over the details later, but for now? It will give you your own space. It's safe, and I'll be close enough to keep an eye on your injuries. Plus, you'll need help while you heal."

She hesitated, so Fox went in for the kill. "You don't want to stay at Dean's, but I think you know that as soon as he hears about what happened, he'll strongarm you there. This is the best way for you to have your own space."

Finally, her shoulders dropped and she nodded, as if finally realizing she'd been outmaneuvered.

Fox set her foot down on the ottoman to help it stay elevated, then got to his feet. "Now, where is your luggage?"

"I can pack my own things." Ell went to rise, but Fox stopped her with a sharp look.

"I'm being extremely reasonable at the moment, princess, but don't press me. You are hurt, frightened and in pain. Every fiber of who I am wants to put you over my shoulder and haul you out of here without any of your things, then tuck you into my own bed where I can keep a very close eye on you. I'm resisting that, for the moment, but you need to stop pushing. I'm going to pack your clothes and anything else you'll need, then you will get into my car, and I'll drive you to the apartment complex. You'll get off your foot, eat something and ice your ankle while you stay put. Do you understand me?" His tone had shifted, had lost that detached voice and drifted into his Dom voice. He knew damn well he was speaking to her like she was a sub of his, but he didn't give a damn. He hadn't been kidding—he was struggling with his own control.

Ell stared at him as if deciding if he was telling the truth. When she finally answered, her tone was sullen and sarcastic. "Is that all, *Daddy*?"

No doubt she meant the nickname as an insult. Was she trying to throw him off balance? Trying to embarrass him?

She'd have to work a *lot* harder than that to manage it.

Fox set a hand on the back of the couch and leaned forward, into her space. "If I was your Daddy, you'd damn well know it, so unless you want me to act that way, I suggest you don't tease."

Her eyes widened, and wasn't the soft whine that left her a thing of beauty? It was almost enough for him to forget what had happened, for him to act on instinct and find a way to ease the tension and fear inside him with her body.

Instead, he brushed his lips to hers as if to reassure her, then pulled away.

Yet, he couldn't get the way she'd called him Daddy out of his head, or how damned much he wanted to hear her say it again...

Chapter Ten

The apartment made Ell uncomfortable. Fox hadn't crowded her, yet she couldn't seem to wrap her head around the place.

It was far nicer than they'd let on and made her previous duplex look like a tiny studio apartment in comparison.

The apartment had two rooms, two bathrooms, a large open kitchen, dining room and living room combo and a balcony that probably had an amazing view of the sunset. It was furnished, as they'd said, which meant that she didn't need to worry about moving her things in right away. The elevator to their floor had a code so no one could use it unless one of them buzzed them up or they knew the code. In addition, the doors to each apartment had a keypad instead of a regular lock, and Ell's code would get her into any of their places.

After spending a bit of time on her phone to determine the general rent amount for such a place, Ell was quite certain she wouldn't stay long. It was in a very nice area, walkable to the busiest part of town, and Ell would guess it cost about double what she'd been paying before.

Still…the fact she could set her things down, that she could breathe for a minute without worrying about who might break in was worth the cost—at least for a while.

Ell looked toward the kitchen, her mouth dry. Fox had told her to text if she needed something and to otherwise remain off her feet. She couldn't get herself to do it, though, to bother him for something so trivial.

Which had Ell getting off the couch so she could get her own water. The meds had started to wear off, as evidenced by the throbbing pain in her ankle and the fact it wouldn't bear weight.

It was funny, since Ell hadn't even realized she'd hurt her ankle at first. She'd felt the man hit her, had felt her face slam into the tile, but she wasn't sure when she'd hurt her ankle. She guessed it had been when he'd grabbed her other foot.

Still, it was by far the most annoying injury she'd suffered.

Ell braced herself on the furniture as she made her way toward the kitchen, knowing Fox had placed water bottles in the fridge for her. He'd also left some crackers and told her he'd be back later with crutches and real food.

"You don't listen well, do you?" Clint's voice made Ell jump, the action causing her to put her bad foot to the ground.

She yelped before lifting the foot and leaning against the counter. That didn't seem good enough for Clint, because he lifted her as if she weighed nothing. It made her feel small against his wide chest.

It also set her anxiety soaring. After that other man touching her, after the threats and her fear, it seemed her body wasn't ready to just move forward as if it hadn't happened.

"Easy," Clint said. "I'm just getting you off your feet before you fall."

He didn't carry her back to the living room, though. Instead, he set her on the kitchen counter, making sure she was steady before moving back and giving her space.

The higher position helped Ell to separate what had happened at her duplex to now, to let her body see that she wasn't in danger.

After a long moment, she let out a shaky breath. "I'm sorry," she said, shame in her voice.

"No reason to apologize. Did you choose to get attacked? Did you choose to panic? No? Then there's nothing to be sorry for." That sort of statement from someone else might have sounded insincere, but from Clint, it seemed obvious.

"I guess I'm still shaken up."

He nodded, then reached into the fridge and grabbed a water bottle. How had he known? He handed it to Ell. "That happens. Our bodies create triggers in our memories, a holdover from when we used to get chased by predators. It's a defense mechanism to try to keep us alive, to keep us from repeating what hurt us before."

Ell nodded, opening the water and taking a drink before responding. "Believe it or not—I do know that. I've worked with traumatized kids for a long time."

"Yeah, but knowing something is true and accepting it about ourselves are different things. I can tell anyone that alcohol isn't good for them, but that doesn't stop me from drinking a beer after a bad day."

Ell risked a look at Clint and wondered for a moment why she'd thought he didn't like her before. She'd thought he was closed off, that he was almost emotionless. It was strange, but now she had no idea how she'd come to that idea.

He was hard to read, sure, but as she got to know him better, she realized he had feelings — they were just harder to figure out. They just weren't nearly as loud as most people's.

"Thank you for the water," Ell said.

"Fox said you were supposed to call us if you needed anything."

"I wasn't going to bother you for something that silly."

He lifted his eyebrow. "If we offered, then why do you think it's a bother?"

He always managed to get her with those simple questions, didn't he? "Because you're busy. You have your own lives. You don't need to be running around and taking care of me."

"Do you believe that I can handle my own life? That I know my own schedule? That I can prioritize my obligations?"

Ell nodded, but they seemed like obvious answers. Clint was a detective, and from what she'd seen, a good one. Everything she knew about him said he was successful, driven and smart. He had no serious life issues she was aware of, nothing to indicate he was unable to handle his own affairs.

"Exactly," he said. "So, if I tell you that I have the time and ability to help, that I *want* to help, why do you choose not to believe me?"

Ell went to answer, but quickly realized she had no response...

He was right, which chafed.

Finally, she shrugged. "I guess it just makes me feel like I'm taking advantage. I don't like leaning on others."

"So it's about you, not us? You didn't call us after it happened, probably wouldn't have told us at all if we didn't find out from the station." He spoke slowly, as if working through it. "You really don't like help, do you?"

"I don't like to be a bother."

He crossed his arms as he leaned his hip against the counter beside her. "That's not it, since we've already discussed that you wouldn't be. You don't like to rely on others because you expect they'll let you down."

His words slapped her, the truth of them, the fact he could read her so easily.

That was *exactly* why she hated to trust anyone, to need them. She'd been down that road before, knew how people let others down, and she'd experienced what that meant when she was left on her own.

It was safer to take care of herself.

She really didn't want to tell that story, so she pressed her lips together instead. She might not want to tell the truth, but she didn't want to lie, either.

Clint snorted softly then shook his head. "Well, stubborn or not, you're going to have a *much* easier time if you learn to listen."

"I'm an adult, you know. I can take care of myself."

"You can, but why do it all on your own if you don't have to? Besides, all that'll do is make us even more overbearing."

Ell glanced down at the fact she was sitting on a counter that Clint had set her on. "Is that even possible?"

"Oh, it is. If you keep getting up for water, we'll buy a mini-fridge to put by the couch. Also, we'll come over more often if we can't trust you're behaving yourself."

Ell's cheeks heated at the way Clint spoke, at the fact he seemed to have no issue admitting to taking over her life, to doing as he pleased no matter what she had to say about it. And yet…as much as it made her uneasy, another part of her responded to it with warmth.

She sort of *liked* the way he acted, the way her safety and wellbeing mattered to him. Even though she had no intention of letting him take over her life, the fact he seemed willing made her smile.

Which was nice, since she hadn't felt much like smiling since the attack.

"Have you slept?" Clint asked.

"No. I was at the hospital most of the night, and when I got home, I couldn't settle. I kept jumping at every little sound."

"That'll happen, but you need sleep to recover. You got hurt, so your body not only had to deal with what happened in your head, but with repairing itself, too. It can't do any of that if you're suffering from sleep deprivation."

"I tried to shut my eyes and I couldn't sleep," she whispered.

Clint nodded, then walked over and lifted her from the counter with the same ease he'd had when he'd placed her there. If he struggled to carry her, he didn't show it. Then again, muscles like his didn't happen on accident. It wasn't like a woman just being thin—he had to work hard to build and maintain them.

Ell breathed slowly, though the panic didn't hit her nearly as hard this time. Maybe it was because she'd had time to reminder herself that she knew Clint, that she trusted him at least this far.

He went to the master bedroom, then set her onto the bed.

Which made her heart speed but not out of fear. Instead, it was from being in the bedroom with a man she was incredibly attracted to.

He went to the dresser and opened the drawers without asking, something that seemed rather invasive. However, he did it as if not thinking about it, as if it were the most normal thing in the world. He pulled out a set of her pajamas that Fox had packed for her. When he came back over to her, he reached for the hem of her shirt.

Ell swatted his hands. "What do you think you're doing?"

"You won't sleep comfortably if you're not in your pajamas."

"So? That doesn't mean you have to dress me."

"As you've pointed out, you aren't all that good at listening. I have a feeling if I leave before you're settled in, you'll just stay up stewing all night."

Which was probably true...

"I can dress myself," Ell muttered in a sullen tone.

"You can, but I like to help."

"Why? Just so you can see me naked?"

Clint pressed his lips together, then shook his head. "No. If I just wanted you naked, I'd tell you that. I enjoy taking care of you, and I'm feeling rather uneasy after you were hurt, especially seeing you with bruises. I can't fix that, I can't remove them, so please just let me help."

The way he spoke stole her fight. It was hard to find annoyance when he sounded so honest, so pained.

Ell nodded, not trusting her voice.

Clint removed her shirt with gentle hands, something surprising given his size and strength. As he'd said, he didn't leer, didn't make her feel as if he were just trying to sneak a peek.

Not that it mattered, since he'd seen everything before.

"Do you sleep with your bra on?" he asked.

Ell shook her head.

He reached behind her and undid her bra with deft fingers, then set it with the shirt he'd removed. He pulled the nightgown over her head, then reached beneath it to grasp the waist of her leggings.

That put all her body on high alert, the action feeling sultrier than him taking off her shirt, as if reaching beneath the clothing were more exciting. Then again, that was probably the same idea as there was behind lingerie instead of just nudity.

He tugged the pants off but took extra time when working them over her bad leg. Even still, she let out a soft hiss when it aggravated the wrapped ankle.

"Sorry," he said softly, then pressed a kiss to the spot. "Do you sleep with your underwear on?"

"Yes," Ell said quickly, not because she really did — she often didn't — but because she wasn't sure how she'd react to him taking those off.

Already she felt hot and on edge. Her skin seemed to react to every brush from his, as if all her nerve endings were on fire. She had a feeling if he reached beneath her nightgown and removed her panties that there was no way she'd stay unaffected, that she'd keep her wits about her.

He made a soft sound that implied he knew she was lying, but he didn't call her on it. Instead, he gathered up the items that he'd removed from her and put them into a laundry basked in the closet. "How many days of clothing did you bring?"

"I'm not sure. Fox packed the bag."

"Then a week's worth. We'll do laundry in a few days."

"You don't have to—"

His sharp look silenced her. Right, he didn't appreciate when she didn't want his help...

"Thank you," she said rather than the denial she'd started on. The reality was that she could argue with him later if she wanted.

Clint nodded, then left the room for a moment. He returned with not only the water bottle she'd had but also with another unopened one and set both on the nightstand beside her.

It made Ell uneasy. She wasn't used to people taking care of her, for them to move around while she stayed put. Everything inside her wanted to get up, to help out, to take some of the burden off Clint's shoulders.

Since she knew that would only cause a fight, she stayed quiet as he set the room up. He retrieved her phone from the living room and placed it on the nightstand, then also placed her pill bottles there. He went into the bathroom and frowned for a minute, then crouched to look under the sink. When he found what he was looking for—a night light—he plugged it into the outlet beside the sink.

Which made her rub at the center of her chest, an odd feeling there. He'd done that so when it got dark, she could find her way in an unfamiliar place. It was one of the times she was reminded that while he might seem cold, he actually thought about others and cared a lot.

Finally, he came back into the room and surveyed the space. A quick nod seemed to say he found his work acceptable. He returned to the side of the bed and pulled the blankets up over her.

Being tucked in was an entirely new experience, and tomorrow she could wonder why she enjoyed it. For tonight, she was too tired to worry. He pressed a kiss to her forehead, something chaste and surprisingly sweet.

"Now, sleep before you get yourself in trouble."

Okay, that is less sweet…

Still, it didn't take away the strange sense of belonging she had there. She should have said thank you again, or something, but Ell's mind refused to work enough to come up with anything worthwhile.

Not that Clint seemed to mind. He headed for the door and turned off the light.

The darkness hit Ell all at once, and she let out a gasp as fear swarmed through her. She had no idea *why* the dark would bother her. It hadn't been dark when the men had broken in, yet the inability to see anything made every shadow suddenly a potential threat.

Immediately, the light came back on.

Ell sat up, leaning forward as she tried to slow her breathing, as she reminded herself it was stupid to react this way.

She *knew* she was safe here, so why the hell was her brain doing this? She'd survived plenty of things growing up, times when she'd seen the worst of people, when she'd suffered horribly, yet none of those had made her panic like this.

Ell twisted, then moved the items Clint had set on her nightstand. She placed the three bottles of pills along the back side of the table, then lined the water bottles up on the edge beside the bed, with the fullest at the back. She shifted the clock so it sat between the others, perfectly lined up with the back.

Yet, it didn't quite ease the pressure in her chest, the way she struggled to take full breaths.

Hands caught hers, and she realized then how bad the shaking had gotten.

And it embarrassed her. She hated having anyone see her like this, see her as weak and lost and hurting. Her little rituals didn't seem to work, couldn't make this better, and now Clint got a front row seat to the entire thing.

"You need sleep," he said in a soft voice.

Ell risked looking up at him, but his gaze was on the way she'd placed the items on the nightstand. It was almost enough for her to want to swipe her arm across it and knock it all to the floor, to erase the evidence, but she knew that would only upset her more.

Finally, Clint let out a soft sigh and released her. Was he going to walk out? Had he had enough of her? A part of her felt relieved at the prospect of being proven right, of knowing that no matter what these men said, they were as flaky as all the rest.

Except, it seemed she'd misread him.

Clint kicked his shoes off by the door, then went over and got into the bed on the other side of her. The bed shifted beneath his weight as he settled himself in.

"What are you doing?" It was funny that Ell kept asking things that were obvious, but she couldn't help it.

"You need sleep, but you're not going to manage it if you keep panicking. I thought company might help."

"Why would that help?"

"Because you'll know that nothing can get you, not while I'm right here. Now, close your eyes." He pulled his phone out of his pocket, and it took Ell a moment to figure out what he was doing.

He didn't strike her as a social media sort of man, who would spend his time scrolling through the newsfeeds. Sure enough, he opened an eBook reader app and the screen was filled with words.

"What are you reading?" Ell asked as she turned toward him, the desire to know something about him. Even though they were…something, she didn't know all that much about his life.

"A mystery story."

"Don't you get enough of that at work?"

"I like books because they always solve the crime at the end. I like the way everything gets wrapped up. Real life isn't like that." He turned toward her, then glanced at the pillow meaningfully.

Ell took the hint and lay down, but she couldn't seem to get comfortable. When she rolled over yet again, he asked, "What is it?"

"I can't sleep," she admitted. She steeled her nerves before speaking again, before asking for something she wanted. "Could you read out loud?"

"Won't that keep you up longer?"

"I like the sound of your voice, and when I hear it, I know you're here." She kept her voice so low, she was surprised he could hear her, yet that was the only way she could even get the words out. When had been the last time she'd asked anyone for something? She was so used to no one helping, to being ignored, that she'd learned to stop asking.

Yet there she was, begging Clint to read out loud. It made her stomach sick, made her swallow down an immediate apology for her stupidity.

Clint looked down at her as if surprised by the request. However, he only nodded and settled his back against the headboard, then reached the hand not holding the phone over to stroke through her hair. The touch was soft and eased her, like some reminder that he was there, that he wasn't going anywhere.

And he was right…him being there let her close her eyes. The shadows didn't seem so scary, not compared to Clint.

"The sky was dark, but enough light poured in through the window for Maverick to notice how the books on the shelf were placed in an odd fashion — someone was trying to send him a message."

The tension drifted from Ell's body as she listened to Clint read, as his steady voice lulled her to sleep. She could go back to being strong tomorrow.

For tonight, she'd take what Clint offered, and in the morning, she'd have the strength to resist them.

Maybe…

* * * *

The clicking of the scooter made Fox grin about a minute before a knock on his door told him Ell had come by.

He'd stopped over first thing in the morning and brought the knee scooter for her to use around the apartment. It let her rest her knee on the padded area and would give her more mobility.

Ethan had scoffed at the thing and asked why he'd gotten it. Then again, Ethan would have preferred Ell entirely helpless. At least then she had to rely on them.

But Fox understood better than Ethan ever would how much getting back some independence would help Ell recover. The feeling of helplessness would only increase the panic that seemed a part of her, that had gotten worse after the attack.

Fox went to the door and opened it, unable to resist a smile at the woman who glared at him. Had she come all the way across the hallway to yell at him?

And why did that excite him?

"Good afternoon," Fox said, pretending as if she wasn't staring daggers at him.

"Don't you good morning me."

He moved back to make room for her, and she rolled into his apartment as if she were already comfortable on the scooter. No doubt she'd been rolling about her own place all morning, doing all the tasks they'd forbade her from before.

She needed to remain lying down more, so her ankle could be elevated, but he'd bet the little bit of time upright was doing wonders for her mental health.

Which was proven by her being there and able to yell at him.

"Aren't you in a mood today?"

Ell used the breaks then twisted to narrow her eyes at him. "My boss called me today and said I was off work for a week."

"Good. A week is the bare minimum amount of time you should remain off work *and* off your feet."

"It wasn't any of your business to contact him!"

Ah, that's her problem... Fox shook his head. "I didn't call him."

"Really? So how did he find out?"

"The police station works closely with the Department of Social Services. I doubt your attack would have been a secret."

"So you're telling me you didn't call him to tell him?"

"I didn't."

"What about Ethan or Clint?"

"They didn't tell me they were going to call him. Ethan wouldn't do that. Clint might, but if you ask him, he'll tell you whether or not he did. My guess is that your boss heard about the attack and, in turn, your injuries. In fact, *you* should have called to tell him yourself and to take off the time needed."

Ell straightened her back as if the subtle rebuke surprised her. As quickly as it happened, though, she doubled down. "I have kids who need me. I can't just ignore that because my ankle is a little sore."

Fox sighed softly before going to the kitchen. He took a tamale from the fridge, wrapped it in a damp paper towel, then put it in the microwave before turning back toward her. "Sprained ankles don't seem like much, but they take time to heal. If you don't give it that time, you can seriously harm yourself. You can even require surgery or prevent it from *ever* healing correctly. The reality is that there are other social workers who can take over temporarily, until you can return, and that is a far better outcome than pushing yourself so you end up needing a cane indefinitely."

She opened her mouth but snapped it shut. She tended to do that often, he'd noticed, as if she were ready to fight only to realize she had nothing to actually say back. It should not have been as adorable as it was.

Finally, she shifted so she could sit on the padded area of the scooter. "I don't know what to do with myself if I'm not working."

The microwave dinged, so Fox removed the plate and uncovered the tamale. He added a container of guacamole, then placed it on the dining room table and gestured for Ell to come over.

She did as he wanted, sliding over the chair. Once she did, Fox moved the scooter, then lifted her bad ankle so it rested on the padded area. It wasn't elevated enough, but it was better than nothing.

"You will be back to work before you know it."

She shook her head. "You don't understand. I have this energy inside me. It feels like it's bouncing off my insides and I can't get rid of it. I keep trying to busy myself, but nothing works."

"Is this just since the attack?" Fox sat at the table across from her, giving her space as she picked up the fork and started to eat in small bites.

"Yes. Well, no, I guess not, but it's worse since then."

"That makes sense. Issues we have get worse after stressful events."

"I don't have *issues*. I just have a low tolerance for sitting still."

Fox tilted his head as he watched her eat. She used the side of the fork to cut the tamale into uniformed pieces, careful to ensure they were all the same size, then separated them until they lined up on her plate.

He hadn't gotten much time to really observe her, but suddenly some of the things he'd noticed before came back to him. In her place, as he'd packed her bag, he'd found her house organized to an extreme degree.

The items in her bathroom had been lined on the counter, divided by size, shape and color. Her kitchen counters had been similarly set up, all with things in their place, nothing messy.

He might not have thought about it before, but watching her eat, hearing her talk, he recognized just how deep her anxiety went. "Have you seen a therapist?"

She froze, her fork halfway to her mouth. After a heartbeat, she took the bite — probably out of stubbornness rather than desire. Once she swallowed, she answered him. "In the past, I have. Why?"

"You know why."

She frowned, as if she didn't care for the answer. Then again, no doubt she wanted to fight with him, to argue, to turn his words into an insult. It was better to not give her anything to slam her head against. "I saw a therapist when I turned eighteen for about a year."

"Did you find it helpful?"

"Not especially."

"Why was that?"

She shifted the food on her plate so the lines were even as she spoke. "She was nice, but she was a big 'tell me about your childhood' sort of person. I didn't feel digging up the past was useful. After a year, I decided it wasn't doing me any good, so I stopped going."

Fox struggled to not take over, to not lecture her. They were in a strange place, an uncertain one.

If Ell were his, he'd set her up for an appointment immediately and drive her ass there to ensure she went. He'd make damn sure she ate, that she slept enough, that she was safe.

But she *wasn't* his. She was staying near them, and she'd somehow become important, but he wasn't able to treat her the way he really wanted to.

Jayce Carter

Ell finished eating her food in silence, giving Fox the chance to observe her, to think. He couldn't kick the idea that he wanted more, couldn't stop the desire each time he looked at her. It was worse after knowing how sweetly she moaned, how wonderfully she responded to each touch, to each demand of her.

When Ell had cleared her plate, Fox took it into the kitchen, rinsed it, then placed it into the dishwasher. Her having eaten made him feel at least slightly better.

Still, when he turned back around, Ell hadn't moved. She kept her gaze on the table, her expression screaming of unhappiness.

He got the sense it was deeper than the attack, or perhaps it was better to say it wasn't *just* that.

"Look at me," Fox said, his tone giving no room for her to refuse.

She did so, looking miserable.

"Better." Fox pulled a chair over so he was at eye level with her. "What do you need?"

She drew her eyebrows toward each other as if she'd never thought about it before. After a long, quiet moment, she answered. "I don't know. I just can't relax."

"And what do you want me to do about that?"

She shifted but kept her foot on the scooter.

Fox leaned until she met his gaze. "I want to help. We all do. I need you to tell me what you need, though."

"I felt better that night…" Her words drifted off, but the night in question was obvious.

And Fox couldn't help the hope that sprang up in him at her saying that. Did she mean…? Still, he one waited, wanting her to come out and say it more clearly.

153

Ell let out an unhappy sound. "I don't know what I need, okay? I always know my plan, I always know what I'm supposed to do, but I don't know right now. I feel like I've just been getting more and more tense, like each month that passes, I'm wound tighter, like I'm more stressed and less happy, and I don't know how to fix that. The only thing I'm sure about is that when I was with you—all three of you—at Sanctuary, I didn't feel like *this*."

Fox kept the smile off his face. "So you're saying you want to try that again? That you want to go back there with us again?"

She dragged her tongue along her bottom lip, telling Fox what she planned to say next wasn't easy for her. "I want to try *more*. You told me that you prefer twenty-four-seven."

"Are you sure about that?"

At least she didn't respond right away. Her shoulders drooped when she answered. "I honestly don't know. When I think about trusting anyone, my brain tells me not to, but what I'm doing isn't working. I guess I didn't realize how little it was working anymore until I was attacked, until I had to come face to face with how little I can handle my own feelings." She set her arms on the table and stared at her hands. "If you don't want to, if I'm not your type, that's okay. You just have to tell me, and I won't be upset. I know I'm asking a lot—"

"Do you really think I wouldn't say yes? Come on, Ell, I've thought about you for a long time, well before we saw you at Sanctuary. If you want to do this, we'll do it."

"Don't you need to ask Clint and Ethan?"

Fox curled his lip into a smile. "I can guarantee they'll jump at the chance. Why don't you roll yourself back over to your place, and we will come over tonight for dinner to discuss the details?"

Ell nodded but refused to look at him. Did she think that gave her some privacy? Some security?

She got to her feet and rested her weight on the scooter. "Okay. I'll make something for dinner."

"You will not. You will go back home, plant yourself on the couch, elevate and ice your ankle until we get there."

"You can't really think I'm going to just wait around and let you all cook food when I'm home all day."

Fox moved closer until his lips were a breath from hers. "That is exactly what I think, but if you want to test it, if you want to ignore me, well, I wouldn't mind introducing you to what punishments are like." He brushed his lips to hers, taking a gentle kiss meant to tease her, to excite her, then whispered softly, "Your ankle may be hurt, but I have no problem adding a sore ass to your list of problems."

In fact…he sort of hoped she did disobey him, because he wouldn't mind an excuse to show her exactly how he handled disobedience.

* * * *

Ethan felt *far* too giddy. He was a full-grown adult man—a cop who had faced down dangerous criminals and risked his life for innocents. He was *not* supposed to be the sort of person who felt like skipping, but that didn't change how he felt.

Fox had messaged him and Clint, filling them in on the conversation with Ell. It was so much more than

Ethan thought the woman would ever want to try. Despite the fact he worried if it was real, if it would last, he had no intention of turning her down.

He'd had too many dreams already that involved Ell for him to risk losing it for anything. Even if it didn't last long, even if she decided two weeks in that she wasn't interested, at least he'd have her for that short time.

He could deal with heartbreak later — that was a problem for future him.

Still, he struggled to keep his excitement in check, to look calm and collected. Then again, he'd never been a calm person. Sometimes people expected Doms to be silent and brooding and moody. Ethan, on the other hand, didn't fit into any of those molds. Eventually, over the years, he'd come to accept himself.

At least, for the most part.

A part of him wished Clint and Fox were with him. It felt strange to be alone, to not have that backup, but he'd understood the reasoning.

Ell was flighty, nervous, unsure of herself or them. She'd react better if she were only dealing with one of them. Besides, they all had their points of expertise. Fox was good at organizing a person's life, at general care. Clint was great at protocol, at making clear expectations.

Ethan?

He was the one that was easier to talk to, the less scary of the three.

While it made sense, though, Ethan couldn't deny that he found it an odd feeling.

His knuckles struck the door, and Ell opened it fast enough he suspected she'd been waiting near it already.

The idea made him smile.

Ell peered around him, as if confused.

"Just me," he said, hooking his thumbs into the belt loops of his jeans.

Was she disappointed? It was hard to tell… Ell had put her ice queen face on, the one he'd grown used to seeing when she was working.

It meant she had her defenses up.

Fine by me.

Ell moved away and gestured for him to enter. It made Ethan glance around while he realized it had been a long time since he'd been to the apartment. They never rented it out because they preferred privacy, so usually they kept it for guests who came to visit them.

Though, Ell being there was a far better use of the space.

"I thought you'd all come," Ell finally said.

"Figured you'd be more comfortable if you only had to deal with me."

Her expression said she wasn't.

Not that it bothered Ethan. In fact, it charmed him. "You don't like me that much? That's funny, because normally I'm seen as the least intimidating."

Ell met his gaze for only a moment before darting it away. "I can't ever tell if you're serious or not, if you're just teasing me. You're charming enough that it sometimes feels like you just say whatever you need to say to get what you want."

Okay, so that *did* sting a bit, especially as she got it righter than he would have preferred. A good joke tended to defuse situations and make them easier to manipulate, to get out of.

He didn't care for the way she said it, though, for the unspoken part — *I don't trust you.*

"Well, don't worry so much. I'm much less fussy than Clint or Fox, so you're less likely to end up in trouble with me."

"In trouble?"

Ethan paused, then grinned at her. "You don't like that idea? Or do you like it and that's what you don't like?"

She shook her head as she scooted back, the tires clicking as they moved over the grout lines of the tile. "I'm not a child—I don't need punishments. When you say things like that, I wonder what the hell I'm thinking."

Ethan pointed at the couch, his meaning clear. Once she sat, he placed the takeout container of food in her lap. "Punishments are a part of life. All they are are consequences to actions to help a person make better choices. It's no different than when I overindulge in sweets and end up having to put in extra time at the gym, or the hangover I get when I drink too much."

"Those things are natural consequences. They aren't controlled by someone else. It sounds pretty abusive, honestly…"

Ethan dropped himself onto the couch beside Ell, having eaten his food in the car on his way home so he could focus on the talk and not his dinner. "Parents punish their children because they love them, because they want them to be safe, to have the best life possible. The fact they have to punish them doesn't mean they don't care. It doesn't make them abusive. In fact, it's *easier* not to punish people, to let things go, but easier isn't always better. When your parents punished you, did they love you any less?"

That flat expression returned to Ell's face, telling Ethan he had just said the exact wrong thing. It seemed she had some issues with her parents that would need to be uncovered in the future.

He again reminded himself to have patience, to go slowly. There was no reason to risk scaring her off now by picking at old wounds.

"I'm not a child," she repeated softly instead of answering his question.

"No, you're not."

"So explain it to me? I don't understand the reasoning why this whole power exchange thing is a good idea."

That made Ethan's smile widen. She'd asked *them* for help, to show her, so clearly she had some idea of what a person could get out of such an arrangement. If she needed him to spell it out, though, that was fine by him.

"Kids get to relax, right? They know that everything is taken care of, that they're safe, that they aren't alone. That's something that gets lost as we grow up, that sense of belonging. In a situation like ours—meaning Clint, Fox and I with our past experiences—we like to let a woman have that feeling again. The women who want that, who crave it, they're happier with those rules, with that feeling of being cherished and protected."

"And what do you get out of it?"

"I like taking care of someone. I like having someone look at me like I'm their whole world, like it when they trust me, when they rely on me. When a submissive looks up at me with this sated, relaxed smile, it just melts me. The world is a hard, dangerous place. I know that better than most. I *need* this kind of dynamic so I know the person I love is safe, that she's taken care of, that the world isn't going to crush her because I won't let it." Ethan's words quieted as he went, as he said more than he thought he'd every told a woman before.

It wasn't that he lied before, but rather that none had ever asked him exactly *why* he craved this. He'd never had to think about it. Most women who came to Sanctuary knew what it was all about, so they didn't ask him such things.

"Besides," he added on, "since you asked Fox for this, since you came back to Sanctuary, since you enjoyed our night there, I have a feeling you understand a bit about the appeal."

"I enjoyed what we did there, and it made me feel…peaceful. I just don't understand why, and I don't understand this whole *baby girl* thing."

Ah, that. Ethan tapped his finger on her food to focus her. "People do get caught on that. Go on, say what you want to."

She pressed her lips together tightly.

"I mean it." Ethan used a serious edge to his tone. "You won't get in trouble for anything you say. Be as mean and blunt as you want. I've been partners with Clint for about all my adult life, and if he hasn't offended me yet, you won't. You need to get it out to deal with it, though."

Ell took another few bites of food, moving slowly as if still thinking. Finally, though, she set her fork down. "It's weird, like some psycho-babble thing, where women want to sleep with their fathers. And it's even creepier because the inverse of that is you wanting to sleep with your *daughter*. Do you not see how twisted that is?"

Maybe if Ethan were new to the lifestyle, that would have bothered him, but he only shrugged, the words ones he'd heard enough times before. "If a couple dresses up and plays doctor, does the woman *actually* want to sleep with her doctor?" He let himself cast Ell a mischievous smirk. "Well, I mean, *you* do, but normally? Just because someone is into pet play, because they want their partner to dress up in cat ears and a tail, does that mean they actually want to fuck their pet? So why do you think that a Daddy kink means the people want to make that real when you accept all those other kinks as a fantasy that is removed from reality? The appeal is in the dynamic, in the trust."

Ell scrunched her face up, as if considering the words, as if trying to figure out if they made any sense at all.

Ethan held his breath. Just because she was interested didn't mean it would last, didn't mean she wouldn't turn tail and run at any time if she decided things were too weird for her.

"I guess that makes sense," she whispered before shutting her food container.

She hadn't eaten enough, really. Fox would have scolded her for it, but Ethan tended to let such things go, to be more understanding. A tense conversation and nerves could ruin an appetite.

"So what would this look like, then?"

"We figure that out as we go."

"But I thought you all were in charge?"

"In a way. We call the shots, but you set your limits. Your needs are important, so we might discover that certain things don't work for you, or that others don't work for us." When she didn't look relieved by that, Ethan pressed. "You don't like that. Why?"

"I get anxious when I don't know what is expected of me."

"You do have trust issues, don't you?" Ethan didn't need her to admit it, so he kept going. "Okay, I understand. First, your safe word still applies, even outside the club. If you ever use it, we stop — it doesn't matter where we are or what we're doing. As far as expectations, I can give you some generals. Rules are pretty simple — be respectful and do not disobey any clear directions. If you don't understand them or have an issue with them, speak up. You won't ever get in trouble for that if you're respectful when you do it."

That one seemed to ease her a bit. So, she was afraid of getting in trouble without understanding why? It made him wonder about her parents, about her past. Clearly, whatever she had gone through still wore on her.

He continued. "For general safety issues, you will keep your phone on you and let us know when and where you go. Do not just get up and leave without telling anyone."

"So you'll let me go places?"

"You're not a prisoner, Ell. You have a week off for your ankle — though how you're doing will determine whether or not you're ready to go back then — but after that, you'll return to your job. We don't expect you to give up your life, to get locked up in this apartment."

"Those women said you wanted twenty-four-seven."

"And you thought that meant some sort of sex slave?" Ethan chuckled, then laughed harder when she glared at him. "Twenty-four-seven means we like to exert control during the daytime hours as well. That might mean Fox sits down with you in the morning to review your to-do list and habits, then later in the evening you two go over how you did. It might mean that you wear the clothing I pick out for you, or it might mean Clint has you kneel by the table some nights as he hand-feeds you. Basically, it means we stay in our roles all the time rather than just during designated scenes, but the amount of control we exert is negotiated. I may want to see you in heels, but if you tell me that your ankles can't handle them, then we work out that rule until it fits both of us."

Ell didn't respond right away, which was probably a good sign. When a person answered too quickly, it signaled that they hadn't really considered it, hadn't thought it through. Then again, Ell was nothing if not careful.

"Okay," she said as if that finished things.

"Okay what?"

"Okay, I understand and agree."

"Do you have anything you want to say upfront? Any rules, limitations or concerns? It won't be the last chance you have—you can always speak up if something bothers you that you didn't expect."

"I won't call you Daddy in public. I have a reputation and career to think of."

"Fair enough. I wouldn't want you coming into the station and asking me for a spanking in front of my coworkers either."

Her cheeks turned red. "I wouldn't," she rushed out.

Ethan offered a wink but moved on. "However, I don't consider Sanctuary public. I'd like to be able to indulge there without concern."

She shifted, but after a long moment, nodded.

"Good girl," Ethan praised her, rewarded when a small smile crept across her pink lips.

Fuck, he liked that. It made him want to praise her more, to worship her body as he lavished affection to each inch of her.

She'd walk that line between uncomfortable and happy, and he *loved* that line.

"So what now?" she asked softly.

"I want you to strip."

That seemed to take her by surprise. "W-what?"

"I've seen you naked already—I doubt there's anything new. Come on, strip off all of it. You should get used to being naked because Clint tends to prefer submissives be naked around the house. It's the advantage of owning the entire floor—you can walk between any of our places without a stitch on." He dropped his gaze to her foot. "Or, I guess, you could roll between our places."

Ell just stared at him, but Ethan didn't push. He waited, the tension thick, the question obvious. Would she obey? Did she really want to do this? It was easy to make a choice, to think a person was interested, but when it came right down to it, would she back out?

She brought her trembling hands to her shirt and undid each button. Ethan didn't rush her, didn't say anything as he watched her.

Item after item was removed, revealing her soft, flawless skin. She was stunning, and the more she showed him, the more he fell for her. It took a long while before she managed to remove each item, leaving her there, her arm crossed over her chest to hide her breasts and a wrap still on her ankle.

Ethan gave her a gentle smile. "You're beautiful, baby girl. You shouldn't be so self-conscious. Now, I'm going to take off the wrap."

"Why? Do you have a kink for ankles?"

"A piece of advice? While I find your bratty comments charming, Clint and Fox wouldn't. Was that something respectful to say?" He undid the metal clasp of her bandage, then rolled it as he carefully removed it from her foot and ankle.

"I'm sorry," Ell said in response.

"Like I said, I like your snark, but I also have a feel I'll like seeing your ass turn red when you mouth off to Clint, so it's a win-win for me." Once he'd removed the bandage, Ethan held his hand out.

Ell took it, then let out a soft gasp when he pulled her to her good foot, then lifted her with ease. She really did fit nicely against his chest, didn't she? Especially when naked.

There was something about a naked woman that excited him. It wasn't just the sight—sure, they were stunning to look at—but it was the innocence, the trust of the action. He loved when a woman had nothing to hide, when she couldn't keep anything secret from him.

So Ell's warm, bare skin was about the best thing he'd ever felt.

Her hands were drawn into fists, her body strung tight. "I don't know why you all like to carry me," she muttered, her voice low.

"Because it keeps you under control. Besides, I don't like to see you hurting, and I'm sure you're putting more weight on your foot than you're supposed to. So quiet down and let me enjoy it."

She huffed, the same sound a dog made when told to lie down when they didn't want to. It was an adorable little rebellion that made Ethan press a kiss to her head. He took her to the master bath, then set her on the edge of the tub.

She remained silent as he worked, as he put the stopper in the tub then turned the water to hot. He added bubble bath that was beneath the sink, then dimmed the lights. Ell said nothing, at least until he reached for the hem of his shirt and removed it.

"What are you doing?" The panic in her tone only made Ethan laugh.

"Nude ice skating."

She furrowed her eyebrows, so it seemed the joke didn't land, at least at first. After a moment, though, she narrowed her eyes.

"What do you think I'm doing?" Ethan added in a mocking tone.

"We are not taking a bath together."

"I had my dick inside you, Ell. I don't think sitting in some warm water together is really any more personal than that."

And the way her cheeks turned bright red was a thing of beauty. The fact she could embarrass so easily made Ethan want to press that, to see just how excited a bit of humiliation got her. It was always a hard line to draw, to figure out the point at while a girl enjoyed it versus when it actually upset them.

He wanted to find that line with Ell, wanted to see the way shame and pleasure mixed into a potent combination.

When she said nothing else, Ethan kicked his shoes off and removed the rest of his clothing. Undoing the zipper of his jeans felt like a miracle, the uncomfortable pressure on his hard cock disappearing.

He'd been hard since before he'd walked into her apartment, since he'd started thinking about her wanting him, since he considered how much he wanted her.

Her gaze locked on his shaft, something between nerves and desire there.

Ethan wrapped his hand around his cock and stroked himself, giving her a show. "I like your eyes on me."

She licked her lips, the mindless action drawing a deep groan from him.

"You haven't gotten much of a chance to just play, have you?"

"Play?" She frowned, then shook her head. "I'm not some virgin."

"Never said you were, but sex is often quick, especially when vanilla. If you'd had partners who let you look, who let you tease and play, you wouldn't look at me like *that*." He approached her until he stood right in front of her, tall enough that in her position, she was impossibly close to his cock. "Stay still," he ordered her.

Ell froze, but her breathing quickened. The red from her cheeks spread until her chest was pink as well, and even her arm dropped from her breasts as if she'd forgotten about modesty entirely.

He didn't grab her hair, didn't force her to be still. Instead, he enjoyed the way she listened, the way she obeyed him on her own. He leaned in and traced her full lips with his cock, leaving pre-cum like a gloss.

She darted her tongue out to taste him, and as much as he enjoyed the sensation, he tapped her chin with his other hand. "I said be still. You haven't earned treats yet, baby girl."

Her eyes were full of lust when she looked up at him, and he was nearly pulled into them. It was so tempting to tell her to do as she pleased, to give in. He could feel her warm mouth around his cock, and she would get what she seemed to want as well.

Ethan reminded himself of his plan. Sometimes a person had to give up what they wanted in exchange for what would come later that was better.

So he traced her lips again, and this time, Ell remained still, her gaze locked on his, letting him drown in the hazel, in the need there. Finally, he tapped his cock against her cheek, then grinned down at her to lighten the mood.

"In." He nodded at the water.

Ell moved as if dazed, having hit the point she was reacting more on instinct. That was exactly where he wanted her, though. After they got into the water, the bubbles of the deep tub reaching up to cover her breasts even when she sat upright, she glanced around as if unsure what to do.

"Face that way," Ethan said, then got into the tub behind her. They'd put large soaker tubs into all the apartments on the top floor, so there was plenty of room for both of them.

Well, not *too* much room. He didn't want it to be a hot tub where she could sit far away.

Ethan reached for a cup that sat on the edge of the tub. "Tip your head back."

It took a long moment for Ell to obey, but it was less time than it had been before. She seemed to be learning. He poured the cup of water careful through her long dark-brown hair, then a second.

When he reached for the shampoo, Ell's voice broke into the action. "Are you seriously washing my hair?"

"Yes," he said as he poured shampoo into his hands, then worked it through her hair.

"Why?"

"Because I enjoy it?"

"I can do it myself."

"Again, just because you *can* do something yourself doesn't mean you have to. You can get yourself off, but that doesn't mean I don't want to do it for you."

She shifted, and he got the sense it was less embarrassment that time and more excitement. In fact, she even let out the softest, sweetest moan when he worked the shampoo against her scalp. The girl might struggle with being pampered, but that didn't mean she didn't like it.

When he finished the job and rinsed her hair, he used a large clip he'd also set on the bathtub edge to secure her hair up, to keep it out of the way, then pulled her back so she rested against his chest.

Each moment that passed, she relaxed more fully against him. Even with his cock aching and pressed between them, even though she was naked and could feel it, the tension eased from her body.

At least, it did until he stroked his fingers along the top of her breast. "I didn't get enough chance to really see these," he whispered before cupping one. He teased the soft, wet skin, then thumbed the nipple. "I think one of these times at the club, I'll need to dress you in a corset with an open chest, so everyone can enjoy the sight of these."

She shook her head.

"No?" Ethan used his nail to scrape over her pebbled nipple. "You don't like that idea? Why not?"

"I'm not that sort of girl."

"What sort?"

She didn't answer at first, so Ethan closed his fingers around her nipple in a light punishment for her trying to keep anything from him.

She hissed softly, then shivered. "I'm not pretty like that. No one wants to see me like that."

That made him pause. Asking her if she was actually an idiot would probably not go well, so he pressed his lips to her neck instead. "Trust me, you're wrong about that. If I stripped you down and put you on that St. Andrew's cross out in front of everyone, I can guarantee we'd have quite the crowd."

She shook her head, as if she couldn't agree with him but didn't want to get in trouble for arguing either.

Which made him smile as he moved his other hand down her front. She snapped her legs closed when he reached her lower stomach, like some defense mechanism she couldn't help.

"Spread your legs for Daddy," he whispered. "I want to feel your sweet pussy."

That shiver she'd had earlier spread, but she obeyed. She parted her thighs for him slowly, and Ethan took advantage by stroking up the length of her slit.

"I think I'll blindfold you," he said as he teased her pussy with gentle strokes, so much softer than she wanted them, he was sure. "You won't know who is looking at you, but you'll know they're there. See, I want to show you off, make sure everyone knows what a lovely, slutty little girl I have. You're worth showing off, especially when you're flushed and excited and embarrassed."

She whimpered, and when she squirmed, it teased Ethan's cock.

Still, he kept speaking, as taken by his words as he hoped Ell was. He could imagine it more clearly, could picture her exactly as he said, her arms bound to the cross, her legs spread.

"I'd let you keep on the corset, but I'd be able to play with your pretty tits while everyone watched. Do you think I'd let them see your cunt, too?"

She shook her head, but that felt like a lie, as if she knew damn well he would.

"Then you have a lot to learn about me. I enjoy people seeing what I have. I like to show off my things. I don't let others touch, but there isn't a hole on your little body I wouldn't display. Hell, not even just when you're excited. Maybe I'll tie you up, fuck your ass, then leave you there with my cum leaking out of you? Can you imagine the breeze, the way everyone would know how filthy you are? Don't worry, I wouldn't go far. I'd make sure you were safe, but I'd love to watch everyone staring at your little asshole while it clenched, so empty and well-used."

She cried out, and that was Ethan's signal. He focused his attention to her clit, rubbed at the erect nub. She shook against him, moving and shifted as if she wanted more.

She did want more, but this was all she'd have for tonight. For tonight, he wanted to make her come, to get her out of her own head, to show her that this sort of thing didn't have to be so bad.

And the sounds she made said she didn't find it bad at all.

Ell wasn't a quiet woman, not one afraid of making noise and letting him know what she liked. Or perhaps it was more accurate to say she couldn't seem to help making the sounds.

Ethan rocked his hips, letting himself grind against her for the friction he needed. "I love using you to get off," he admitted. "I want to use every fucking place on your body, to own it all, to cover it all in my cum to claim it. Will you be a good girl and let me do it?"

She nodded, the gesture telling him she'd broken, that she'd passed that point where her brain was telling her she shouldn't want things or that things weren't smart. Instead, she operated on instinct, on desire and need.

He nipped her shoulder as he rubbed harder at her clit, his own end close. "When you come, I want to *hear* you say it."

"Say what?"

"You know what."

Even in her state, she knew exactly what he wanted from her, what he needed to hear, what she needed to say.

"If you don't," he warned, "I'll consider that disobedience, and I have more than enough toys to make you wish you'd just given in."

"You'd hurt me?" A tremor to her voice broke his heart.

Ethan kept his mind in the game, though. "I'd never hurt you, baby girl, but your pussy would be sore, overworked and exhausted by the time I finished having my fun. I wouldn't hurt you, but that doesn't mean you'd enjoy it nearly as much as I would. So it's your choice. Say what I want to hear, or I'll find my fun another way."

She made a soft sound of frustration, as if caught between two options when neither sounded good.

Ethan gave her no chance to think her way out of it, though. Instead, he ground against her clit, knowing it was probably too much but not caring, especially as he thrust against the tight space between them.

Ell arched her back sharply, and when she parted her lips, her voice came out broken and mindless in need. "Please, Daddy," she begged.

The moment she said Daddy, she came. It was as if that word broke the leash she had on her own body.

Her knees snapped shut around his hand and she went wild. That made it all the better for him, though. He used his strength and his arms around her to restrain her, to hold her against him as he fucked between their bodies. Sure, he'd have loved to be inside her, to have taken any part of her, but he couldn't complain as he fell over that edge right after her.

When they both calmed, when the bathroom was filled with their panting, when the hot water of the bath soaked into them, Ethan took a deep breath and settled in.

He wasn't sure he'd ever felt as fulfilled as he did right then, with Ell's soft and sated body against his.

He'd never really thought this sort of thing was possible.

Chapter Eleven

Ell sat on her balcony, amazed by just how good the view really was. It wasn't *just* the view, either, but the way the place felt private. She didn't feel like she was on display, like everyone was looking at her.

Instead, the space, which had a swing on it, overlooked a nice outdoor area that all the apartment building shared. There was even a garden in the corner, and the green plants inside said it was well cared for, since the heat of the desert could quickly wither anything left unattended.

A tall, corrugated steel fence surrounded the large back yard, making it feel even more secluded. In fact, Ell thought she might go down later and actually take a look at the garden. It had been a long time since she'd lived anywhere that she could plant things beyond a pot or two.

She glanced behind her, through the large sliding glass door, and spotted the paper on the table. The words were written by Fox, and she had to admit, he wrote the way most people expected doctors to write. Even still, she knew every item listed.

It had felt strange when he'd come by before leaving for work, when he'd brought the notebook and pen, then sat down with her. She'd expected an arrangement like theirs to have her with expectations like cleaning their apartments or owing them one blow job a day.

Which was why it startled her when instead the list had things such as drinking water, eating three healthy meals, icing her ankle every two hours and using a stopwatch Fox had brought to time how long she was upright between resting, along with the upper limit of no more than an hour at a time.

In addition, he'd brought her an eBook reader preloaded with books and access to more if she found nothing that was interesting.

She'd stared at the rules, unable to formulate an exact response to explain how she felt. He'd only offered her a smile that said he understood before telling her that he expected her to write it down in the journal he'd brought and review her feelings later that night when they went over the list.

The fact that he'd taken over so much of her day chafed. Ell had planned her time for as long as she could remember. She'd been on her own and in charge of herself, so having anyone looking over her shoulder made her uneasy.

Yet…there was a security in it also. She spent so long trying to make her life fit a certain mold, so much energy wondering if she was doing things right, that it was oddly soothing to have a list she didn't have to question. So long as she completed that, she'd done well.

The only point they'd argued on had been a location tracker on her phone. Fox had explained that given the jobs of all three men, they tended to be paranoid. Knowing where she was would help alleviate that from them.

However…Ell just couldn't seem to get past that one. It felt like a tether she wasn't sure she could tolerate. Fox had understood, though he hadn't looked happy about it, and said they'd address it again later.

A knock on her door made her frown, but she refused to let it make her fearful. She reminded herself no one knew where she was, that she was safe here, that it *could* be the same men who had broken into her place.

Even still, a part of her wanted to call Ethan or Clint. She wanted to do something that made her feel more at ease with opening the door, a way of telling herself she wasn't alone.

Her phone rang, which *did* make her jump. Ell only cursed at herself for the reaction before answering the call.

"Take a breath for me, baby girl." Ethan's voice relaxed her, something that annoyed her. Why was it that just that one line, offered so quickly, got her to comply? Why did it make her feel better?

Still, Ell did as he said, her fingers wrapped tightly around the phone. It made her realize just how rapidly her heart was pounding, how lightheaded she felt. She'd known she was anxious about the knock, but she hadn't realized she was nearly *that* upset.

After a long moment, Ell's chest eased. "How did you know?"

She could see Ethan's smile even when he wasn't there, knew the way his lips would curl into a smirk. "We have cameras in the elevator and the hallway. Don't worry, only we have access to them, but they trigger when there's movement in the hallway."

"So you have cameras in my apartment?" She turned, peering at the corners, searching for them. How could they have been watching her in her space without telling her?

"Of course we don't." Did Ethan sound offended at the question? "We wouldn't put them inside your apartment, not without making that clear ahead of time."

"Why didn't you mention the ones in the hallway?"

"Because they're standard practice, no different than cameras on the outside of a house. The hallways are the space between our living quarters, so if someone broke in, if someone attacked any of our places, those cameras would show." He paused, then spoke with a soft voice. "I'm sorry if that bothers you or you felt we were being dishonest. I just didn't think about it."

Now that Ell's heart had started to slow, now that she was able to think straight, she realized that perhaps she'd been overreacting. "Sorry," she offered. "I guess I'm more anxious than I realized."

"It's fine." The funny thing was…it seemed to be. Ell had grown used to people being dishonest, to them telling her what they wanted her to think rather than the truth. Ethan sounded as if he wasn't bothered by her accusations, as if he really took her apology and let it go. "Tonight I'll get it set up so you can see the doorway without opening the door. Then you can access the cameras whenever you need. For now, though, it's only Donnie by the door."

"How does he know where I am?"

"He was at the station, and I could tell he was worried about you. Poor kid couldn't concentrate on his work, so I gave him the address and sent him to check on you."

"He shouldn't see me like this. He'll just worry."

"He's already worried. I think knowing you'll be okay with help."

Ell sighed but nodded. She'd bet her reaction, her desire to send him away, had more to do with her not wanting to be seen as injured then it did about not wanting *him* to see her injured.

"I'll let you have your visit. Call me if you need anything." Before Ell could hang up, Ethan tacked on, "And stay off your feet."

She offered the phone a glare before ending the call.

He *had* helped, though. Ell felt better, and the ability to fix her attitude before answering the door made her feel more in control. She didn't want Donnie to see her upset, to see her as a frightened person. She wanted him to see her as someone he could trust, someone who would take care of him.

When she opened the door, Donnie didn't look her in the eye, instead staring at his own feet. While she might have told him not to come if she'd been given the option, actually seeing him made her realize she would have been wrong.

"Ethan gave me the address," Donnie said. "Sorry I didn't call — he said I shouldn't."

Of course he did, the meddler...

"It's fine." Ell moved back so he could enter.

He peered around the space, his eyebrows drawn together. "This is really nice..."

"Yeah, it is." Ell used her scooter to go back, then went toward the kitchen. "Water?"

"You sit, please. I'll get the water."

Ell paused and turned back toward him. Donnie was sweet, but he normally didn't offer to help much. "Are you okay?"

He nodded, gesturing for the couch before he moved past her and into the kitchen. He opened the door to the fridge, and when he came out again, he held two water bottles in his arms. After handing one to Ell, he took a seat in the chair that sat perpendicular to the couch where she sat.

Still, he refused to look directly at her. His gaze darted everywhere else, though it didn't seem like he was gathering much information. Instead, Ell would guess it was just an attempt to not look at her.

But why?

"I really am okay," Ell said.

Donnie nodded. "Yeah, Ethan said that."

"I'm safe here."

"Yeah, with those cameras, especially."

Ell frowned. It wasn't concern for her wellbeing, or worry that she'd be targeted again. So what was it?

Donnie tightened his cheeks, lines etched between his eyebrows.

So that's it?

"It's not your fault."

That hit home. Donnie huffed an angry sound. "It's my fault."

Ell straightened her back. Donnie shouldn't carry that much responsibility on his young shoulders. "What are you talking about? Some men broke into my apartment. It had nothing to do with you."

He got to his feet, and the thud of his boots against the tile was loud. "You shouldn't have to worry about people breaking in. I should have kept you safe."

That hurt her chest. "I'm an adult. It's *my* job to keep myself safe—no one else's. Furthermore, you're a kid. It's my job to take care of you—not the other way around. Where did you get it in your head that it's your job to protect me?"

Donnie had drawn his hands into fists, and the tight press of his lips said he wasn't close to done carrying that guilt. "You helped me a lot, especially when I was too little to do it myself. Well, I'm not a kid anymore. I can take care of myself, and well, I should watch out for you, too."

Ell warred between feeling warmed by his statements while also being bothered. The fact Donnie cared about her, that he wanted to help her, it made her smile. Others had written Donnie off so many years before as being a lost cause. They'd said that all the traumas he'd endured, the things he'd seen, that no child could possibly grow into anything worthwhile.

They didn't know this boy, though. They didn't know the one who could be so sweet, who wanted to help others even though he'd grown up in a world where no one did anything for anyone else.

Yet...Ell knew what that sort or guilt could do to a person, how carrying those expectations wore on people. That wasn't what she wanted for Donnie.

"I know you're not a little kid anymore, and I appreciate you more than you know. What happened at my apartment was a random attack. They happen. No one can predict them, and no one can stop them. Tell me you understand this isn't your fault."

He pressed his lips into a thin line before he spoke. "I understand that you think it isn't my fault."

"Nice try, but I haven't fallen for that for a long time. I want to hear you say it."

Donnie narrowed his eyes, then finally looked up at her. "I don't lie to you, Ell, so I can't say that because it isn't true."

Ell let it go. Why waste her time to visit arguing about that? If anyone understood how hard it was to let go of a need to control things, it was her.

"Tell me about how working at the station is," Ell said instead, trying to give Donnie something else to focus on.

He blew out a slow breath, one that said he was still bothered by what had happened, before he took a seat in the chair again and started to tell her.

Ell smiled, listening intently, especially since Donnie seemed excited. Maybe it had been a good idea, maybe this was the thing that would change everything for him.

The idea made Ell gaze around the apartment, made her think about the men who had put her here, and she had to wonder…

Could they do the same thing for her?

* * * *

Fox had found that there were parts of the BDSM lifestyle that caused friction rarely dealt with outside of it. One of those?

Jealousy.

Sure, there was jealousy elsewhere, but it wasn't the same, and when it occurred inside of close groups, it usually tore them apart. There were reasons people laughed about dating drama, when someone had relationships with more than one person in a family or friend circle. It often destroyed the group.

In Fox's life, that wasn't the case. In a place like Sanctuary, people often moved between different partners. It meant jealousy wasn't the same sort of thing.

It was far more complicated, and as Fox watched Dean exit the front of the apartment building, he had to admit it was more difficult to navigate.

What was Dean to Ell? She'd said just friends, but the idea of another Dom having anything to do with Ell made Fox uneasy. Even if platonic, dynamics could exist that blurred lines, that caused issues.

Dean spotted Fox, then offered a stiff nod. The other man wasn't nearly as friendly as usual, as if his mood weren't any better than Fox's.

"How is she?" Fox asked.

"Don't you already know?"

Fox shook his head. "I just got off from work, so I haven't seen her this evening. Besides, you know her better."

That seemed to make Dean still, and the way he stared at Fox said the man might seem jovial, but he had a darkness inside him as well. After a long moment, Dean sighed. "Sorry. I don't mean to be a dick. This is...strange for me."

"Are you in love with Ell?" Fox didn't bother to nice-up the question, to make it more subtle. While he could speak with tact—unlike Clint—he knew when to be direct.

Dean let out a soft laugh. "No, not the way you mean."

"So how do you know each other? What is this all about? I'm not trying to pry, but I think it's fair to understand before I get myself into a situation that goes badly. The last thing I want is to step on any toes or end up with some sort of rivalry."

Dean took a seat on the small retaining wall next to Fox. "I've known Ell since we were kids. We sort of grew up together—hell, we sort of raised each other."

"Raised each other?"

Dean nodded. "We were both in foster care, shuffled around the city to different homes. It's not easy to grow up that way, so I guess we bonded. Ell is about five years younger than me, so when I aged out, I tried to see about adopting her."

Fox knew the story without asking, but he still did to give Dean the chance to explain. "Did it work?"

"No. They weren't about to let an eighteen-year-old adopt a thirteen-year-old. I get it, now, but back then? It was so frustrating. Come to find out, part of it was her objecting. She didn't want me to get saddled with having to take care of her, wanted me to be able to go out and do what I wanted." Dean stared at his hands. "The thing was, I *wanted* to take care of her. She was like my little sister, the only family I had. Still, it let me finish up my education, get a good job, get settled. By the time I did that, though, Ell was an adult, already out on her own."

Fox listened to the story, to the things Ell would never have told him. A part of him felt guilty, as if he were prying her secrets out of someone else, invading her privacy, but he also knew they'd both benefit from him understanding her better. "The way the two of you interact makes a lot more sense now. It is very much like siblings."

That drew a tired smile from Dean. "I'm not in love with Ell but I do love that girl with all my heart. I want the best for her. It's why I brought her to Sanctuary, because I was hoping that would help her."

"Help her how?"

"She's gotten worse recently. She's always had issues with anxiety, with perfectionism, with trying to control everything around her. The problem is that life is chaotic—it's impossible to control. So she's just tried harder and harder until she's nothing but this ball of nervous energy trying to organize her way out of that chaos. I guess I was hoping she'd see something different, and it'd make her realize she didn't need to hold on that tight."

Fox remained silent for a moment, letting Dean's words sink in. When they did, Fox let out a quiet laugh. "You know, a Dominant complaining about someone else wanting control is pretty funny."

Dean joined in on the laughter, then shook his head. "Fair enough, but I don't reorder the items on my counter twelve times a day because I'm afraid one might be a centimeter to the left. Ell is so terrified to rely on anyone, to let anyone else help her because she thinks the only safe way to live is by holding on to that control at all times. Living like that will kill a person, though. It'll hollow them out, and I don't want to see that for her."

"I don't, either," Fox admitted. "I can't say what's going to happen with Ell. You know as well as anyone that a lot of that is up to her. I can just tell you that I want the best for her, that Ethan and Clint do as well, and that as long as she's with us, we'll do everything we can to protect her and give her what she needs."

Dean let out a long, drawn-out breath, before nodding. "I can't say I like the idea of letting her go, of letting anyone else step in, but hell...I haven't exactly done much good. Maybe you can get through to her." Dean stood, but before he left, he looked directly at Fox. "I know people see me as fun and lighthearted, but let me make myself perfectly clear. If you do anything to hurt her, you'll find out I wasn't always like this." Dean didn't wait for Fox to respond, instead only nodding his head then walking away.

Fox sat there, watching as Dean rounded the corner having probably parked down the street. All the things Dean had told him, all the new information about Ell swirled in his head as he tried to make sense of it, tried to wrangle it into a plan.

The way Ell liked her routine, the way she resisted help, the fact that giving in seemed to terrify her all suddenly made more sense. The girl might be desperate for what Fox and the others could give her, but history had taught her that leaning on anyone else was a surefire way to pain and disappointment.

Which meant it was about time for Ell to learn that she *could* trust them, that she needed that release, and for her to realize that if she stopped clutching things so tightly—even for a moment—the whole world wouldn't fall apart.

Ell wouldn't want to learn that, of course, but Fox had never been afraid of a difficult case.

Chapter Twelve

Ell pulled her shoulders back and tried not to look so anxious. She'd been to Sanctuary twice now, so why was it that she struggled with nerves the moment she walked in?

Because you're not alone this time...

Sure enough, Clint walked beside her, looking larger than life. He should have made her feel safe, yet that was almost worse. The idea that she'd feel better with him around burned.

At the reception area, they signed in. She spotted Ethan's and Fox's names already on the list, telling her they'd arrived before she and Clint had. It made sense, though, since Clint had returned to the apartments to pick her up for their...date?

She wasn't sure a sex club counted as a date, but they hadn't exactly done anything else, had they?

Her cheeks heated as she thought about the fact that they'd done *plenty* of things, but none of them normal dating activities. At best, they were after-date activities.

Still, being checked in as their guests felt so much more serious than she'd been signed in as Dean's guest. There had been a clear line before, one that made her just a friend.

She wasn't friends with Clint. What she was, well, she didn't know exactly, but she didn't feel or act this way with her friends.

In the car, before entering the club, Clint had fastened a pair of cuffs to her wrists. They didn't have locks, which made her feel better about it. She could remove them herself if she needed by undoing the buckles, and she felt herself tempted for a moment. They'd put a boot on her bad ankle, which she'd thought would ruin the entire outfit, yet it was a fair enough compromise. It would let her hobble, at least, rather than using a scooter to make her way through the club.

"You're fidgeting," Clint said as they passed the receptionist and fully entered the club.

"And?"

"And you have no reason to be so nervous. You've been here with us twice and enjoyed it each time."

She blew out a long breath and kept to herself that things were different. The first time she hadn't known who they even were. The second time, she'd just been trying it out. This time, though?

This time felt real, like the difference between two people just running into each other and eating lunch versus them actually setting up a date. She didn't feel like they were strangers, and worse? She felt like she was *theirs*.

Clint shook his head. "One of these days, you'll learn to stop lying to us. Your life will be far easier if you simply behave and talk to us."

Ell didn't mean to let out a derisive snort, but it seemed to happen all on its own, as if her very body were allergic to the bullshit he spouted.

In reaction, Clint caught the collar at her throat and stopped, the action forcing her to look up at him. "I am not a difficult man to get along with, little one, but I do not put up with disrespect. Have I disrespected you in any way?"

Ell wanted to say yet, but she couldn't seem to recall a single time he had. She might not *like* what he had to say, but he always treated her with respect. An unexpected shame bubbled up inside her, and eventually, she whispered softly, "I'm sorry."

Clint nodded, then pressed a kiss to her forehead, a gentle touch that both relaxed and wound her up. She already knew how good the press of his lips could be, how talented his tongue was, so even that chaste kiss made her thoughts wander along in that direction.

His lips curled on one side, that half-smirk beyond sexy. "You are adorable when you blush." His gaze moved down from her cheeks to her throat, then to her chest. "And I know from experience just how far down that red goes."

That reminded Ell of exactly how she'd dressed. She'd forgone the frumpy clothing she'd worn the last time—it wasn't like it had worked to keep her head on straight—and instead put on a sweet sundress. No heels—she wasn't good enough in them to risk that. Instead, she wore white sneaker on the bootless foot and had curled her long dark hair. All in all, it made her appear softer than usual, sweeter. She hadn't been sure she liked the look, but the way Clint had stared had reassured her.

He ran his thumb along the top of the collar once more before releasing it and taking her hand in his. The touch was surprisingly intimate, which was hilarious since it wasn't as if they hadn't done much more than that.

Yet, holding hands made it feel as if it switched from being just about sex to something more, and she wasn't sure she liked that.

If Clint noticed her unease, he said nothing. Instead, he only moved forward, guiding her toward the back room where they'd met that first night. Sure enough, at one of the tables, Ethan and Fox sat. The moment Ell neared them, both men turned their attention to her.

Fox was silent, but Ethan ran his thumb across his bottom lip. "You look awfully sweet in that outfit."

Ell used her free hand to smooth down the front, as if that made any sort of difference. The pink fabric was feminine, something she rarely aspired to be, yet when the three of them looked at her like *that*?

She told herself she'd have to wear such things a bit more often. Clint released her hand as he slid into the booth, but when Ell went to follow, Ethan caught her wrist. He pulled her toward him, then into his lap.

"This reminds me of the night we met," he said, his breath warm against her ear, his voice quiet.

"I wasn't sitting in your lap," she argued.

"You were, just not for long enough. Now relax—I like you this close." He set a hand on her thigh, something that made her jump.

Still, when he did nothing else, Ell managed to relax.

"Did you reserve a room?" Clint asked.

"No."

"Why not?"

Ethan started to move his fingers over Ell's thigh in gentle strokes. "I was thinking we'd use a place in here."

That made Ell take notice. She twisted so she could look back at Ethan's face, to try to gauge if he was joking. "Excuse me?"

He grinned, but that told her *nothing*. He always smiled like that whether he was joking or not. "I wanted to play with you a little more public – see what you think."

"Do I get a say in that?"

His smile lessened. "Of course you do. You can put that as a hard limit if you want, but I'd suggest you think it through, first. It's easy to say no to something right away without really figuring out if you want it or not."

Ell opened her mouth to tell him *hell no,* but the words wouldn't come out. She settled back in his lap, breaking her gaze with his, giving her a moment to really think.

Did she really want to say no?

So far she'd enjoyed everything they'd done... They'd never ignored her feelings or made her unsafe.

So why was the idea of being in public so bothersome to her? She wasn't at a library or a park, here. She was at a sex club that had places for this sort of thing exactly, so why was it that Ell couldn't seem to get herself to consider it?

She tried to picture such a thing, to let her brain work through it. The thought of the men touching her, that was easy. The memory of their kisses, of their hands, those things made her blood heat and her heart speed.

Then she thought about others watching her, about the way they'd see her in that state, the way they'd see her so vulnerable.

She gulped, unable to decide if what she felt was positive or not.

Still, she couldn't bring herself to tell them no.

"You can stop it anytime you want," Fox said, as if he could read her mind. "If you give it a try and decide it's too much, all you have to do is talk to us."

Ell nodded, knowing they were right, that if she just told them she didn't like it, they'd stop. It gave her courage, made her feel as if she could handle it.

"Besides," Ethan said, whispering into her ear again in a way that made her shiver in anticipation, "the second I saw you in this dress, all but *begging* us to fuck you, I couldn't imagine depriving anyone of that sight. You're about the prettiest girl I've ever seen when you're drunk on us, when you're moaning and whimpering and breathless. I can't *wait* to get you to that point while everyone watches." With that, he shifted her over to the seat and rose.

Clint and Fox followed suit, with Fox pausing before leaving. "We'll get the spot set up. Why don't you mingle a bit first?"

Right, mingle. Because Ell was in a good mindset to go and make friends after what Ethan had just said.

And yet, she couldn't deny the way him calling her pretty affected her.

I really am in over my head, aren't I?

Ell didn't have to think about that long, because no sooner had the men disappeared from view then two women appeared.

One of them, Ell recognized.

Toya, the owner of Sanctuary. She'd seen her for a meeting when she'd come the first time, with Dean.

The woman terrified Ell. She was confident and no-nonsense. All the things Ell desperately wanted to be, but whereas with Ell, it felt like armor, like a role she was trying to play, Toya wore it with ease.

"May we join you for a moment?" Toya asked.

Ell nodded, not sure what else to say, taken off guard. She hadn't shown up to make friends.

Toya sat on the bench, and the other woman sat beside her. Where Toya was regal, the other woman seemed frantic, chaotic. In fact, in any other setting, Ell would have avoided the other woman at all costs.

"It's nice to see you returning," Toya said. "Often we have guests who never come back. This is your third visit, is it now?"

Ell again nodded, then felt stupid for not speaking so came up with something to add. "Yes, third time." *Real useful addition…*

"I'm Kat," the other woman said, blurting the words out as if she couldn't stop herself. She stuck her hand across the space, then waited until Ell shook it.

"Nice to meet you. I'm Ell."

Kat nodded, sitting back in the seat. "I know. I always make it a point to know the repeats. The guests? I ignore them unless they look like they need a bit of help, because they just come and go so fast it's too much to keep track of. The ones who come back, though? Well, I'm nosy."

"She really is," Toya acknowledged. "Are you enjoying your time here?"

"Yes, thank you." Ell wasn't sure what the women wanted. She hadn't ever been great at making friends.

It always felt too dangerous, too close to baring her weaknesses.

"Are you interrogating Ell?" Dean's voice made Ell able to breathe again. Even if seeing him *here* was still slightly uncomfortable, she suddenly didn't feel abandoned, especially as Dean sat to Ell's other side.

"I'm introducing myself," Kat said, attitude in her tone.

"So you're the official welcome party?"

Kat stuck her tongue out like a petulant child. "Well, you didn't show her around much, and Clint is about as friendly as a frozen-over lake, Fox is too busy with his work to help her and Ethan is…well, Ethan. She needed to get to meet other women here."

"Sorry," came a soft voice Ell didn't recognize. A woman with red hair and freckles walked up, looking frazzled. "I'm sorry I'm late. I told Connor I needed to get here in time to meet you guys, but he said I was 'rushing' him."

A clear red sprang up on her cheeks, one that screamed of exactly how this Connor person felt about being rushed. She took a seat beside Kat, which filled about all the space at the small enclave.

"That's why I warned you about them. Remember when you hid Trent's flogger? Those men don't find jokes that funny," Kat said.

"That was *your* idea!"

Kat's grin said she'd been involved in the prank, but neither of them looked worried. "Well, I guess someone forgot Trent is a sadist who has no problem using his hand."

The newest woman offered a playful glare before turning her attention back to Ell. "I'm Sunny. Sorry for sort of ambushing you, but it seems like you might stick around and so we wanted to make sure you felt welcome. I know how *overwhelming* this place can be, and finding friends here really helped me."

Ell frowned at the statement. "Are you new here?"

Sunny nodded. "Sort of. I've been coming here for about five months. It's funny how quickly it goes from this terrifying place to feeling like home."

Ell glanced around and struggled to believe that was possible. This place felt uncomfortable and scary and chaotic. None of that felt like *home* to her. Was it possible, though? Could it change and turn into something that felt safe to her?

It wasn't the lighting or the music or the many strangers wandering about. Instead, it was the sight of Ethan, Clint and Fox across the room, setting things up. It was Dean beside her, and Kat and Toya across from her, and even Sunny's smiling face. Those things didn't seem quite so bad, which made Ell wonder if they might not just be right…

Maybe this place had the potential to become important…

When Ethan spotted Ell sitting there between Dean, Toya, Kat and Sunny, he wasn't sure if he should smile or curse.

Sure, he wanted her to have friends, but another part of him worried that those particular people would cause problems. Dean had always struck Ethan as being overly jovial. Ethan tended to be as well, but Dean had a darkness inside him Ethan had never fully trusted. Sunny was sweet as could be—a new coming to their little family—but Kat and Toya were another story.

It was funny to think they were so similar to each other yet so different. Toya was confident, tough and willing to put any man in his place with a withering glare. She didn't ramble, rarely smiled and watched over the club—and especially the subs—with the sort of attention that would make about anyone think twice before displeasing her. Kat, on the other hand, was chaos made flesh. She talked constantly, seemed always about half a step into some disaster. She was tough, but in an underhanded way.

Ethan still recalled a few years before when he'd let down a girl who had wanted more with him than he was ready to give. Kat had made his life hell for a good two weeks, screwing with his bags, changing the music when he tried to use a private room to a popular kids show song and basically being a nuisance.

Meaning Ethan really didn't think he wanted his sweet girl spending too much time with bad influences. Before they knew it, she'd end up getting into trouble right along with Kat, who usually managed to pull Sunny into the mess anymore.

Yet, after seeing how damned alone she seemed, he couldn't help but feel a warmth inside his chest as well.

"It's time, baby girl," Ethan said as he walked up to the table, settling his gaze on Ell. He ignored the rest of the people there because his focus was on Ell, on the woman he was intending to pay much closer attention to.

Ell rose, the action fast enough for Ethan to grin. There was something about a woman who responded right away, who followed an order before she thought about it, that had always gotten to him. She avoided the gazes of the others as she came over and took Ethan's hand.

Kat and Sunny smirked, a sign that, despite their bad influence, they supported Ell with Ethan, Clint and Fox. Dean was harder to read, somewhere between suspicious and cautiously optimistic. Toya, on the other hand, was basically impossible to figure out. The sharp way she moved her gaze over the two of them said she was deciding what she thought.

Not that it shocked him. She was nosy when it came down to it, and she was more than willing to say or do whatever was necessary to protect those she felt were under her care.

Which was every person inside that club.

Ethan offered a nod to the table before pulling Ell with him, away from that crowd and to the one he was far more interested in. "Nervous?" he asked Ell, keeping his voice down.

She swallowed hard then nodded.

"Good." At her sharp look, he grinned. "Sorry, baby girl, but I like when a girl is nervous. They get more sensitive, and they jump at every little touch. Plus, there's this sense of power, a feeling like for that moment, I'm your whole damned world."

"That sounds horrible," Ell said. "What sort of man admits he likes making a girl nervous?"

"Nervous isn't the same as afraid. Nervous is anticipation. It's a little bit of 'what if' without actually being scared. Scared is no fun."

She nodded, though if she really understood the difference or not yet, Ethan didn't know. It was one of those things people got as they went forward, as they spent more time in the lifestyle.

The spot where Fox and Clint stood was the one they'd already prepared. A rectangular metal frame stood there with hooks around it, and a table to the side had their toys. As soon as Ell caught sight of the frame, her feet stopped moving.

Ethan could have pulled her forward, but he paused there at the boundary line, the place where she wasn't actually *in* the scene area but rather in the spectators' spot. And that anxiety inside her looked as if it might vibrate right out of her body.

"What are you going to do?" she whispered.

"You need to start trusting us," Ethan answered instead. "I'll tell you that we aren't going to hurt you, that we'll respect your limits, but beyond that?" He squeezed her hand gently, trying to draw her attention away from the frame and to him. Once she looked into his eyes, he went on. "Beyond that, I need you to trust us."

Ell chewed on her bottom lip for a moment, then nodded once in a decisive move of her head. She released Ethan's hand and walked forward—her steps were slow but she moved, and that was what mattered—until she stood in the frame and turned back toward Ethan. A tremble in her shoulders made him smile and lean in to press a kiss over the strap of her dress.

Clint held his hand out and waited for Ell to give him hers. He took one of the tethers from the table and used it to hook her wrist to the frame. Fox repeated the action on Ell's other wrist while Ethan knelt in front of her. He slid her cute sneakers off first, then her socks, and handed both to Clint. Fox gave him to cuffs for her ankles, and Ethan went about securing them around her then to the frame, the one band loose enough to go around the boot.

Of course, getting her to spread her legs enough to hook them required a few quick taps to the inside of her ankle, and it didn't take Ethan looking up to know her cheeks were bright red.

After he finished, he rose and moved back to study his work.

She really *was* beyond lovely, wasn't she? Ell's long hair had curls in it from about the chin down. Even with the curls, it reached past the curve of her breast, and the darkness of it stood out against the sweet pink color she'd picked. She looked innocent and delicious, and he wanted nothing more than to have her.

Ell shifted after a moment, as if the longer they stared at her, the more uncomfortable she grew. The metal latches on the tethers scraped against the hooks, groaning as she moved. She didn't struggle, not exactly, but instead just squirmed and shifted.

"Are you just going to stare?" she finally snapped.

Fox let out a soft laugh at that. "You do make a pretty ornament like this. Maybe we don't need to decorate around our apartments anymore. We'll just tie you up in different spots and you'll bring all the beauty we need."

Ell narrowed her eyes, and Ethan was pretty sure she'd end up saying something she didn't want to say — or, better put, something she'd regret later. For this reason, he pulled the next item from the table. He held up the gag, using one finger. It was a ring gag, one that would fit behind her teeth and keep her mouth open. He preferred them because it not only kept her mouth open and useable, but it allowed for better breathing and less risk.

"Not a chance," she said.

"No? Why not?"

Ell licked her bottom lip, and the sight of her tongue did what it always did for him, making him all that much more aware of his need. "You said I could use my safe word. How can I with that?"

"Good catch," Clint said. "I'm proud that you thought about that."

Ell damn near *glowed* at the praise. What was it about a 'good girl' that could turn a submissive into a puddle?

Fox held up a small, round item in front of Ell. "This will go into your hand. If you want to stop, you just drop this." He tossed it up, then caught it again. When the clear ball hit his palm, lights inside it turned on and flashed and a loud, sharp clap went off easily heard above the music and noise. "We'll stop immediately, remove the gag and check in. I also expect you to drop that if your ankle starts to bother you."

Ell stared at it for a long moment, then finally nodded.

"Brave girl," Fox whispered as he pressed the ball into where her right hand was, then ran his fingers under the cuff another time to check the tightness.

Ethan tapped her lip. "Open up."

Again, Ell didn't obey immediately, but Ethan just waited. Finally, she did so, after prompted, opened wider so he could fit the rubber ring behind her teeth. He used his finger to feel, to ensure the ring didn't strike her teeth anywhere, that nothing would catch or rub wrong. After he was cure of the fit, he brough the straps around and ducked beneath her arm to fasten the buckle behind her head. Finally, he checked the tightness and fit again. "Does that feel okay?"

Her eyebrows drew toward enough other, and she made a sound impossible to make out, one that went *straight* to his cock. There was something beyond sexy about a woman making those noises.

She shook her head as soon as she seemed to realize she couldn't speak.

She *hadn't* dropped the ball, though, so Ethan moved right into her line of sight. "Does it hurt." *No.* "Are you afraid?" A longer pause, then she shook her head again. "Do you need to stop?"

This was the big question, the one she needed to figure out. After about ten seconds, she let out a long, slow breath then shook her head again.

Ethan smiled and leaned in offered a few gentle kisses to her lips, to where the gag held her mouth open. No doubt it embarrassed her, but that made it all the more better. He also reached in and ran his hands over her waist, then up to cup her breast.

And boy did that seem to ignore something in her. She jerked, probably because that's nerves did. Anxiety could prime a body, make it so they were just waiting for any touch, so a person reacted so violently and powerfully to *anything*.

Tonight was going to be *so much* fun.

Fox couldn't stop his need to touch Ell. Sure, he felt that need a lot, but seeing her bound like this, offered up like some sweet virgin sacrifice, got to him. It turned his want to need, made him feel ravenous and desperate.

And worse? Ell had worn what could have been a fantasy for him. She looked like the best gift, like everything he'd ever wanted torn right from a dream.

And since she *was* theirs for the night, he had no good reason not to indulge.

He moved behind her and reached down, dragging his fingers against her thighs just below the hemline of the dress. "I like you wearing this," he whispered to her. "You look like a princess, just like I call you." He moved his fingers slightly beneath the fabric, teasing her soft skin. "I like to reach beneath your dress, as well. It feels naughty. I could strip you out of everything, have you naked when I take you, but I like the idea of fucking you while you're still clothed, of having you while you're still wearing this sweet dress."

She made those muffled, broken noises again. He had no idea if they were asking him for more, to stop, but it didn't matter. So long as she held that ball, so long as she didn't drop it, nothing else mattered.

So Fox let his fingers move up higher until he stroked along her pussy through the panties she wore. They weren't lace, not satin. Instead, they felt like incredibly soft cotton.

And they were damp.

He grinned and pressed a kiss to the nape of her neck. "Already wet, hmm? Well, I think we can take care of that. Are you going to be a good girl for us tonight? Are you going to let us use your pretty little body right here? In front of everyone?"

She shivered, but damn if he didn't feel her cunt move, as if she tightened at the idea. Clearly, she enjoyed some level of exhibitionism. Exactly how much, well, they could find out.

Fox slipped his finger beneath her panties so he could touch her wet heat directly. When he brushed her clit, she arched her back and yanked at her bindings. *What a pretty reaction…* Fox repeated the touch, wanting to see her struggle again. He wanted to see the sweat drip down her back as she realized she was entirely trapped and at their mercy.

"Your pussy is *so* wet, princess." He sank two fingers deep into her, forcing her to adjust, to take him.

He turned his wrist, making sure she felt him, before he withdrew and pumped his fingers into her again, more roughly. "I've wanted to fuck you for days, now, and I'm looking damn forward to tonight being the night, to getting to sink into you and feel just how snug your pussy really is. Do you want me to fuck you here? Like this?"

She shook her head, but again, the ball remained.

It posed a challenge, one Fox was only too happy to respond to. "No?" He pulled his fingers from her warm pussy and from her underwear. "You sure? Because your pussy says otherwise." He held his fingers in front of her, the ones coated in her sweetness. "See? See how wet you are?" He pressed his lips to her ear. "I'm pretty sure your little pussy knows exactly what it wants." Fox dragged his drenched fingers across her bottom lip.

And Ell yet again surprised the fuck out of him when she darted her tongue out to taste herself, to lick her own wetness from his fingers. His cock *throbbed* at the sight.

Ethan chuckled, still standing in front of her. "Sharing is caring," he said before leaning in and dragging his tongue first over her bottom lip, then against Fox's fingers. Ell couldn't close her mouth, couldn't kiss, but that didn't stop her and Ethan from sharing the wetness that coated Fox's fingers.

And the feeling, the sight, the anticipation all mixed together until Fox knew he needed to feel Ell's cunt around him.

He groaned as he pulled back and unfastened his pants. He didn't like getting undressed in public, not beyond what was needed. Where neither Ethan nor Clint had hang-ups about it, Fox had always been a more private person. It meant he didn't remove any articles entirely.

Though, fucking Ell while they were *both* still mostly dressed was hot in its own right. It felt like he'd found her somewhere, had pushed her into a dark corner to ravish her because he couldn't wait another moment.

Which was pretty close to how he actually felt.

He grabbed one of the condoms on the table and tore it open, then rolled it onto his cock. Even that contact made him grown.

Clint had moved closer, crouching beside her to reach beneath her dress and pulled her panties down. When he got them off, though, Fox chuckled.

They were white and cotton with *Daddies' Little Girl* written across the ass.

Which was a level of brat Fox hadn't known the girl had. In fact, the look she gave him held an edge of fear, as if she wasn't sure it would be taken well.

Clint handed them over to Ethan, who let out a boisterous laugh when he read them.

"Oh, you're cute," Ethan said, holding them up so she had to see them. It made her squirm.

So, she enjoyed playing the game, but getting called out embarrassed her? She drew him in, and he shouldn't enjoy that struggle of hers, the point between what a person wanted and what they thought was best. She *wanted* to play with them, but she was still afraid of what it might mean.

"If I'd known you'd had these, I'd have rotated you around and left them on, so everyone could see."

She shook her head, as if to tell him no. That only made Fox hungrier, so he moved in closer and reached beneath her dress against, finding her cunt even wetter, even puffier and more sensitive. He offered a rough stroke to her clit, and the noise she made through the gag was better than the most popular music.

Because they'd set up the frame properly — preparations were something new Doms too often missed out on — Ell sat at the perfect height despite being shorter than any of them. Fox stroked his cock before shifting closer and dragging the tip along her folds. "I'm going to fuck you now, princess. You're going to take every inch, aren't you? In front of everyone here? You're going to be such a good girl while I fuck your little cunt, while I ruin you in your pretty dress?" The words slid from Fox without him even thinking about it.

And Ell just nodded as she made more of those broken sounds.

So Fox did as he'd said, sinking into her tight heat, into the perfect grip of her pussy. It was everything he'd wanted and more, just a molten vise that teased every part of his dick.

He didn't hide his groan of pleasure, wanted to make sure she knew *exactly* how good she felt to him. "You're so well-behaved," he said. "Daddy's little girl is so good for him, aren't you?"

Again, she nodded, her body trembling as if already on the edge.

Which Fox understood perfectly. He was hardly new, hardly some untested youth who risked getting to the finish line before ever actually getting inside a girl.

Yet Ell seemed to tear his control away, made him feel on edge right from the start, forced him to fight himself not to come yet.

He grasped her hips so he could fuck her harder, so her could sink deeper into her heat. He didn't try to talk anymore, just lost himself in her body, in the sensation of her wrapped around him, in her scent and the sounds she made.

She was *perfect*. He'd never felt this way, never felt so lost and sure while unsure. It had always been so easy to know what to do before, yet he was confused when it came to her. He had this overwhelming need for her, but that only served to make him uneasy, to make him doubt himself.

Instead of questioning it, he slid one of his hands forward until he could reach her clit, until he could sneak beneath the fabric of her dress and stroke that hard nub that would drive her as crazy as he felt.

She exploded around him when he touched her clit. Her cunt tightened even more in waves that took him over that edge with her. He rested his forehead against her shoulder as he came, as he fell into that pit along with her.

And he wasn't sure he'd ever be able to pull himself from it, or if he even wanted to…

Ell felt as if she couldn't possibly be expected to stay awake as Fox pulled out of her. Even his softening cock stroking against her cunt walls was so overwhelming that she whimpered and cried.

Not that Fox seemed to care. His dark chuckle said he probably enjoyed the panicked noises she made, the way she squirmed. When he pulled away, her dress dropped to cover her again.

Ell raised her eyes to Ethan, expecting him to undo her wrists, to take her home. At least, she thought that until she saw the way he smirked. That was *not* the look of a man who was finished.

"Poor, tired little girl," Ethan said, his words holding an almost cruel edge to them. "You want to go to bed?"

Ell nodded.

"It's not time, just yet. You see, you took good care of Fox, but what about Clint and me? Don't you care about us, too?"

This time Ell nodded without thinking about it, then cursed herself. She *did* care, and it annoyed the hell out of her.

"So you'll let us use your tight cunt too, won't you?"

Like there was any way to say no to that...

Though, Ell wasn't sure if she could take all three of them. They weren't small men, nor were they all that gentle. It made her question if she could handle that.

Before the fear took hold, Ell reminded herself that she trusted them, that they'd been careful so far. If she really couldn't, they'd stop.

Ethan pressed a kiss to her forehead before he moved behind her as well.

Which made her aware of something she hadn't been before. When Fox had taken her, Ethan had remained in front of her, blocking her from the room and making it feel as if it were just them.

Now, with Ethan behind her, Ell could look out at the entire room. It made her blood heat, made her stomach clench and she wasn't sure if she liked those feelings.

Ethan shifted behind her, and the tear of foil told her he was putting on a condom, that he was going next.

When the thick head of his cock pressed against her cunt, he paused. He brought his lips to her ear, and his voice was pure sin when he whispered to her, "I'm going to fuck you in front of all these people. Some will just glance this way, but others? Oh, they'll gather, standing right there, *wishing* they were me, that they got to have you."

Ell shook her head, but the gag prevented her from arguing with him like she wanted to. The words inside her head screamed that *no one* would want to watch, that she wasn't the sort of girl anyone would line up to see.

Ethan reached around her with his free hand and dragged his fingers across the neckline of her dress. He curled his fingers around the top and gently pulled down, careful to not damage the dress.

He tucked the fabric beneath her breasts, and she cursed herself for not wearing an actual bra. The dress had a built-in shelf bra, so she hadn't worried, but now that the cold air blew over her exposed nipples, she wished she'd done more.

Not like that would have deterred Ethan… If the man wanted her bare, there was likely no number of layers that would have kept him from it.

Ethan didn't *just* expose her, though. No, what he did was so much worse. He then stroked his fingers over her bare nipples, teasing them to tight points with *nothing* to block her from anyone who looked at them.

Just as Ell's tension became too tight, as she shook, Ethan plunged his cock into her in a single hard thrust. Ell didn't make a soft sound there, didn't moan or whimper, but let out a cry that drew more than a few looks their way.

If Ethan cared, he didn't show it, since he set a hard pace before moving both hands to her front, to her breasts that he teased and pinched. "I like fucking you in front of everyone," he admitted.

And that made it all worse. While Ethan's hands and cock could drive her wild, his words were so much more potent, and he seemed perfectly willing to use them to his advantage.

"Look out there, see people looking? You know how long they've been here based on how much they look. New people just glance, but those who have been here a while?" He pinched her left nipple especially hard, using the edge of his nail. "They're the ones who come closer, who take a spot to watch everything. Do you know how many are going to leave here and masturbate thinking of your pretty tits? Of your snug little cunt?"

A wave of pleasure rolled through Ell, her body tightening as she came again. When they ran so close together, though, it felt almost impossible to figure out what was another orgasm and what was just another aftershock from the last.

Not that it mattered, since Ethan seemed to be using her as he wanted no matter what.

A man and a woman walked up, standing on the outside of the scene, watching without the least bit of shame. The woman's lips were curled into a smirk, and the man, who wore a collar that said, 'Puppy,' across the front, held the woman's hand. They didn't stare at her as if she were filthy, as if they though she were shameful. Instead, it was lust in their eyes, pleasure.

"See?" Ethan said as he took her harder. "You look like the perfect little slut right now. So wonderfully messy. Maybe one day in the future, we'll do this again when we can forgo condoms. You have a cunt I'd love to see painted in cum, that I'd love to display to everyone. My sweet little whore."

The *whore* name threw Ell over an edge she never saw coming. It was the sort of word she'd have punched him for if her hands weren't bound.

However, it was the combination of words that confused her mind, the way he mixed up insults and praise until Ell couldn't separate them. He called her a slut and a whore but he did it with *such* affection that she couldn't make herself angry about it.

It made her feel happy, which freaked her out all the more.

"You like hearing me talk, don't you? Each time I say anything, you tighten up again. Fuck, one of these times I'm going to call you while you're out and tell you all the things I'm going to do with you. I'll make you have on earbuds so you have to walk around turned on and drenched. I'll keep you on the edge and won't let you come until you can't take it anymore and have to find some private corner where you can finger yourself like the naughty little girl you are."

Ell cried out, not giving a damn who heard, or about the crowd that had gathered, or the way Ethan teased her breasts as if putting on a show. She was so locked inside her own head, inside the feelings he forced out of her, that nothing else mattered.

"Of course, naughty girls get punishments, so when you get home, I'll have my fun. You'll be sensitive from being denied all day, so maybe I'll tie you up in the hallway like a present for Clint, Fox and me. I'll have you hog tied and waiting so we can use whatever slutty little hole we want as we get home. You'll get to sit out there just waiting for whichever one of us wants to use you."

The idea tore through Ell, made her whine, made her tug at the cuffs around her wrists. She imagined being totally at their mercy, just waiting for one of them to decide to use her. She could picture the way Clint would get off the elevator and see her, that surprised smile he got whenever he saw her unexpectedly. Of course, then he'd fuck her.

"Wouldn't even say a word to you, either. Whoever it was would just unzip and use you however we wanted. No orgasms for you, though, since you were bad and got off on your own."

The pleasure that ran through Ell terrified her, and yet another crashing sensation pulled her under, made her feel pushed far beyond her ability to cope.

Ethan only groaned and stilled for a moment, as if the squeezing of her cunt was almost too much. He nipped her bare shoulder before taking both her nipples between his fingers. "You're fucking perfect, baby girl. Look how many people are watching me fuck your sweet cunt? How many wanted to see?" He let go of one breast, but her moment of reprieve was short-lived as he used that hand to gather the fabric of her dress and pull the front up. It exposed her cunt, the way Ethan fucked her.

Not that at this angle or distance they could see *much* but it still overwhelmed her. It felt like her last defense stolen away, taken from her.

"Fuck," Ethan said in her ear so low that it felt like a growl. "Do you know how much I love others seeing me fuck you? They can see your pussy stretched around my cock, and they *know* you're mine, that you're Daddy's little girl, that this cunt is mine." His thrusts were erratic and broken and rough. He fucked her as if he'd die if he didn't, as if driven by some deep need to procreate or to claim that was written inside his DNA.

So when he released her other breast to grab her hair, to force her eyes to the crowd, to see just how many watched them, Ell shattered.

It was Ethan's words, his touches, the raging feelings inside her. It all mixed until she broke apart beneath the weight, when she came so hard, it felt like a mockery of anything before.

The world felt as if it went black around her, and Ell sank into the darkness of it.

* * * *

When Ell stirred again, Clint smiled softly at her grumble. The girl didn't seem to care for coming to.

She frowned as she sat up, pulling her face away from the passenger-side window.

"You were sleeping," he said, wanting to help her place her surroundings before she panicked. Anyone who woke somewhere other than where they went to sleep could react badly.

"Oh." She wiped at her face as if afraid she'd been drooling.

Which was far more adorable than it should have been.

"Are you sleeping enough?" Clint asked when she yawned again.

"Yes," Ell said as she moved her jaw, then rubbed at the joint.

"Your jaw will be a little sore," Clint explained. "It should go away pretty fast. If not, let us know and we'll use heat to help ease it, and we can forgo the gag in the future if it's bothersome."

Ell nodded, then dropped her hand as if self-conscious. She peered down at herself, a moment of relief crossing her face when she found herself dressed.

"We wouldn't carry you out undressed," Clint muttered.

"Sorry," she said. "I'm just still getting used to all this." She frowned, then peered to the side at him. "Wait...you didn't...?"

Clint huffed softly at the question she didn't ask. "No."

"Why not? Just because I was tired?"

"No. Well, I mean, you were tired, but that wasn't the only reason. I don't care for public play."

"No?" Ell twisted slightly, but Clint kept the bulk of his attention on the dark road. "I thought all guys enjoyed that sort of thing?"

He shook his head. "I don't like feeling like I'm on display, or like I'm being studied."

She furrowed her brows. "Did you not want me to—"

"No. If I had an issue with you up there, I would have come out and said it. I don't mind—and I even enjoy watching it."

"Then I don't understand," Ell admitted softly.

Clint sighed, struggling between her question and what he wanted to come out and say. He'd *always* had trouble with that, with knowing the right way to phrase something, with admitting his own issues. In the past he'd mostly kept it to himself, but with Ell?

He didn't want to do that.

So he spoke while pinning his gaze to the road ahead. "You know I'm not always great at social settings, at dealing with people. Public play feels like others are judging me. It makes me anxious, makes me unable to relax or enjoy myself because I'm wrapped up in wanting to ensure I speak the right way, that I say the right things, that my expression is what it should be. That's exhausting."

"You don't do that with me," Ell said, the words a statement and not a question.

"No, I don't. I'm able to let my guard down with you, and you seem to understand that I will tell you what I think, that you can ask me if you're unsure. Other people aren't always so accepting. It means I like to enjoy you in private, when I don't have to think about those things."

Clint knew that was enough, but for some reason, he kept speaking. Perhaps he knew there were things he'd never really admitted, and somehow, in the darkness of the car, with only Ell there, he felt safe enough to say them. "I've had a lot of issues with people misunderstanding me, with them thinking I am cruel or unfeeling. Women — submissives specifically — often would assume I was something I wasn't, that I was sadistic or some game for them to play, to push buttons with. I'd grown used to accepting that people wouldn't understand me. Even Ethan and Fox struggle, at times, so I thought if they couldn't fully accept who I was, no one else could. You're…different."

Warmth on his forearm made him drop his gaze to find Ell's hand there. She squeezed gently, as if she knew that would mean more than any words.

"Are you hungry?" Clint asked. "I can stop and pick something up on the way back. There are a few places left between us and home."

Ell shook her head as she ran her hands over his arm, the touch stirring a desire inside him that hadn't been satiated. Still, the touch didn't stay there. She danced her fingertips along his arm, then over his side, then to the top of his leg. Even through his slacks, her touch was like fire.

Clint let out a deep groan. "You've got to be sore," he said. "Maybe playing with me isn't your best idea."

Ell moved her hand toward the inside of his leg, then up his thigh until she cupped his erection. The touch was blatant, and the fact it came from Ell, who rarely took control, made it all the better.

When she squeezed, Clint knew his control was all but shot. He pulled the truck to the side, not caring as it bumped over the dirt and into an empty lot tucked away behind some trees for just enough cover.

He reached down and pulled the lever that slid the seat all the way back, then hauled Ell into his lap. She didn't fight him, even though the position didn't give her much room. In fact, if she leaned back at all, she'd hit the steering wheel.

He caught her chin and pulled her toward him, taking a deep kiss as he pushed the fabric of her dress up. She still wore no panties—Ethan had tucked those into his pocket and decided she hadn't needed them— which meant when he ran his fingers between her thighs, he found her wet heat.

Ell gasped, jerking back, her body no doubt still sensitive from earlier. Even still, she didn't break the kiss, didn't stop him. If anything, she spread her thighs more in a surrender.

And Clint about came from that—or maybe it was the way she reached between them and undid the fasteners of his slacks, the way she dragged down his zipper as if she needed him right then.

"You sure?" he asked just as he pressed two fingers into her, testing.

She whined, which made him pause.

The last thing he wanted was to actually hurt her.

"You're too sore," he said softly.

Ell shook her head, breaking the kiss. "I'm not. Please?"

He stared down at what he could see of her cunt, at the outline of her pale thighs. Fighting between what he was desperate for and what was best for her was a hard battle.

Ell set her hands on his cheeks and rested her forehead against his. "Please?" Her voice was softer than he'd ever heard, sweeter. "I'm a little sore, but it's not bad. You always tell me to trust what you say, so you should trust me, too. I need you."

Need.

That was what did it, what made it impossible to deny her. If she'd said she'd wanted him, that would have been different. Need was a whole different matter, though, and something inside of him had no choice but to give in.

"I'll take good care of you," he swore to her while he reached behind, to the bag on the back seat. He took a condom from the zipper pouch, struggling in the small amount of space to roll it over his cock.

Ell rose when he finished, her hands still on his cheeks, giving him room to position the head of his cock at her entrance. When he started to press in, Ell took her bottom lip between her teeth and seemed to try to stay quiet.

"I want to hear you," Clint said. "Don't hide the pretty noises you make from me. Hell, don't hide *anything* from me. I want it all, every little piece of you, everything you hide, everything you want to keep secret, I want it all." He punctuated the demand by grasping her hip and pulling her down so he filled her entirely.

And he now understood what the others had meant—Ell had a cunt that could make the most sure man question himself. She was hot and tight and wonderfully wet. She responded, so each word he uttered, each touch he offered her caused her pussy to tighten like some barometer to her mood.

Ell moaned, something sultry and deep in her throat. It was a sound of complete satisfaction, something that warmed him and made him want to puff out his chest. *He'd* made her make that sound, he'd caused it, and he'd bring out plenty of other similar noises from her.

"I've never had anyone understand me," Clint admitted as he leaned his seat back to give her more room, as he let her set her own speed and ride him to prevent him from being too rough. "Even when I'm with Ethan and Fox, I feel like an outsider, like I'm there but they don't really *get* me. I've never felt like I have a place, like I belong anywhere..." He paused when the next few words stuck in his throat, when he had to gain his courage before he said them out loud. "Except with you. I don't know why, but I don't feel different with you. I don't feel like the outsider."

Ell let out another of those moans as she rose and fell over him, as her tight cunt enveloped his cock each time she came down. "People think I'm cold," Ell admitted softly, her words broken by her shallow, rapid breathing. "They think I'm some sort of ice princess."

"Because you like making them think that." He brushed his thumbs over her nipples, then tugged down the neckline, wanting to see the way her breasts would sway as she rode him. "You want to keep people at a distance so you feel safer. I get it, but I don't plan to give you that, not with me. I like the woman you are beneath that, the one only we get to see, the one that's all for us. You're anything but cold, Ell, once you get past the nonsense in your head."

"It's not nonsense," she argued.

Clint leaned in and dragged his tongue over one of her peaked nipples, knowing she'd feel it all the more after Ethan's rough treatment. "Yeah, it is. I get it — you couldn't rely on anyone when you were younger, so you think that if you lean on anyone now, you'll just end up disappointed, right? But we weren't there — we've never let you down. You can trust us — *always*."

Ell gasped, and the squeezing of her cunt said she was close. It again made him excited to sometime take his time with her, because so far, she pushed his control right out of the window. She made him crazy and impatient and desperate. Would there ever be a time when he didn't see her and need her right then?

Maybe the trick could be to fuck her once quick, to take the edge off, then get to toy with her all night?

Another time.

Instead, of focused on the moment, on how her pussy surrounded him, on how he teased her erect nipples, on how she trembled.

"Rub your clit," he told her. "Move the dress when you do it — I want to watch. I want to see you come apart on my cock, see you get yourself off using me."

She whined, that soft sound that said she loved the idea every bit as much as she hated it. Still, she did as he asked. She pulled her dress up, rolling it so the fabric remained rucked up around her waist. With his seat leaned back, Clint had a great view, especially with the glow from the instruments in the truck.

Her cunt was spread around his thick cock, and when she stroked her clit, he groaned while holding himself back. Her hands looked so small, so delicate, as she rubbed her clit while leaving the hood in place.

No doubt because she was still so sensitive.

But Clint wanted to make an impression, wanted to make sure she remembered him as much as she did Ethan and Fox—which was odd, since he'd never felt competitive with them before.

"Harder," he ordered her. "I want you to move the hood out of the way and touch your clit directly."

"That's too much," she said, her tone broke when she stroked from the bottom of her clit up, when the touch was more direct. "I'm too sensitive."

"Good," Clint all but growled out. "Be a good girl for me and show me that sweet little clit of yours. Bring your fingers here." When she obeyed, he sucked two of her fingers into his mouth and slid his tongue around them, getting them wet before releasing them. "Now show me what a good girl you can be, how good you can be for me."

"Okay," she said softly.

"Okay what?" he pressed, wanting to hear it.

"Okay, Daddy," she whispered, though it turned into a soft whimper when she did as he said. She pulled the hood out of the way, and Clint *almost* felt bad for her when he saw just how swollen her clit really was. They'd teased and played with her all night—no doubt it was nearly painful.

The first time she touched it directly, it was as if she'd touched a live wire. Her back arched as she pulled away from him, and her pussy tightened around him, forcing her to stop riding him as she could only tremble and whine.

And that was beyond sexy. It was Ell hitting a limit she thought she had, it was her choosing to push past it to please him, and it made him put his hands behind his head to watch.

He wanted her to use him, to get off on his cock, on his demands, to do what he said because she wanted to.

Ell stroked her hard clit again as she set a rhythm, as she rode him. Her panting breaths filled the cab of the truck, and Clint had never seen a better sight, never wanting anything more.

"You're perfect," he said. "You're the best girl any Daddy could ever hope for. You're so damned sweet when I tell you to do something, and you work so hard to make me happy." He gritted his teeth when she twisted her hips, when the friction nearly drove him over the edge.

You aren't going to come before she does, damn it.

Clint took a deep breath, but he couldn't make himself close his eyes. He didn't want to miss a moment of this.

Ell looked like some sprite there, rising and falling above him, taking his cock into her, stroking her clit harder than she wanted…all because it pleased him. He grasped the headrest of his seat to stay still, to try to tame the desire inside him, to hold out.

"Come on, now, no more playing. You're enjoying my cock—you're squeezing down on me like you're a breath away, so let go. I want you to come all over Daddy's cock, right here in the truck on the side of the road because you needed it and I'll *always* give you want you need. You don't ever have to be afraid of shit, not with me here, because I'll never let you down."

Ell sounded like a trapped animal as she came, her voice almost hoarse, as if all the sounds of the night had made it hard to speak anymore. The walls of her pussy clutched him, as if she didn't want to let him go.

Clint let himself follow her, allowed his own orgasm to rush through him.

The truck was filled with their tired, sated breaths, with the scent of sex, of their sweat, and Clint did the only thing he could think of.

He wrapped his arms around Ell and pulled her down so she rested against his chest, so every inch of her pressed against him, then closed his eyes.

After believing for so long this was impossible, he was terrified of losing it.

Clint wasn't sure how he could possibly go back to a life without this sweet woman in it.

Chapter Thirteen

Ell was in *so much* trouble. She knew it in the sharpness of Ethan's text message, in the way it had lacked any of his normal humor.

She couldn't even blame him. There hadn't been that many rules, but she'd gone ahead and broken their main one.

She'd left without telling any of them, without talking to them about where she was going. She'd told herself it was only a quick outing, only to attend a hearing at the courthouse that she was too afraid to hand off to another social worker.

And, *yes*, maybe it hadn't gone quite as planned... The father, Lee, had screamed at her in the hallway. He'd nearly taken a swing at her, but security had intervened before anything happened.

That was what she kept telling herself, over and over again, but none of it fixed the ache in her chest. It wasn't fear, not really. It was so much worse than that. She was terrified to see that disappointed look on their faces when she came back, when she had to explain why she'd done it.

Why did I?

No matter how much she reviewed it in her head, she couldn't figure it out. She'd trusted them, she cared about them, but when she'd looked at her phone, when she'd thought about calling them, this area in her chest felt like ice and she'd put her phone away.

Her phone buzzed in her pocket as she sat on the small half-wall outside of the apartment complex, stalling for time.

The words made her shoulders droop, and she let out a long sigh. It was time to face the music. Still, Ethan's text stayed in her mind.

You might as well get in here now. The longer you wait, the worse it'll be.

* * * *

Ethan grinned as Ell walked into his place. He was still pissed, of course, but the fact that she'd followed his last text and come to his apartment pleased him.

As did the idea of what was to come.

Ell had fucked up, and by the look on her face, she knew it. Of course, when she walked in, leaning heavily on her cane, he let out a sound of frustration.

"Strip down and kneel by the foot of my bed," he ordered her as he turned away from her, not bothering to watch and see if she'd obey.

He went to the hall closet and took out a few ibuprofen, knowing they'd help with her ankle since it seemed she'd overdone it. He also brought a water bottle, then gave Ell another five minutes before he walked into his bedroom.

He gave her the time both to ensure she had enough to follow through—he didn't like setting a person up to fail—but also to give her time to stew. Sometimes silence, sometimes kneeling there and having to just wait, not knowing what was coming, could get someone to really consider what they'd done, to think about why they'd done it.

Anticipation was a hell of a weapon.

In his room, Ell was exactly where he'd requested. She knelt, entirely bare, on the cushions at the foot of his bed.

She'd never actually been into his room before, he realized. More than that, though, how much he liked her there surprised him. Her gaze remained on the floor, her expression pinched.

She really was sweet, wasn't she? Even when she didn't want to be, when she wanted to play the part of a woman who didn't give a damn about others, that wasn't who she really was.

He took the two pills and held them out. He shook his head when she reached. "Open."

Color spread across her cheeks, but she listened and opened her mouth. He set the two pills on her tongue, then opened the water and held it for her as she took a drink and swallowed.

"You need to take better care of yourself," he said. "You're mine, and I don't like my things to be poorly cared for."

Still, Ell only huffed, as if she wasn't pleased with the rebuke.

Ethan sat on the small chest at the foot of his bed, the place where he stored all his toys, then stared at her.

Ell still kept her gaze down, her back straight, her posture good. She had her knees spread and she rested on her heels, her hands on the tops of her thighs. He knew he hadn't ever taught her that position, which meant she'd probably looked it up during one of her many study sessions.

"Does that position hurt your ankle?"

She shook her head, which made her hair—pulled back and into a ponytail—fall forward and over her shoulder. She glanced up—not into his eyes, but just at his body—and seemed to get stuck at his crotch.

And, really, who could blame Ethan for his reaction? He had a beautiful sub naked and kneeling in front of him. Any man who didn't get hard at that needed to visit a doctor. Besides, he rather enjoyed punishments, and he had every intention to make this a good one.

Ell reached toward him and scooted closer until her fingers went to the button of his jeans.

Ethan caught her hand to stop her. "Did I ask you to do that?"

She shook her head again. "I just thought..."

"Don't think, then, since thinking got you to leave without telling us, and that didn't go so well. Why don't you just listen and obey, instead?"

Her shoulders drooped, a sure sign that while Ell might have ignored their rule, she gave a damn that they were disappointed.

"Look at me."

Ell closed her hands into firsts before she lifted her gaze to his.

"Better," Ethan said. "Why did you go out without asking?"

"I got a call that there was an emergency custody hearing, and I was afraid if I didn't go, the father might win."

Ethan understood that perfectly well. He'd pushed himself plenty of times all because of fear of what could happen if he didn't. Still… "But why didn't you call us? Do you really think any of us would have told you no? Would have stood in the way of what you needed to do?"

She frowned, as if that hadn't even occurred to her. "I guess not," she admitted.

Which was good. Her answering him said she trusted him, though the confusion on her face implied she didn't understand her own choices any more than he did.

"We wanted you to contact us to we know you're safe. Most likely, Clint or I could have driven you ourselves. If that wasn't possible, at least knowing you were there would help us relax. How would you feel if you knew I went somewhere, had no idea where or why, then you couldn't get hold of me?"

The color of her lips blanched as she held them together tightly. Finally, she answered softly. "I'd be worried."

"That's right. We were worried, afraid that the people who had attacked you before might have come back, afraid you'd been threatened or targeted or tricked. We're pretty understanding, will bend on a lot of rules, but your safety is not up for discussion." He reached out and stroked his fingers over her cheek, glad to see the darkness from the bruise had mostly faded. "Do you understand that? Your safety is the most important thing to me. I was worried sick about what could have happened to you. That's why we wanted to turn on the location on your phone, to prevent issues like *this* from happening."

Even still, she didn't offer to change that, to allow them access to her location. Ethan pushed that aside, tried to tell himself it *was* a difficult line to cross for her. Not that it soothed him much, given his stress from today.

"I'm sorry," she said softly.

"Not yet," he told her. "You will be, though. See, that's the whole idea. Punishments are to make sure lessons sink in. People tend to remember only the very pleasant or the very unpleasant. So to make sure this sticks in your mind, a punishment makes it unpleasant enough that your brain won't let you forget it."

A slight tremble started in her shoulder, but Ethan refused to be swayed. If they were talking about a breach in basic protocol, if she'd screamed and insulted them, if she'd done about anything else, Ethan might have let her off easily. However, since they were talking about her safety, he just couldn't seem to get himself off that track.

"Come on, baby girl." Ethan took Ell's arm and helped her up so she wouldn't put weight on her bad ankle. "I'd normally have you lean over the bed, but I want you to stay off your foot, so hands and knees on the bed."

Ell moved — slowly, but she kept going — until she was in the position he'd asked for. Looking at her, it wasn't *quite* right. He set his hand on her back and pushed until her chest touched the bed.

Which was one hell of a sight.

He moved his hand over the curve of her ass, beyond tempted to spank her until she understood the point they were making. Her ass would look lovely pink, after he swatted it just as long as it took to make her understand. She'd whimper and beg and —

Ethan shook his head. No. Maybe another night, but for tonight, he had something else planned.

He opened the chest at the foot of the bed, but since Ell was positioned facing the other way, she had no ability to see what he was getting. No doubt that anticipation made her more nervous.

Good. A little worry did wonders for a sub.

He took out the items he'd already had ready, but left the chest open to make her more uneasy. Ethan sat on the bed beside her, the things he'd gotten from the chest hidden still.

"I know we ask for your trust, but this *is* your first punishment, so I'll let you know what will happen and what is expected of you."

She let out a long breath, her body sagging slightly as if him understanding and giving her that was worth everything.

He took the items he'd gotten and set them in front of her, and there went her ease.

She shook her head, but a hand to her back kept her in place when she went to sit up.

"Easy," Ethan reminded her. "Have I ever hurt you?"

Funny how well that question worked with her. Often times it didn't work, when people were too caught up with their own past, when they struggled to separate the actions of one person from that of another. With Ell, however, she always seemed grounded by the question, by the reminder that *he* hadn't shown himself to be untrustworthy or dangerous to her.

"Do you know what these are?" At her nod, Ethan grinned. The girl *did* like to do her research, didn't she? While he had to admit he enjoyed the surprise of a sub when he showed them something they didn't know, he also adored the nervous anticipation Ell had since she'd already researched so many things. "Good, that makes this easier, then. You'd said before you'd never tried anal, but that you might be open to trying. So your punishment—and your lesson—tonight is that we're going to train your ass."

Her gaze shifted over to his groin, a fear dancing in her dark eyes.

He shook his head. "No one will fuck your ass tonight, baby girl. There's a reason I'm saying 'train.' You'll need to get used to it, and it's better to do that slowly."

"So what are you going to do?"

Ethan tapped the butt plug he'd set in front of her. "I'm going to use my fingers first, then I'm going to slide this into your ass. After that, I'll bring you to Fox, then Clint, for you to apologize properly to them as well."

She bit her lip, but Ethan knew she looked *far* too happy with that.

"Oh, baby girl, you don't quite understand, do you? You're not going to get to come. You're going to keep that plug inside you while we use any other hole we want, but no one will touch your clit or your sweet little nipples. No one will let you get off. Then, after we're done, I'll remove the plug and you'll have to go to sleep with me to make sure you don't try to be naughty and take care of yourself. This is a punishment, after all."

Her dark eyes looked absolutely miserable as she stared at Ethan, as if pleading him to reconsider. It was funny that she was already begging for future orgasms that they were denying her. She really was something…

Still, Ethan kept his mind on the task at hand. He picked up the plug and the lube, then shifted so he was comfortable beside her. He ran his hand over the curve of her ass, enjoying the softness of her skin, the way she jumped slightly at each touch.

Keeping her from coming would be a challenge in itself. She seemed ready to go off at any little touch. Which was the reason for the other small container on the bed…

Ethan took the lube and flipped the cap open, having already placed it in the warmer before Ell had come over. He dripped some on his fingers, glad he'd set the large towel out on the bed so he didn't have to be as careful.

Something about the smell of the lube they used always made his cock throb. It was as if it called him forward, made his brain ready for whatever was next. It was one hell of a Pavlovian response.

The moment he touched his lubed finger to her ass, Ell tensed and went to rise again. Ethan was ready for it, though, and cleared his throat in warning.

A soft whine escaped Ell as she took her spot again, even with the tension inside her.

"There's my brave girl," Ethan praised before again circling her ass with his finger. He wasn't interested in edging her, in trying to purposely bring her to the precipice of release only to keep it from her until they were ready. That was a different sort of game.

Since the point tonight was to deny her entirely, he had no intention to tease her much, to make it any harder to keep her from coming than it already would be. For that reason, he pressed against the tight ring of muscles even as she tensed against him.

"Relax," he told her. "It'll go easier if you just try to loosen your muscles. The plug isn't too thick, so you can take it, but it'll be better for you if you don't resist." He leaned in and pressed a kiss to the curve of her hip. "Or you can keep fighting, keep trying to keep me out, but it won't work. Trust me, you'll tire before I will, and you still have two more men to apologize to today."

She whimpered, then buried her face against the blankets and gripped the fabric in her hands. He almost felt bad for her.

Almost. Because then he recalled why exactly she was in this position, thought about how that other man could have hurt her and Ethan wouldn't have been able to do anything about it.

His pity drifted away and he pressed harder, rewarded when his finger sank into the tightness of her ass.

They *both* groaned. Ell no doubt due to the foreignness of the sensation and Ethan because he could now imagine how it would feel to take her sweet ass, to have all that tight heat wrapped around him.

"See?" he said with a chuckle. "Not so bad, is it?"

"Because it's not your ass," Ell snapped, though the words were muffled because her face was still pressed against the blankets.

"Get that out now while you can, because I like your snarky attitude, but Fox and Clint don't find it nearly as charming. I don't think you want to annoy them any more, do you?"

She shivered, then shook her head.

Ethan chuckled at her sullen response before focusing on getting her ready. He took his time, sliding his one finger deeper then retreating. The moment she seemed to ease, when a moan left her that said she was starting to enjoy it, Ethan switched it up. He pulled out, then pressed two fingers together and plunged back into her.

And *there* was that whimper again. Why that made him so much harder, he wasn't sure, but he liked it. It said he'd taken her to a place she hadn't realized she'd wanted, that she hadn't known about, that she'd resisted. It happened when he pressed her past the limits she'd imposed, all because she'd chosen to trust him.

It was the epitome of a power exchange, when a woman gave herself to him, trusted him to take care of her.

"Oh, Ell, you're so responsive. Do you have any idea how much I wish I was fucking your ass tonight? If you get this wet from just this?" He clicked his tongue softly. "Too bad that's a treat and bad girls don't get treats."

The noise she made then was made of frustration, of unmet needs, and it made Ethan grin.

Poor girl.

The moment Ell started to get into it again, when her hips moved just a bit, he withdrew his fingers from her yet again. He picked up the butt plug — he'd chosen a small one, not much bigger than his fingers — and added enough lube to it to ensure it didn't hurt.

He wanted her uncomfortable — not in pain.

"Deep breaths," he told her as he pressed it against her, just as he had his fingers. A part of him was jealous, the part of him that wanted to feel her wrapped around him and not some toy, but he again reminded himself he needed to stay focused.

Ell did as he said, taking a deep breath, then releasing it slowly. As she did so, she relaxed, and the plug slid into her. At least, it did about halfway, as which point it seemed her brain had decided hell no and she clenched again. She even shook her head.

"Almost there," Ethan reassured her. "It's widest near the back, then narrows again. You've already been a bad girl — don't you want to be good now?"

"Yes, Daddy," she whispered.

Ethan groaned. "That isn't playing fair, you know? And calling me that isn't going to get your out of trouble. What sort of Daddy would I be if I let my baby girl do dangerous things without addressing it? Now, I'm going to finish sliding this into your ass, so I suggest you try to relax again."

She nodded, but he wasn't sure she managed much relaxation. He pulled the plug back, then moved it forward again in tiny little thrusts until it sank in deep enough to reach the thin area near the end, when the bottom flared out to keep it in place.

And she looked amazing like that, bent forward, surrendering. The butt plug ended in a heart-shaped pink jewel that looked like a decoration for her. Ethan couldn't help but press his thumb against the end — it wouldn't make the plug sink in deeper, but just moved it enough to make her all the more aware of it.

She gasped, then turned her head to the side, toward him, and had he ever seen such lust-drunk eyes?

Damn, Ell really was a thing of beauty.

"How does it feel?" Ethan asked.

"Weird."

He laughed, then flicked the end of the plug once more before standing. "Bet it does. Plugs feel stranger in some ways, because the fullness is deeper inside you. Still, it's not entirely weird. You've managed to drip onto the towel, so you're enjoying it plenty."

The red on her cheeks was almost too much, but Ethan reminded himself that there was plenty of time ahead.

Which reminded him...

"Roll over onto your back and spread your legs." He didn't soften the command, didn't give her reasons.

He wasn't sure if Ell was already so far gone that she obeyed without thinking, but she followed the order without hesitation. Even the modest woman who always went slowly when naked spread her thighs for him as if it were nothing.

And again, he was reminded just how pretty she was—especially the tight lines in her face as the plug no doubt felt odd when she moved, each shift reminding her of it there.

Ethan used the wipes he'd set on the bed to clean his fingers off, then picked up the last thing—the small container of white cream.

"What's that?" Ell asked, suspicion coloring the words.

"Well, given that you seem one good breeze from coming right now, I think the only way you'll make it the night is with a little help."

"Help?" She frowned, narrowing her eyes as if that would help her read the tiny writing on the glass container.

Ethan screwed off the lid, then placed some on his fingers. "Yes. See, I want every part of your body to be available to us, but if we so much as touch your slutty little clit, you'll get off. We can't have that, can we?" His fingers tingled for a moment before he brought his fingers to her clit.

She gasped at contact, a sound of relief as if she thought he'd changed his mind and finally touched her where she really wanted.

The girl would soon realize that wasn't the case.

He spread the cream onto her hard clit, going gently to make sure she didn't come just from this. When he was sure he'd placed enough, he repeated the motion on her nipples, both of them already erect and darkened to a lovely rose color.

Ell lifted her hips, and her desperation from such a small amount of contact told Ethan that, A, he'd been right to use this and, B, he really was going to have fun tonight.

He pulled away reluctantly and put the lid back on the container, then replaced all the items in the chest. When he turned back toward Ell—who was still right where he'd left her—his heart about stilled in his chest.

She was *gorgeous*. He knew that, of course, but somehow seeing her there, surrendering to him entirely, trusting him entirely, drove the point home. She didn't submit because she was confident in herself, because she'd done this all so many times that it didn't faze her.

She submitted because of *him*, because she trusted him, because she believed he would keep his word and take care of her.

A tightness in his chest made him rub circles there as the reality hit him. He didn't just like her. He didn't just find her pretty or interested or anything else so trivial.

Fuck...he was pretty sure he was falling in love with her.

And that was something he hadn't expected at all.

* * * *

Ell couldn't stop thinking about the plug inside her. She'd never felt *anything* in her ass before, but this seemed far worse than Ethan's fingers.

When he'd teased her, when he'd sank his fingers into her, it had felt personal. Plus, the friction had felt good. The plug only shifted a tiny bit as she moved, just enough to remind her it was there but not enough to get her anywhere. It just helped to keep her on some edge—too far from an orgasm to hope to reach it but not far enough to ignore wanting it.

After that, he'd brought her to Fox's apartment, still naked, and each step of hers was slow because it forced the plug to shift. The first few steps, she'd stopped, frowning, until Ethan had actually *laughed* at her.

The asshole...

Still, it was walking into Fox's apartment that really threw her. Ethan was still dressed, as were Clint and Fox, whereas Ell was entirely naked.

No, *worse* than just naked—she was aroused and on display with a butt plug nestled inside her, its jeweled pink end a visible invitation. Her face felt as if it might catch fire.

Fox rose from the couch, his gaze moving over her in a slow perusal. "How is your ankle feeling?"

"It's okay," Ell answered, her voice small and uncertain. Had there ever been a time when she felt the difference between them more than now? When she felt less powerful and smaller than them?

Fox lifted an eyebrow as though calling her a liar.

"It was sore, but Ethan gave me some medication and put a brace on it," she amended.

He nodded. "Good. If it starts to bother you, I expect you to tell us."

That made her frown.

"What?" he pressed.

Ell shifted her weight, the action reminding her of the plug and only throwing her off balance more. Finally, she blurted out the truth. "Why? If this is some sort of punishment, don't you want me to suffer? Shouldn't I just deal with my ankle then?"

That seemed to throw all three men, who went silent.

Fox was the one to answer. "Punishments aren't about suffering—they're about teaching you something. I don't want you hurting, though, or potentially further injuring yourself. Even if something is a punishment, we expect you to communicate with us, to tell us the truth. If you're in pain, if something is too much, if you don't feel well, those are all things you need to say."

Ell had no idea how to do that, how to admit to a weakness.

Fox slid his fingers into her hair so she looked into his blue eyes. He waited, and Ell knew what he wanted. "I'll tell you if my ankle starts to hurt."

"Good girl," Fox whispered before he leaned in and brushed his lips to hers. The kiss was passionate and deep and made her whimper in pleasure. Maybe tonight wouldn't be so bad... Maybe Ethan had just been talking a big game to scare her...

Fox trailed his hand down her front, over her stomach, her mound, then ran his finger along her slit.

And...nothing.

Ell pulled back and stared down, confused.

Fox let out a laugh, and when she met his gaze, he seemed beyond amused. "So, it seems the cream worked well."

"What?"

"Ethan put something on your clit and your nipples, remember? It's a numbing cream. It removes most of the sensation from your more sensitive areas, making it much easier to keep you from coming."

The tingling she'd felt when he'd applied it came back to her. She'd assumed it had been something to increase sensation, not something to remove it!

"Why would you do that?" she asked as if personally offended by the fact they'd stolen her orgasm.

"I told you," Ethan said from across the room. "We want to be able to enjoy your body without worry about you coming. Now, if you can get off with that on, well, you've earned your orgasm, I guess."

His chuckle heated her blood, made her twist to glare at him. He should *not* find this so funny. It wasn't fair, really. Ell was suffering and there he was, looking as if they were on the best date.

Clint huffed, and when she looked his way, he didn't seem nearly so amused. "I suggest you not turn that look my way, little one. I'm not nearly as easily charmed by disrespect."

Ell immediately blanked her face, knowing damn well that if she annoyed Clint, he wouldn't take it as well as Ethan did. The corners of Clint's lips curled up as if her reaction pleased him.

"So what now?" Ell asked, again acutely aware of the fact that she was naked and between the three of them. Did they want her to clean? To suck their cocks? She felt adrift and unsure without direction.

"We're going to watch a movie," Fox said as if that were the most obvious thing in the world.

Ell remained in place as the other three took their spots on the couch. They'd gotten her naked, teased and tormented her, just so they could watch TV?

Except it became clearer when Fox patted his lap after sitting. Ell went over, and when close enough, Fox caught her wrist and tugged her into his lap. The roughness of his pants scraped at Ell's bare thighs and further emphasized that she was naked and he wasn't.

Plus, sitting pressed the butt plug in more, moving it around and making her very aware of it.

Fox pressed a kiss to her shoulder. "Why didn't you call us?"

Ell wanted to turn around to glare at him, but she figured she was in enough trouble as it was. There wasn't a reason to compound her problems, was there?

He laughed, then reached around her. She jumped when two of his thick fingers sank into her cunt.

At the same time, Clint hit the button to the remote and the TV turned on. They put a show she didn't recognize on, one about people who turned vans into little houses they could live in. She got the feeling the men didn't care much about what was on either — and she sure couldn't stay focused on it, not when Fox fucked her with his fingers.

With the numbness of her clit, she didn't seem to get any closer to release. It was as if her body were stuck in this horrible place where she wanted something she couldn't seem to reach.

The show went on, and after a while, she jumped when someone touched her breast. Clint sat to the side of she and Fox, and he stroked his fingers over the curve of her breast. She shivered in response, but when he neared her nipples, the sensation fizzled to just a whisper of what she should have felt. She watched as he took one nipple between his fingers, as he tugged softly as if proving a point, only for her to feel next to nothing from it.

"You knew the rules," he said. "And you did well following them before. So why did you break that one?"

Ell opened her mouth, her body on fire and her lungs struggling as though she couldn't draw in enough air. "I don't know," she said.

"You know the worst part?" Fox asked. "I don't think you're even lying. I don't think you have any idea why you did it."

She shook her head, wanting that to be the end of it, wanting them to accept that and move on. She wanted things to feel like they had before, when she wasn't bad, when they weren't upset with her.

Or…maybe that wasn't the case, but she couldn't get her brain to work through it.

Fox tsked softly before having her rise slightly. He reached between them, and when she twisted to stare back, she found him rolling a condom onto his cock. That was the benefit of wearing sweats, she supposed — easy access.

She had no time to think much about it, though, before Fox's hand on her waist pulled her down, and he plunged into her drenched cunt. The feeling was strange. With the numbing cream, the sensation was lessened. She felt him inside her, felt the way his cock stretched her pussy, but it didn't send the same sparks of pleasure through her that it normally did. Everything was diminished.

Which was beyond frustrating.

"You might not know exactly why you did what you did," Ethan said from his spot, sitting on the chair next to the couch. "But you can call us what was going on in your head at least."

Ell pressed her lips together, but the way disappointment spread across his features made her chest ache. She didn't like that look on his face, didn't like the way he didn't tell her she was good or brave or any of the other things that always made her smile.

Fox used his grasp on her hips to take her, fucking her hard, but it still got her no closer to her release. "You need to learn to talk to us. We want to help you, Ell, we want to take care of you, but we can't do that if you don't *talk* to us."

Ell closed her eyes, blocking them out, refusing to let them into her head, into her heart. It felt too dangerous.

Fox let out a low, unhappy sound, but that didn't seem to matter. He lifted his hips just as he came, and Ell nearly sobbed at her own denied orgasm.

Just as quickly as he finished, she was shifted again, into Clint's lap. He didn't face her toward the TV, though. Instead, she faced him, though her eyes were still closed. Clint took her face between his palms and pulled her closer, pressing a kiss to her forehead. "Poor little one, so tied up in knots in your head you can't even see straight."

And that was true. Ell nodded even if it wasn't a question, then let out a thin whine as his thick cock filled her. It reminded her of how nervous she'd been before at the idea of having sex with him, and how quickly that had fled. Clint was a lot of things, but she couldn't picture being afraid of him anymore, not a single part of him.

"You just have to talk to us," Clint said, though his gentle words were a stark contrast to the way he took her. He fucked into her with powerful, deep thrusts, ones that forced a small gasp from her each time. They were perfect—wild and passionate and just on the edge of pain.

And yet they *still* didn't get her where she needed to be. Even when she shifted her hips, when she arched her back, when she tried to get closer to that orgasm she wanted, nothing worked.

Damn them!

Ell whimpered as she accepted each thrust from Clint, as she wrapped her arms around his shoulders and buried her face against his neck. She breathed him in, felt the way his pulse thundered just beneath his skin. It was so much more than she'd ever thought she had, and yet this fear wouldn't stop inside her, this feeling that it was dangerous, that it would only end up hurting her.

Clint shook his head but held her tighter. "You really are a mess."

And she nodded at that. *I really am.*

He groaned as he came, and the twitching of his cock inside her cunt was just another reminder of what they'd stolen from her.

He kissed her, a gentle brush of his lips to hers, but it teased her as much as his cock had.

She didn't get time to think about it, though. Instead, the scraping of something heavy being moved over the tile made her turn to find Ethan pushing the large ottoman over, against the couch. It meant both Fox and Clint lifted their legs so they could rest them out straight on it.

Ell didn't understand the point at first, not until Ethan took her arm and twisted her, moving until she was lying flat, the ottoman giving her enough room so her head was on the couch—between Fox and Clint—and her body rested out straight.

Ethan took the spot above her, his heavy body caging her in, his lips finding hers for a deep and passionate kiss.

"You're going to tell us," Ethan said as if it had already been decided, as if it were obvious to everyone except her.

Or, maybe it was obvious to her as well. She couldn't imagine keeping anything from them, but that didn't mean she understood yet, that she even had an answer for them.

Ethan took her thigh and lifted it, wrapping it around his hip, then pressed his cock—when he'd put on a condom, she wasn't sure, but she wasn't following their movements all that well—against her. He sank into her with a deep, masculine groan, as if he'd felt nothing better.

He covered her with his body, pressing close to her so not an inch of space existed between them. It let him speak softly and his whispered words found her ear. "Didn't you think we'd worry?"

And here comes the guilt...

Ell nodded.

Ethan fucked her hard, but not fast, each thrust plunging him deep into her, but it wasn't nearly enough for her. It broke her resolve, turned her raw so each breath of his against her ear, each thrust, each time his body pressed tighter against hers further wore down any resistance she had.

"I'm sorry," she gasped out.

"This isn't just about sorry." Fox ran his fingers through her hair. The way he touched her while another man fucked her set her off more, kept her off balance. "It's about figuring out *why* it happened so it doesn't happen again."

"I don't know why."

"So don't try to figure it out. Just tell us what you were thinking."

Ell struggled, that feeling like so long ago she couldn't seem to figure it out. Ethan slowed and gentled, made his thrusts go from frantic to languid. It helped her to think straight, though the friction still kept her on edge. "I knew I should call you, but I couldn't."

"Why not?" Fox asked her, his tone gentle. "Why couldn't you just talk to us, Ell?"

The use of *Ell* instead of princess deepened that ache, made her feel as if she'd already lost them, as if she'd really screwed up and they'd walk away.

And as much as that hurt, it also made her chest loosen, as if she was okay with it.

That realization was what got her to speak again, to answer, the words leaving her before she could think about it much. "No one ever cared where I was."

Ethan slowed more, lifting off her enough to stare down and at her face. It made his green eyes bright, intense. "What?"

Ell licked her bottom lip, then allowed the words to spring from her. "I grew up without anyone giving a damn. I had to take care of myself, always. It was just me."

Fox's hand paused in her hair for a breath, then after a soft breath, he continued the gentle touch. "So you don't like us asking where you are?"

That didn't seem quite right, so she shook her head. "The few times I had anyone, they always left, and I was worse off for it. Every time I relied on sometime, it screwed me over."

Ethan paused entirely, his eyebrows furrowed.

It was Clint who spoke while he ran his fingers over her cheek. "So you're afraid of letting us in, of trusting us because it's hurt you in the past?"

She nodded, realizing wetness tracked down her face from the corners of her eyes. "I stared at my phone, but I kept thinking that it was only a matter of time until you didn't want this, until you walked out, then I'd have to pick up the mess. I'd have to stand on my own again and I didn't know if I could do that."

"Baby girl…" Ethan said, his voice soft. He leaned in and brushed his lips to hers. "You might think we're going somewhere, but we aren't. No matter what happens, we're not going to just drop you, won't screw up your life and leave you to pick up the pieces. You probably walked out thinking we would, huh? That we'd get so mad that we'd kick you out?"

She nodded, the tears coming harder until she felt as if she'd crack apart. At least, she did until the men didn't pull back, they didn't retreat from her tears or her panic or her stupid choice to ignore their rules.

Fox let another of those sighs, the ones that made her want to curl into a ball and disappear. Still, his words after were gentle. "Maybe that's the lesson you really need right now, princess, that we're going nowhere. You can test your limits. You can push us all you want, but we're not going to break."

Ell frowned, the words making no sense to her. Others in her life had taken off at the slightest provocation, at the smallest problem to come up. The idea that these men wouldn't, that they'd stay even when she did things to push them away, it just didn't seem to compute.

"You don't believe us?" Ethan's blue eyes met hers, shining brightly as he smiled. "Well, let's see just how long you can keep up with that stubbornness."

When he plunged deeply into her again, when she arched her back, Ell had a feeling he was more than ready to spend just as long as it took making his point clear.

And even though she should have been worried, she wasn't sure she'd ever felt more cared for…

* * * *

Clint groaned softly as he shifted, wondering why the hell he was asleep on a couch. It took a long moment for him to come to fully, to look down and see the naked woman spread out across his lap.

Right. Ell… The night came back to him, the way they had played with her for hours, how they'd kept her from coming, how sweat-drenched and desperate she'd been. The woman had cried more than a few times, but each time she'd broken apart, they'd been there.

They'd gathered her against one of their chests, kissed the tears away and reminded her that no matter what happened, they'd help put her back together each time.

And Clint wasn't sure he'd ever felt as happy, as content. The world felt peaceful, quiet in a way it normally didn't. Just how she did that, he had no idea.

Ethan slept in the chair, his feet on the ottoman, and the scent of food from the kitchen said Fox was cooking.

While Clint was sure he'd pay for the late night and poor sleeping posture through the day, he couldn't be sorry about it, not when Ell snored so softly against him.

I'm in love...

There was no other explanation. He couldn't stop thinking about her, couldn't stop smiling when he did.

He dragged his fingers up her arm, rewarded with an unhappy grumble before she cuddled in closer against his chest.

All night they'd had their fun, but the poor girl hadn't gotten off. It had killed him, near the end, that desire to see her break apart, but punishment was punishment. They'd agreed at the start that to drive their point home, she wouldn't get what she wanted, not that night at least.

It isn't the night anymore...

Clint pressed a kiss to her head, then repeated the stroke over her bare arm.

Ell stirred, the movement dragging her hard nipples against his side. It made him smile, knowing she was still wound up. When she repeated the motion, she let out a low, desperate moan.

So sensitive...

"Little one," he whispered.

The words seemed to wake not only her, but Ethan as well. The other man looked over, then grinned as if understanding the game.

Ell lifted her head, sleep clouding her dark eyes, a confused question there. Still, when he dipped his head down and took a kiss, it seemed her body got with the plan quickly enough.

She moaned again, then slid an arm around him and dug her fingers into his side. That hungry edge pleased him, made him want to take care of her, give her everything she needed.

Which, judging by the way she thrust against his leg, was an orgasm.

Clint slid away from her, kicking the ottoman out of the way, then sank to his knees in front of her. It had been *far* too long since he'd gotten a taste of her, and this sounded much better than whatever Fox was cooking.

He set his hands on her knees and spread her thighs. Ell didn't resist, didn't try to hide. He wasn't sure if they'd gotten through to her or if she was just that desperate.

"But I thought…" she asked, her voice trailing off.

He paused, then fit together what she just meant. From her history, he had no doubt people held grudges, that they blamed her for things long after it should have been let go. He shook his head. "Your punishment is over. You handled it well, and you're forgiven. I think you deserve a treat, now."

The smile she gave him melted him. If he'd ever thought he could resist her, he was an idiot. He couldn't say no to that face, not when she looked so damned sweet and innocent and *his*.

Fox came into the living room. "Breakfast is ready." He paused, as if realizing the situation.

Ell's smile lessened. Was she worried Clint would stop, that now that she almost had what she wanted, it would get taken away?

Silly girl.

Clint stroked his thumbs over the insides of her thighs and gave her a rare and honest smile. "Let the food get cold. I've got everything I need right here."

Ethan chuckled, and said, "Fuck yes," behind him.

"But Fox—" Ell started, as if to mention the fact that Fox had spent time cooking, that it would be rude to not eat, but Clint silenced her when he leaned in and dragged his tongue up her cunt.

"Food reheats," Fox said as he took a spot beside Ell then stole a kiss. "But I think Clint's right—spending the morning tasting every spot on your sweet little body is a much better start to the day."

And just like that, Clint knew he never wanted to lose this woman.

Chapter Fourteen

Clint hung up the phone, his jaw tight and his teeth about aching.

"Bad news?" Ethan asked as he paused near the kitchen.

Fox was cooking dinner, with the scent of sauteed onions filling Clint's apartment. They tended to like to cook there, since Clint kept his place the cleanest, and he didn't mind them there. While he didn't care for most people coming into his private space, Fox and Ethan were almost a part of him already.

And Ell would be by in another half an hour or so — another of the rare people he didn't mind. In fact, he rather enjoyed the nights she crawled into his bed to sleep beside him.

Ethan lifted an eyebrow, which reminded Clint of the question.

The call.

"It was Kat," he said.

That made even Fox pause and turn around. "Did she get herself arrested again?"

"Jane is in town."

That drove the tension in room up, the name seemingly ripped from the past. It brought up the memory of the woman it belonged to, her short blonde hair, her large blue eyes, the soft cries she'd let out when they'd —

Clint shook his head. It was easy to remember the good things, but that wasn't the whole truth. It never was.

"Shit," Fox said, then shook his head and turned his focus back to the food.

Then again, that one word was pretty much a good explanation of the truth. It was all that could be said after the massive wreck of that relationship. The relationship between Clint, Ethan, Fox and Jane was the equivalent of a six-car pile-up on the freeway.

No one walked away without their share of scars.

"Is she coming back to Sanctuary?" Ethan asked.

Clint shrugged. "Kat said she is probably going to come back, but she isn't sure when. I think she's a little gun-shy…"

Fox spoke from the kitchen. "Maybe we should stay scarce for a while, if she wants to go there."

Clint wanted to argue that point, but he struggled to. He didn't want to lose his place, didn't like the idea of being run out of Sanctuary, but at the same time…

He didn't want to cause any more pain for a woman they'd already done enough to. Clint sat at the bar, staring down at his phone, as if that item was at fault for the way his chest tightened. Still… "Why should we give up a place we have gone to for years just because someone else might want to go there?"

"Because she might not feel comfortable with us there," Fox said. "I don't want her to feel unwelcome or like she can't go there anymore."

"So that means we can't go?"

Ethan sighed, the sound the men often made when Clint just didn't understand what they meant. "You remember her when she left, I'm sure."

Clint nodded.

"Well, with how upset she was, do you really think she wants to see us?"

Clint pressed his lips together. "Probably not." After a moment, Clint dropped his phone to the bar. "I get it. Believe it or not, I'm not stupid. I know Jane was upset. I know that what happened wasn't what any of us wanted. We didn't do anything wrong, though."

"Didn't we?" Fox asked. "We should have realized sooner she didn't want that life, that she was doing it to make us happy. If we'd been paying more attention, things wouldn't have gone so far and she wouldn't have ended up so…" Fox paused, then shook his head. "So hurt. We can't pretend like that had nothing to do with us, with our actions."

Clint couldn't argue with that.

The memory of how things had gone with Jane had plagued him just as it had the others. It had started out so easily, seeming like everything they'd wanted. Jane had been sweet, pretty and new the lifestyle. They hadn't been in it for that long, either, but longer than her.

Yet, no matter how it had started, it sure hadn't ended that way.

"It doesn't matter right away. Jane won't show up for at least a few weeks, I'd bet."

"What about Ell?" Ethan asked.

"What about her?" Clint countered.

"What if it's the same issue with her? What if it goes the same way?"

Fox again turned, this time pointing at Ethan with his spatula. "Ell isn't Jane. You can't take every submissive we meet and think it'll end the same way." Fox went back to the food, then paused. "Should we tell Ell about Jane?"

"Why do that?" Clint asked. "She doesn't need to know."

By which, Clint was fairly sure he really meant that she might not like it, and that telling her would only risk what little trust they'd built thus far.

"Because we ask her to be honest. How fair is it to keep this from her?"

"She hasn't told us about every person she's dated or slept with—I don't think we need to do that, either," Ethan said.

The tension in Fox's expression said he didn't agree. No doubt he wanted to spill everything to Ell, to prevent any chance of a future misunderstanding, but Clint saw no good reason to offer up potentially damning information on a whim.

The chime inside the apartment said the elevator had opened on their floor, causing all three of them to go still and look toward the door.

A moment later, the lock clicked just before Ell opened the door and walked in. The look on her face said she noticed the way everyone stared at her.

"Is everything okay?" Ell asked, patting her hands down her front as if she worried she might have forgotten something.

Ethan recovered first, though he'd always been the best at saying whatever needed to be said. "Yeah, of course, baby girl. Come on and have a seat. How was your day?"

Ell narrowed her eyes, saying she probably didn't quite believe him, but nodded and did as he said.

Clint couldn't help but rub at his chest for a moment. He hadn't wanted to tell Ell, but damn it, he didn't like the guilt he felt now over it.

It felt far too much like breaking her trust…

* * * *

Ell snuggled up against Clint's side. It was funny that he seemed so unapproachable, because she was the first to admit he was amazing at cuddling.

Perhaps it was his size, the fact he made for a very large and solid pillow, but Ell never failed to be comfortable when she leaned against him.

Dinner had been wonderful, as usual. She'd taken care of a side salad while Fox had cooked the spaghetti, making the sauce from scratch. The whole apartment still smelled of onions and garlic.

After that, Ethan had put on a movie, and all four of them had spread out in the living room. Fox sat in a recliner, Ethan on the floor since the man never sat long enough to deserve a better spot and Clint on the couch with Ell pressed against him, her legs up and over the length of the couch.

The movie was stupid, and Ell hadn't honestly paid much attention. She hadn't given a damn what they'd picked to watch, because what she really wanted was the time with the three of them.

It was strange, because weeks before she'd been happy with her life. She'd been content with the way everything was organized, with how quiet and carefully planned each part of her day was. The very thought of sharing space, of not knowing what would happen would have driven her to panic.

So why was it that when she got a message from Ethan telling her to come over, that he had a surprise, she smiled each time? Even when she knew it was nothing much, that it was something silly, she still happily crossed the hallway to his place? And when Fox stopped by in the evenings to go over her list of tasks for the day, Ell didn't balk anymore. In fact, she felt downright giddy to hear him call her a good girl, to praise her for the completion of her lists? Even Clint, who she had been so sure hated her, made her comfortable, and she crawled into his bed at night more often than anyone else's because his temperature always ran high and she slept soundly by his side.

The movie ended, the screen changing over to credits, but Ell found herself reluctant to sit up, to let the evening end.

Clint ran his fingers through her hair, the touch relaxing her more, before his rough voice interrupted her thoughts. "What do you want, Ell?"

She frowned but didn't look up at him. "For what? Dessert?"

"No. What do you want in general? We've done this a while, tested it out, so I think it's fair to check-in, to ask what you think, where you think this is headed?"

Ell pushed herself upright, her stomach feeling off at the unexpected questions. How was a person supposed to answer that?

Which was funny, since Ell had always relied on plans, had always dug into them and enjoyed the way they made her feel safe. So why was it that when asked what her plans were, what she wanted, she couldn't seem to formulate any sort of answer?

"Why?" she asked instead.

"Because it's important for us to know that this is still what you're wanting. We need to know you aren't just forcing it," Fox said.

"But why? If you're enjoying it, why does that matter?" Ell struggled to wrap her head around why they cared. "I'm doing what you've said, I follow your orders, you get everything you want from me. Why does anything more matter?"

Fox leaned forward in his recliner to meet Ell's gaze. "You really still don't get it? You think subs are just interchangeable and Doms don't give a damn which one they have?"

Ell didn't answer that, because…yeah, she did. Especially if she was the sub in question.

Fox shook his head. "No, princess. You are no more interchangeable than we are to you — or at least I hope that's the case. The fact is that we *like* you here. I need to know if you feel the same, if this is serious for you or if you're just scratching an itch still and plan to walk away." He paused for a moment, then let out a long breath. "For this sort of relationship, we need communication, and it's only fair for us to all understand where we are — how we feel."

Ell pressed her lips together and dropped her gaze as she considered it. What would a future look like? She had to admit…she really liked being here, with them. It was the first time she'd felt…at home? In her old life, she had been constantly trying to organize her world in such a way that she felt safe, that she felt at ease, but it was something she'd never quite grasped.

Here, though?

Ell felt relaxed, happy, at ease. The rest of her life, she'd always felt as if she were moving toward some future point. She'd felt like she wasn't happy then, but if she kept moving, if she did these specific things, she'd get to the place she wanted to be. She never reached it, though, she just spent all her energy trying.

Here she had those things, though. It wasn't some future place for her, not something she thought she could achieve but something she'd *found.*

The thought of losing that made her breath short.

"I want you," Clint said, his voice soft. When Ell looked at him, he was staring down at his own hands. "Maybe it's not fair to expect you to put your cards on the table first, so I might as well go. I want you—I want *this.* I like falling asleep with you beside me. I like coming home and seeing you here. I like the sweet way you look at me, the way you make me feel, the way you look at me like I'm not strange, like someone finally really understands me. I'm not in this for just a few weeks—I don't want to lose this."

His words made Ell both melt and freeze. They warmed her, were exactly what she wanted to hear, but they were also dangerous.

"I want you to stay for good," Fox said. "I feel...fulfilled with you here. It makes me happy to plan your day with you in the mornings, to start my day that way. I've felt adrift recently, like I didn't have purpose, like something was missing. You were what was missing."

That feeling increased inside Ell, the nerves. They wanted something from her, were talking about this as if it could go on, and she had no idea what to do about that.

"Guess it's my turn, right?" Ethan let out a chuckle that was full of more than a bit of anxiety. "I know we started this all with an idea that it was just for fun. Nothing ever stays just for fun, does it? I want you, Ell, more than I think I've wanted anything else. It's one of those things I didn't even realize I needed, not until you got here, not until we've done this. The thing is… I don't want to keep feeling this, keep sinking deeper into it only to find out you don't want it, that it isn't for you. That's fine, it's got to be your choice, but I can't keep going down this path if you don't feel the same way."

Which put Ell on the spot, made her shift in her seat as she tried to sort out her thoughts and figure out what to say. She followed a seam on her pants with her finger to distract her as she spoke softly. "I don't know what I want," she admitted. "I've liked being here, I have. I just don't know…"

When she trailed off, Fox offered up an end to her sentence. "You're not sure if you can do it long-term?"

She nodded. "I don't know if I can be what you want all the time. I don't know if I want this all the time. Just playing, that's one thing, but twenty-four-seven?" Even as she spoke, something screamed in her head that she was letting labels define what she wanted.

Her actual day-to-day life was everything she could have asked for, so why was it that when she actually thought about it, when she tried to define it, she stumbled?

"You never turned on the location on your phone," Clint said.

"Why is that such a sticking point for you?"

"Because it's a sign of trust. It's you saying you put yourself into our care. The fact that you still resist that feels like a sign that you don't want the same things we do." Clint spoke softly, his voice low as if he didn't care of saying that any more than she did.

"Are you going to kick me out?" Ell's words wavered as she asked them.

"Of course not," Fox said. "First of all, we wouldn't kick you out even if you said you never wanted to see us again. We offered to let you stay here, and we aren't going to take that away. Furthermore…this wasn't intended to be some discussion that needs an answer this second. There's still time for us all to figure out what we really want."

"So why ask me now?"

"Because you needed to think about it, to really dig into yourself and sort through your own past, your own needs. People tend to go on through their life without really thinking about anything, just going day-by-day."

"So if I'm never sure about this, that's okay?"

"I didn't say that," Fox said. "We aren't going to accept 'maybe' forever. Eventually, it'll reach a point where maybe means no, where you don't really want this. It isn't fair to force you into anything, but it isn't fair to string us along, either. I just want you to think about it, to decide what it is you really want, because at some point you'll need to know."

"Or what?"

"Or we'll have to walk away."

The sharp pain in her chest at those words surprised Ell, made her realize just how important these men had become to her. Even the idea of not having them, of not waking up and seeing them each day, it seemed impossible, like going backward to a pit she'd finally crawled out of.

Clint slid his arm around her and pulled her against his side again. He pressed a kiss to the top of her head. "We can talk again later. Just relax, for now."

She couldn't, though. Even when they turned on another movie, the tension inside Ell remained.

She couldn't lose them…but she wasn't sure she was brave enough to fully give in to them, either.

Which made heartache seem inevitable.

Chapter Fifteen

It had only been a week since Fox had gone to Sanctuary, yet the moment he walked in tonight, he realized how much he'd needed it.

The club was sometimes too much—too loud, too demanding, too busy—but it was still home. It was a place where he felt welcome, where he didn't feel the need to hide or pretend anything.

It was one of the only truly safe places in his world.

And what made it better was Ell beside him.

Though, really, she did that with everything. No matter where he went or what he did, Ell's small, soft hand in his always made it better.

More fun, more exciting, all of it.

She wore what Ethan had picked out for her, which was another schoolgirl uniform. It reminded Fox of the first night they'd met there, when they'd spoken to her in the darkness, when they'd had no idea who she was. He still recalled his shock when the lights had come back on, when the girl he'd thought about so many times had turned out to be the mystery girl.

That had been a lifetime ago, though. They'd been almost strangers back then, and now?

Now she basically lived with him, with Ethan and Clint. Now Fox knew every inch of her skin, had seen her struggles and her strengths, had kissed the birthmark on her left thigh enough times that he could have drawn it from memory. Before she'd been a fantasy but now, she was his reality.

And yet she still couldn't quite accept what they had between them…

Which was part of the reason for their trip to Sanctuary that night. Ethan, being ever the proactive one when it came to what he wanted, had thought maybe coming here would make her remember how much she enjoyed being with them.

Fox held less hope…

Ell paused on the way in, seeing all the people she knew, the friends who used to be Fox's but had taken in Ell now. Again, he hoped those connections would help her realize a life with him, with Ethan and Clint, wouldn't be so bad.

Or maybe he was hoping for nothing…

"Fox…" The soft, feminine voice just about stopped Fox's heart. It had been years since he'd heard it, but it seemed time hadn't dulled it at all.

He wanted to tighten his hand around Ell's to ignore the woman and just leave, to keep her and the painful memories in the past.

However, he knew better than to try it. He wasn't a coward.

Fox steeled himself and turned to find a short, thin woman standing there, her blonde hair cut into the same pixie style she'd had years ago. "Jane," he said softly.

Ell's gaze darted between them, but Fox didn't introduce her. He wasn't sure how, wasn't sure what would happen.

Would Jane cry? Would she scream? Would Ell ask what had happened, and would Fox have to bare those wounds to her?

"It's been a long time," Jane said softly, her gaze dropping to where Fox and Ell held hands.

"Yeah. How are you?" The question slipped from Fox, the inane sort of small talk people made when there was too much pain between them for anything real.

"I'm good," she said. "I moved back a few months ago."

"Kat mentioned it."

Jane smiled, which felt like a sucker punch to Fox. "Kat has a big mouth. It's a good thing I love her so much."

"Jane." Ethan's voice interrupted the conversation as he walked up, Clint standing beside him. Both men offered Jane a wary look.

Even as she stood there, it was impossible to ignore the tension in Jane, the way she didn't look comfortable. It was strange to think back to years prior, to the times when Jane had been there with them, when she'd been happy.

As happy as Ell looked...

Jane had flitted from group to group, talking to all the friends she had, smiling and as at home as Fox felt in Sanctuary.

Then it had all gone wrong, and Jane had run away, leaving Fox, Ethan and Clint to pick up the pieces, to try to figure out what went wrong, to bear the weight of what had happened alone.

"I can leave," Jane said softly. "I don't want to cause problems."

"What?" Ethan asked quickly, as if her offer had woken him up from a daze. "No, you don't need to leave. This place is as much yours as it is ours."

One side of her lip curled up. "This place was always more yours. I hadn't planned to come back, but between Toya and Kat, I guess I just couldn't stop thinking about it."

Fox squeezed Ell's hand, an unconscious action. He wasn't sure if it was to reassure himself or to reassure her. When she squeezed back, he knew that was all for him.

"I should get going," Jane said, gesturing back toward the bar. "Kat's going to get here in the next twenty minutes or so, and I promised I'd grab us a good table." She took a step back, then paused. "It's good to see you." Her words didn't sound true, though.

Fox doubted very much that it was good to see them, that she'd hoped to run into them at all.

When she left, Fox stood there dumbfounded for far too long.

"Who was that?" Ell's voice shook him back to the present, pulled him from the memories of years before.

"No one," Ethan said, his tone sharp enough to be suspicious.

"But—"

"Drop it," Ethan added.

Ell went silent, then pulled her hand from Fox's. The loss of her warmth was like a physical blow, like something he hadn't been expecting. In fact, when he turned to look right at her, Ell had seemed to entirely withdraw into herself.

We're screwing it all up again...

"Come on." Fox nodded toward the private rooms. He wanted to get Ell away from prying eyes, away from the past and the memories and everything else. He wanted to strip her down and lose himself in her as he swore to himself that history wouldn't repeat itself again.

Even though he was terrified it already had...

Ell couldn't shake the feeling that she'd suddenly become all of two inches tall. Between that beautiful woman she'd seen talking to her men and Ethan's sharp words to her, she couldn't get her bearings.

Even so, she followed them into one of the private rooms, then took a seat on the couch where Clint indicated as Ethan closed the door. The click of the latch was loud in the silent space.

"Sorry," Ethan said after a long moment. "I shouldn't have snapped at you like that."

"Who was she?" Ell asked again.

"Can't you just leave it be?"

She shook her head. "You ask me to trust you, but you won't tell me about someone you know, someone you obviously had a relationship with?" As she said it, the hurt inside her, the part that had shriveled up at their denials, swelled. Anger replaced hurt. She'd given them *everything* and they couldn't even tell her who that woman was?

"It's in the past," Fox said. "I don't really want to go digging up the past for no reason."

Ell rose, tired of sitting there, of listening to them when they refused to listen to *her*. "You talk about what

I need — well, I need this. I need to know that you tell me the truth. I guess you just talk a big game when it's easy for you."

Ethan let out an unhappy sound, then crossed his arms. If Ell had any real fear of the men, it would have sprung up from the way they looked at her. "It was a relationship that went badly. There's nothing more to know."

"So you're going to lie now, too? I saw the way you looked at her, the way you looked over at me. That wasn't just some breakup, and it wasn't all in the past."

Clint took one deep breath, as if to stay calm. "Everything comes back around, doesn't it?"

Ell frowned at Clint, having no idea what that meant. Was it just an attempt to muddy the answer?

No, Clint was nothing if not honest…

Fox rubbed at his eyes, then spoke slowly while his gaze was locked on the table. "Jane was our sub years ago, back when we were all new to the lifestyle."

"Did you love her?" Ell asked the question with a laugh, unable to believe it. Somehow, the idea of them loving someone else hurt.

"Yes," Clint said without hesitation. Another reminder that Clint didn't save people's feelings…

Ell's knees gave out, and she sat back down on the couch, the room suddenly feeling far smaller with the new information.

They'd *loved* that woman. The word submissive told her that they'd probably done the same sorts of things that Ell had done with them. Worse, she thought about just how pretty Jane had been, could almost picture all of them together.

"We knew what we wanted, and Jane said yes. She'd never done that, never had that kind of relationship, but she never said no. Time passed, we thought we'd settled into something good, but we didn't see what was really happening."

"What was happening?"

Ethan answered, pacing in the small amount of space. "She didn't really want what we did. She tried to force herself, to twist herself into something she just wasn't, all to make us happy. I didn't see it, though, not until it was too late." He paused, his hands pulled into tight fists, his gaze on the far wall. "Came home to find her passed out in bed beside an empty bottle of painkillers. Fox called an ambulance, and the hospital was able to save her. She did that because of *us*, because we didn't take good enough care of her. We didn't see that she didn't want what we did, that she wasn't happy."

Ell ached for them as Ethan told her the story. She knew these men—even if she was angry with them at the moment—and they'd never hurt a woman on purpose. She might feel like screaming at each of them right now, but even with that she had trouble blaming them for what had happened. "I know if you'd realized, you'd have done something. You can't blame yourself for everything—"

"We can," Fox said, "Because that's our entire job. What good is being a Dom if I can't even take care of the one person I'm supposed to?"

Clint hadn't spoken again, but his words continued to simmer in the back of her head until they mixed with the story. She peered at him. "What did you mean about history repeating itself?"

"You won't turn on the location on your phone."

"That again?" Ell threw her hands up, the frustration eating away at her that they would focus on such a trivial detail.

"Seeing Jane, it made me think, we're in the same place again but this time we know enough to not let it go the same way. I think what we want is not what you want."

Goosebumps rose on Ell's skin, the same way it happened during a lightning storm, when she knew a strike was coming but not when. "What do you mean?"

Ethan took over, and the way the men spoke implied they'd had this conversation before. "You said from the start this wasn't what you wanted, but somehow you kept sinking in deeper and deeper. You kept giving up more and more. Is that even what you want, though?"

Ell nodded, her throat tight and unable to get the actual words out.

"I don't know if it really is, and I've been down the path of watching someone do something they don't want for other people. It doesn't ever end well. The location isn't the end all, but it's a tipping point. I don't think you're ever going to really want this life, and I don't want a vanilla life, and that leaves us at an impasse."

Each word felt like another strike, like life kicking her and not letting her catch her breath. She'd expected to go into the back room and argue, to get some sort of closure on the fight, but she hadn't expected to hear what was quickly sounding like a breakup. "You aren't serious, are you?"

Fox finally looked at her, and the set of his expression said he was completely serious. "I wanted this to work—I really did. We *all* did. But I think it's time to stop pretending, to stop hoping that we'll just magically start working."

"I don't want to stop." Ell swallowed hard when she heard the tears in her voice, the way her voice wavered.

"And I don't want to see you suffer just because you're trying to force yourself into something that doesn't fit you. I've seen where that ends up."

"I'm not Jane!" The explosion of anger surprised even Ell, but she couldn't help it. They'd offered her something she wanted so badly then turned around and wanted to tear it away, now. It was just cruel.

"And I can't survive coming home and finding *you* unconscious!" Fox yelled back, the first time she'd ever heard such real anger from him. Not just anger, though—it was impossible to miss the fear beneath it. Still, he quieted his voice after a long moment with his eyes closed. "It almost killed me to know I'd done that to her, that I'd pushed her to that point, and I won't do it again. I can't risk that again. The fact you don't want to turn on the location tracker is fine—you get to set your limits. It's just…seeing Jane in person tonight feels like the universe reminding me not to make the same mistake again. This…" He paused, then moved his hands between them and Ell. "It can't continue."

It can't continue.

How could three words hurt so much? How could they make her chest feel empty, make her eyes sting and her lungs burn?

"I'm sorry," Ethan said, his voice so soft it was almost worse. "We shouldn't have let this start, shouldn't have let it go this far." He reached for her, setting a hand on her shoulder.

And that broke her. If they'd been mean, she could have handled it. She could have packed it all down and moved forward, pissed but solid. Instead, Ethan had said *sorry* for what felt like the only good things she had in her life. He was apologizing for some of the best days she'd ever had.

It was like pouring heaps of salt on a dessert. He ruined it, tainted it so she knew she couldn't ever look back on their time together without tasting that bitterness.

"How dare you," Ell said as she knocked his hand away.

"Ell—" Clint started.

She pointed a finger at him. "Don't. I've listened to you three and I've been honest with you and now it's your turn to hear me. How *dare* you apologize to me! How dare you take everything I've given to you, everything we had and spit on it by saying sorry for it all? If you wanted to break my heart, you didn't need to be so cruel about it."

Silence met her, and for a stupid moment, Ell thought they'd take it all back. She thought they'd look at her, realize they'd made a mistake and they could go back to how it had been.

Hope was a dangerous thing, though, and one look at them let her know that wouldn't happen. Their minds were made up.

"I'm sorry that I ever met you," she whispered before turning and rushing from the room.

They didn't call after her, didn't try to stop her, and that was perhaps the worst part of it all. They'd broken her heart, stomped on everything they had together and hadn't even cared enough to try to stop her when she ran off.

It really was all over, wasn't it?

* * * *

"Drink up, brat."

Ell jumped at the voice, even though she knew exactly who it was. What the hell was wrong with her? She couldn't seem to center herself, to ground herself. Even though she knew there were people over, anytime one tried to actually talk to her, she reacted as if she'd been home alone and a ghost had popped out.

Dean handed her a water bottle, but behind his normal grin sat worry.

He wasn't the only one, either, judging by the multitude of people in her new apartment.

Dean had found her a place in his building, then had hired movers for her. While Ell would have fought with him over the location and movers any other time, she lacked the energy to do so now.

Besides, they'd managed the job so quickly that Ell had only needed to spend two nights at Dean's place before her things were all moved into her new apartment on the ground floor.

It meant all her visitors had shown up with housewarming gifts like some party Ell hadn't thrown.

Toya had brought a bottle of wine, Sunny had brought a few different frozen meals so she wouldn't need to cook and Kat brought a box labeled *Breakup Survival Kit*. Inside it was a vibrator, a dildo and a bottle of whiskey.

In addition, Sunny's Doms, Garrison, Connor and Trent, were doing small repairs to the place as the rest of the guests all sat in the living room. The place wasn't that large, which made it even more obvious how many there were.

Dean crouched down so he met Ell's gaze. "Drink your water."

"I'm not thirsty," Ell said.

"I didn't ask if you were. I've put up with your nonsense for two days now — enough. You're going to drink your water or you're going to see that I'm more than willing show you my scarier side."

Ell gulped at the tone Dean *never* used with her. It didn't scare her, not really, but damn it made her chest ache worse. It reminded her of *her* men, reminded her that she wouldn't ever hear them rumble out a threat like that again. She opened the lid and forced herself to drink some.

Dean's expression softened and he sat his warm palm on her cheek. "Poor Ell, you really did have it bad, didn't you?"

Ell nodded, because even if she wasn't sure what exactly he meant, the answer was still obvious.

Dean shook his head and rose. "I'm going to go help Garrison with the security system."

Once he left, it seemed like everyone took a deep breath. What was it about Doms that could change the tension in a room, even when they didn't mean to?

"So now what?" Sunny asked.

"Now," Kat said. "We open the survival kit!"

"You are *not* going to use the toys while I'm here," Toya said, her voice stern.

"What sort of girl do you take me for?" Kat looked insulted, but a playful edge to her words said she wasn't. "No, I figured we'd indulge in the other part of it. No better way to get over something than drink until we no longer remember it!" She lifted the whiskey from the box like she'd found a hidden treasure.

Ell didn't really care for the idea, but hell…she didn't care for much of anything right then.

"Sure," Ell said, knowing damn well her tone was about as lively as she felt.

If she could forget, it would all be worth it…

One hour later

"All over a stupid program on my phone!" Ell grimaced at the way a hiccup brought the taste of the whiskey back up into her mouth.

"Doms are jerks," Kat slurred out. "They think they're so smart, but they *aren't*! They think they know everything, but they don't."

"They're not so bad," Sunny said as she teetered around despite sitting cross-legged on the floor. "They're a little annoying sometimes, but they're not so bad."

Kat stuck her tongue out at the other woman. "You only say that because you're still in that smitten, honeymoon stage. Trust me — it ends. It always does. And when it does, *this* is your future." Kat pointed at Ell.

"Hey," Ell objected.

"I think everyone has had enough," Toya said as she stood. She didn't waver, but Ell wasn't sure she'd seen Toya drink any at all. Instead, she'd sat there like some mother hen, watching over the wayward chicks.

Which felt like a pretty accurate statement given the level of inebriation of Ell, Kat and Sunny.

"I'll take you home," Toya said to Kat.

"No. I'm staying."

"What?" Ell asked.

Kat looked at Ell. "We're having a sleepover. It's your first night here, and I'm not leaving you alone. If I don't stay, Dean probably will, and he'll make you drink water and eat healthy food. If *I* stay, we'll drink more and order a billion pancakes with syrup and whipped cream."

Which was a hard offer to reject...

Garrison, Connor and Trent came in to gather up Sunny—who by that point was sleeping and snoring loudly. Toya walked out with Dean, leaving Ell and Kat alone.

"I still love them," Ell admitted softly once it was just the two of them.

Kat came over and took a seat just beside Ell, then put her arm around her. "I know. I've been there. The thing is—it's easy to love someone, but despite all the stories that tell us otherwise, love isn't all it takes."

Ell grabbed her phone, her fingers moving without her even thinking about it. She opened the program Clint had installed on her phone, the one she'd never authorized to work, then gave it permissions.

"Ell..."

"I know it won't change anything," Ell said, her vision blurring from tears. "I know they aren't going to see that and suddenly change their minds, but..." She sighed softly. "I just want them to know I do trust them. Even if it doesn't make anything different, I want them to know."

Kat nodded and hugged Ell tighter, and for a moment, it felt like the only thing holding together Ell's crumbling world.

Chapter Sixteen

Ethan scowled at his cup of coffee as if it were personally responsible for his bad mood.

It wasn't, of course. Instead, it was Ell.

No, that's not right. It wasn't Ell but her absence that had done it. He hadn't realized just how attached he'd gotten to seeing her, to hearing her laugher, to pressing kisses to her forehead and smelling the strawberry from her shampoo.

A knock on the door got the same level of annoyance Ethan had given his coffee, but after a deep breath, he called out for them to come in.

Of course...that didn't prepare him for who walked in.

Jane.

She looked so much like she had back then, and that same old nostalgia hit him.

But...it also made him admit that what he felt was different than what he did with Ell. Maybe it was that he was older, that he had a better idea of what he wanted, but he saw now that Jane didn't fit him — not like Ell did.

Jane kept her gaze down, looking unsure of her welcome.

Which was what broke Ethan from his shock. "Jane, come on in."

She nodded, then entered his apartment. The way she looked around was strange, as if she were as trapped by the past as he was, as if she noted each thing and recalled how it had all been a part of her life so long ago. "Could you text Clint and Fox and ask them to come over? I think we need to have a talk."

Ethan nodded and did as she asked, partly because he wanted the backup. Facing Jane felt impossible, but doing it alone?

Not a chance.

Within ten minutes, Clint and Fox had come over, but no one broke the silence.

At least, not until Jane spoke. "I'm sorry about what happened at Sanctuary. I shouldn't have come back."

"That's not true," Ethan answered. "It was your place, too."

"I know that, but the looks on your faces? It wasn't fair to just show up out of the blue like that."

"Stop apologizing," Clint said. "This whole thing is our fault. You were the victim. You shouldn't be saying sorry about anything."

Jane furrowed her eyebrows. "Victim?"

"Let's not go down this road," Fox said. "It's in the past."

Jane shook her head. "No, I want to know what you mean by me being a victim."

Again, none of the men spoke. It was a question they didn't like to answer, one that hurt to think about.

When no one else spoke up, Ethan did. "We pushed you into something you didn't want. We didn't see the way it was hurting you. You almost *died* because of us, Jane."

She frowned, then let out a soft laugh at the end. "Is that really what you think?"

"It's what happened."

She shook her head. "No, it isn't."

Clint crossed his arms. "You can rewrite history if it makes it easier for you to deal with, but I was there. I know exactly what occurred."

"You told me before that even Doms aren't mind-readers, so maybe instead of deciding you know what I was thinking and feeling, you *listen* to me?"

Ethan stood straighter at the not-at-all-subtle rebuke.

And worse, at the fact she was right about it...

Still, Jane seemed to take the lull in the conversation as a win. "I did almost die, but not *because* of you. It happened because of me, because of what I did. You're right—what we were doing didn't work for me. I just kept telling myself it did, that I loved you three so much that it had to be enough to make it work. It wasn't your fault that I put myself in that position, that I ignored my own feelings."

Ethan still struggled to accept that. Jane didn't understand—she wasn't a Dom, she wasn't in charge of someone else. She had never taken on that responsibility, didn't know how much it meant to someone who had to properly care for a sub. "You don't understand."

Jane gave him a hard look, one that was nothing like the woman he'd known before. She'd been soft, gentle and all but terrified to speak up against them. It seemed she'd grown quite a lot. "Don't tell me I don't understand. I've had years to figure it out, to look at it all, to work through it."

"You *told* us it was our fault," Fox said.

"Because I didn't know better. I thought it was your fault, wanted to blame you for all the confusion in my head. I wanted you to know what I didn't even know myself." Jane's shoulders dropped. "It took a lot of time to realize it was just easier to blame you than it was to do the work to dig into my own head. I did it, though, and I realized that I put myself there. I wanted to believe I could be something different so badly, I thought if I was what you guys wanted it would make me worthy, that if I played that part, it would prove that I was a good enough. The thing is, it only made me realize I *wasn't* good enough, because that wasn't who I was. It was just a part I was playing, just a role I'd taken on, so even if it was everything you needed, it wasn't me—it wasn't real."

"You should have talked to us," Clint said.

"Yeah, I should have, but I wasn't in a place for that." Jane hesitated. "I saw that girl you were with run off after I saw you in Sanctuary. Was that because of me? Because of what happened?"

Fox shook his head. "It wasn't your fault. We just realized that it was the same sort of thing all over again."

She frowned. "It didn't look like that woman was unhappy…"

"No, but we didn't realize *you* were so unhappy, either."

Jane let out a soft laugh, the sound taking Ethan back. "You all looked happy. Kat told me a little about Ell, when I pressed, and she said you all fit really well."

"I thought we did," Fox said. "But she's new to this all."

"So? Everyone is new at some point."

"So...she's resistant to some of the rules," Fox continued, no doubt being vague to give Ell some privacy. "She never thought this was the sort of thing she'd want."

"It's a hard switch to make in a person's mind — more so for some than others."

Clint spoke up, again reminding Ethan that while he could easily offend people, he also said things others danced around. "She doesn't trust us — I don't think she ever will. Even if she is interested in a power exchange, she has made it clear she isn't interested in the level we are. She's broken rules, hesitated with requests and generally shown she doesn't know what she wants."

Jane lifted her eyebrow. "And have you all been clear? Because the look on her face said she didn't know about me, and your reactions said that wasn't because you'd forgotten me or what had happened. Plus, given how heartbroken you three look, I'm going to guess the breakup was the last thing you wanted. Did you explain any of that to *her*?"

"Why do that?" Fox asked. "It would just hurt her more, and it wouldn't change that she doesn't want this."

"Why is that your choice to make?" At the silence, Jane went on. "Why do you get to decide that *she* doesn't want something? Why do you get to ignore what she tells you? Is it really about her at all then?"

Ethan went to tell her yes, obviously it was about Ell! The girl meant the world to Ethan, to the others, and the last thing they wanted was to have her out of their life. That wasn't about them, it wasn't selfish.

278

Except, he couldn't get the words out. It made him pause, forced him to think about it.

Fox's words came back to him. *"I can't survive going through that again."*

Fuck...

Jane was right. It wasn't really about Ell, was it? It was about their own fears, their worries about losing her, about not being enough for her, about not taking good enough care of her. They'd broken her heart and for what?

All because they were the ones afraid.

"Shit," Clint said softly.

Jane let out a soft laugh. "That's what I thought. You know what I figured out? No one walks away from a hard situation without their own scars. I know you want you to make everything your fault, but the truth is that none of us escaped unscathed. The important thing, though, is to not let those scars keep you from a future, from what you want. It's why I came back, because I *want* that future—but it looks like you needed that same lesson. So...what are you going to do?"

Finally, a question Ethan could answer easily. "Now? We're going to go get our baby girl."

* * * *

Ell groaned when she woke, still in that stage where she was rather drunk, but her head had started to ache. It seemed rude for the hangover to show up before she'd sobered, but there she was.

She peered beside her, a weight in the bed along with her, but it wasn't the faces she'd wanted to see. Ell ignored the pain in her chest as she pictured rolling over to find Clint there, or Ethan or Fox.

Instead, Kat slept, her mouth parted and loud snores escaping her.

Right...she'd stayed over and they'd polished off the whiskey, then had snuck into Dean's apartment to steal his alcohol as well.

Kat really was a bad influence, wasn't she?

A creak made her frown. *Stop being paranoid. New places always sound different.*

She recalled the first night she'd slept at her old duplex, when she'd called Dean over because of a sound she couldn't identify. When he came at two in the morning, they'd found there was a coyote in her covered porch area off the back door, one that seemed to have made a little home for itself there.

While she doubted it was a coyote again, she knew that change always put her on edge.

And there had been so much change in her life. More of it than anyone should have expected her to deal with, to adjust to. She cursed Dean for taking her to Sanctuary, for showing her a world that she couldn't have.

Talk about cruel...

Another sound made Ell sit up because she would have *sworn* it was footsteps on the hardwood in the hallway.

"Dean?" she called out. Maybe he'd come over with his spare key to make sure neither Ell nor Kat had thrown up in sleep and asphyxiated?

No response, but Kat muttered and rolled over.

Ell got to her feet, peering into the darkness through the doorway. Fear gripped her, but she shook her head. She would *not* turn into a coward, not because of what had happened before and not because she didn't have her men anymore.

She'd been through hell growing up, had proven herself strong and resilient.

She closed her hands into fists and walked slowly toward the living room, needing to check, to show herself she wasn't afraid, that she wouldn't allow anything to affect her. She was still dressed in her slacks and top from the day before, since dressing for bed had been too much work given her drunken state. The weight of her phone in her pocket tempted her, made her want to pick it up and call Ethan or Clint before she shoved the idea away.

They left you, Ell. You don't need them.

With the curtains drawn, Ell could see nothing. The inside of the house was pitch-black, and she didn't know the layout well enough to move around easily. Hell, she wasn't even sure where the light switches were…

She went around the corner of the hallway, into the kitchen, but ran into something.

No…someone.

She peered up to find a familiar set of eyes staring down at her, one she'd never forget.

It was the man who had broken into her house before, the one who had threatened and hurt her.

She went to scream, but a hand wrapped around her mouth from behind her, and the voice of the man who had been in charge before whispered into her ear. "You should have stayed hidden."

Chapter Seventeen

Ell pulled in a deep breath when the cloth in her mouth was removed. The fibers still stuck to her tongue, but with her hands bound, she couldn't do anything about that. Getting moved while unable to see or speak turned out to be terrifying, and all Ell had known for sure was that after the men had bound, gagged and blindfolded her, they'd thrown her into the back of a vehicle — possibly a work van, given the hard floor and open space.

The blindfold came off next and relief swamped Ell when she turned her head to find Kat there, bound and on the floor but breathing. She had bruises on her, and Ell had remembered the horrible sounds from the bedroom when one of the men had gone in there.

Kat wasn't the sort to go easily — the scratches on the man's face said she'd put up a hell of a fight.

Of course, that was also likely why he'd carried her out, and why she hadn't woken again yet.

"What do you want?" Ell asked, trying to steel herself. If it had just been her, she might have crumbled.

Kat gave her courage, though. She had someone else to think about.

When the men ignored her as they sat at the table in what looked like a motel room, Ell spoke up again. "This is the second time you've come after me, so clearly you want something. What is it?"

The man who was in charge turned his head toward Ell finally. "Does it matter?"

"Seeing as I'm tied up, yeah, it matters to me."

The man snorted before twisting in his chair to face her directly. "You have more balls than I was expecting. When I first saw you, I was so sure you'd just shatter at the first stern word you heard. Imagine my surprise when you actually gave us a fight."

Ell didn't speak, just stared at the man. She didn't want to get into a conversation about how brave she was or wasn't. Dissecting her personality wouldn't help her at all and only give them more ammunition to use against her.

The man laughed. "I'm Jerry, and you recall my friend, Paul."

"And what do you want from me?"

"From you? Nothing."

"So why risk attacking me *twice*?"

"Because you know someone who has access to things we need. They've been reluctant to give it over, but I'm pretty sure they'll do it for you."

Clint or Ethan? It couldn't have been Fox, because Ell doubted they'd want medical files on kids.

Unless they wanted drugs of some sort?

Ell shook her head. "No one will give you anything for me."

"We both know that's a lie."

But...Ell really wasn't sure. A part of her couldn't believe that anyone would risk their life for her, but another part feared he was right, that those men would come if out of nothing but obligation.

All because of her, Clint, Ethan, Fox and Kat were in danger. Hell, if the men said anything, she had no doubt Dean would come as well.

Which meant Ell had to find a way out of it before anyone else got hurt. "Whatever you want, I doubt it's worth this. I mean, you've abducted two people. That isn't the sort of thing that goes over well."

Jerry let out a laugh that was cold. "I don't think you get it. See, as long as we have you, we'll keep getting whatever we want."

"Let Kat go, at least," Ell pressed. "She has nothing to do with this."

Jerry peered past Ell and toward Kat, who still hadn't woken up. "She is a hellcat, you know? I can't do much to you, or you'll stop being a good piece of blackmail, but her?" The look he had was terrifying, and the fact it was directed at Kat made Ell all the more fearful. "It's good to have something to pass the time with, and after the fight she put up when grabbing you two, well, she can take it."

Ell couldn't stop herself from shaking as she heard that, as the reality of her situation hit her. Even knowing her phone was still in her pocket, that Jerry and his lackies hadn't searched her, didn't ease her much. If she tried to use it, Jerry would notice, and even if she *could* get it, who would she call? She had no idea where she was and the last thing she wanted was to have any of the people she cared about rushing in and getting hurt because of her.

It all led to the same reality — Ell was trapped, and she had no idea what to do now…

* * * *

Ell's apartment seemed nice, but damn it, it wasn't where Clint wanted her. She belonged in her place next to his. The thought of her being so far away, of her being alone, it annoyed Clint more than anything.

Mostly at himself, at the fact he'd been foolish and short-sighted.

They'd wanted to go over right after their talk with Jane, but the reality was that showing up at a woman's apartment at midnight was not the best idea. Instead, they'd agreed to wait for morning.

After knocking for the fifth time without answer, Clint glared at the door. Was she ignoring them? Could she have left for the day already?

"Everything okay?" Dean walked up from around the corner, his expression hard.

Then again, they *had* just broken the heart of his good friend. Clint supposed he couldn't be that mad about Dean's reaction to them.

"She isn't answering," Clint said.

"That sounds like a pretty good boundary there then, doesn't it?" Dean crossed his arms, staring down the three men.

"We had some time to think and some good advice from an old friend. I just want to talk to her, to apologize."

Dean lifted his eyebrow as if surprised by the statement. "And if she doesn't want to hear it?"

"We'll leave," Ethan said. "If she still doesn't want us, we'll go. Even if she decides she wants nothing to do with us ever again, it's important for her to hear what we have to say, to hear *why* we did what we did, that it wasn't about her."

Dean pressed his lips together before nodding. "I have a key. She's probably passed out drunk with Kat."

"Drunk?" Fox asked.

"Yeah. They had a get together last night. Sunny and Toya were here, too."

Clint rubbed at his chest at the discomfort there, at the idea that Ell had been devastated and had to rely on others for that, for pain that Clint, Ethan and Fox had inflicted on her.

He pushed that down. That was far from the most immediate issue.

Dean opened the door, the spare on his keyring, then called in. "Drunk Sleeping Beauties, rise and shine!"

Nothing came back from the dark apartment, and the lack of light said all the curtains had to be drawn — and had to be blackout ones to manage that level of darkness.

Dean's expression changed, as if he'd just realized something might be wrong.

They're probably just passed out...

Even as Clint told himself that, Fox pressed past Dean, no doubt his doctor mode, wanting to ensure that both women were safe.

The apartment wasn't that large — only a one-bedroom — so it was easy to navigate despite them having never been there. Dean turned on the lights, but nothing looked out of place in the living room. Then again, unless it was destroyed, Clint wouldn't know where anything was supposed to be.

"You need to come in here," Fox called from the back of the apartment, drawing the others to leaving any clues from the living room and head toward the bedroom.

The sight Clint found stopped him dead, made his entire body freeze as if ice crawled through his veins.

The bed was empty and messy, with the blankets and pillows thrown off the side and the dresser knocked over. That wasn't the most terrifying part, though.

Instead, it was the blood on the sheets, and the splatter on the headboard.

Ell and Kat were both gone, and the blood said they hadn't gone willingly.

Where are you, baby girl?

* * * *

Ethan paced in the large conference room as other officers spoke, as they went back and forth with ideas and plans and nonsense.

None of it was *finding* her, though. Never before had police work felt so slow, so monotonous. Normally a case seemed to rush, discovering clues, chasing leads.

Those times they weren't personal, though. This was. Each minute that passed, Ell could be hurt. No doubt she was terrified.

Unless she was dead already…

Ethan shook his head, unwilling to consider that option. These people had attacked her *twice*. If they did that, they wanted something from her. They wouldn't go through so much work just to kill her.

And Kat?

He had to think it was a wrong time, wrong place sort of thing.

Dean was there as well, despite being told to leave more than once. His position as a lawyer had given him a bit of leeway, especially since he knew Ell so well.

Not that it had helped. Nothing made sense, nothing gave them anymore clues.

Neither Ell nor Kat's credit cards had been used, their cars remained outside of the apartment building, and while police had taken lots of prints from the apartment, the fact it had just been moved into meant they had a *lot* to go through, between the cleaners, the maintenance people, the movers and the office folks from the building who had done the walk throughs.

None of it gave them any clues.

Ethan rubbed his eyes, frustration eating away at him. This was *all* their fault. They'd broken up with Ell, which had sent her to a different apartment building. Maybe these men had tried to get Ell while she lived with Ethan and the others, but with the security on the elevator, they hadn't been able to. They'd gotten their chance since Ell had moved out.

"You should get some sleep," another officer, Olin, said.

Ethan shook his head. "I'm not going anywhere, not until we find her."

"You know how this works. That could take time, and you won't be at your best if you're falling down from exhaustion."

Ethan couldn't argue with that reasoning, but it didn't change his mind, either. "Could you go home if the woman you loved was missing? I *need* to be here."

Olin sighed but nodded. "Why don't you at least go sit in my office and close your eyes for a bit? If we hear anything, I'll get you immediately."

Ethan offered a quick thanks, because he couldn't deny that he was tired. Besides, maybe if he has just a little bit of quiet, he'd think of something he'd missed.

Or maybe he'd just have nightmares about Ell, about what she might be suffering while he did fuck all about it.

Olin's office was large. The man headed the gangs department, and he was a nice guy for the most part. He was dedicated to his work — obsessed, even — but he cared. Sometimes it was hard to find that with cops who had worked the job as long as Ethan and Olin had.

Ethan took a seat on the couch, then turned the lights off, wanting to close his eyes, to just try to calm his mind for a minute.

The door creaked, but when Ethan snapped his eyes opened, he realized he must have fallen asleep. The person didn't turn on the lights, and Ethan frowned as a small figure entered the room.

Not Olin...

It took him a moment to place the person.

Donnie, the kid Ell worked with, who volunteered at the station.

Ethan remained quiet, unease prickling at his senses because of the way Donnie moved, the way he tried to stay quiet. He went into the office, his steps light, then got to the filing cabinet. He pulled out a set of lock picks and popped open the cabinet so quickly, it was clear he'd used those things before.

The cabinet opened, and Donnie thumbed through the files. He paused at one, then pulled it out and closed the cabinet quietly. He tucked the file into his jacket to hide it.

Ethan rose and went to the door. He flipped on the light switch, and when Donnie spun, his expression full of fear and shock, Ethan just stared back. "I think we need to have a little talk…"

Finally…a clue.

Chapter Eighteen

Fox watched as Donnie crossed his arms, the kid tougher than he should have had to be. Donnie was one of those cases that pulled at Fox's heart.

He wasn't a bad kid, but he'd lived a hard life in a world where good people didn't live long. Fox understood why Ell cared so much for the boy.

Given that he'd been stealing files from the station, it seemed clear he had something to do with what had happened.

The set of Donnie's lips said he didn't plan to talk, though.

"Why did you want these?" Ethan asked and tapped on the files the kid had taken.

Ethan, Clint, Dean and Fox were all in the small conference room. Normally they wouldn't have allowed them to interrogate Donnie but given they all knew him — and hadn't directly said that's what they were doing — the men had a little time before anyone else interfered.

"Nothing," Donnie said and crossed his arms, sitting back. The kid was tough, but he was terrified as well. It was there, in the depth of his eyes, and it told Fox this was worse than he'd thought.

He'd patched up Donnie one time after someone had attacked him, and he hadn't seen Donnie so much as flinch. What was it that had him in this state now?

"Ell is missing," Dean said, breaking in.

Ethan gave the other Dom a glare, but Dean didn't appear sorry in the least.

Donnie's frown said he knew, and Donnie didn't strike Fox as the sort who would hurt Ell.

Which meant it was connected, and while he likely knew, he wasn't behind it.

"We want to help her," Fox said. "She's got to be scared. We found blood at her place, so she might be hurt, too."

Donnie licked his lips, the conflict clear in his dark eyes. "I don't know what to do," he whispered.

"Let us *help*," Ethan said. "Tell us what you know and help us to help Ell. After everything she's done for you, you owe her that."

"Don't you think I know that!?" Donnie got to his feet, the action knocking his chair backward so it clattered to the floor. "Why do you think I got those? Why do you think I'm risking everything to get him what he wants?"

"Who?" Clint asked.

Donnie paused, and Fox had to remind himself that in Donnie's words, snitches didn't live long. They weren't asking him for something easy.

Yet, Donnie showed that despite his age and background, he was stronger than he seemed. "Jerry."

"Who is that?" Ethan asked when the name meant nothing.

"Jerry Historn is the leader of the Eight Card gang, right?" Olin's voice made the tension in the room climb as he entered.

Would he call off their talk? Take over? Get in the way?

Donnie nodded. "They've wanted me to join for a while, but I told them no. When they heard I was volunteering at the station, in the gangs division, they said I needed to steal files."

Olin's expression gave nothing away as he stared at the kid. "But you didn't steal anything, not before today. We keep a close eye on you—I'd know if you had."

"I told them no."

Ethan's voice was soft but dangerous when he broke into the conversation. "That's why they targeted Ell, isn't it? To get you to do what they wanted?"

Donnie nodded, his gaze on the table. "They attacked her the first time just to prove to me they could get to her. I almost did what they wanted then, but Ell moved to your place, and I thought she'd be safe. I didn't know she moved again, not until I got this." He pulled out his phone, then turned it around toward them.

On the screen was a picture of Ell, bound and gagged. No sign of Kat in the image, though…

"I didn't know what to do," Donnie said. "I couldn't just let them hurt her. Even if everyone knew I'd stolen the files, even if I went to jail or Jerry killed me or whatever, I couldn't just do nothing. Ell helped me when no one else would have—she deserves better."

Fox rubbed at his temple. He understood that perfectly, the need to do something even when no good plan came to mind. He didn't envy the boy, who was far too young to have so much on his shoulders.

"Did they tell you where to meet?" Olin asked.

Donnie took the phone and tapped the screen. Afterward, he handed it back. "They want me to bring the files here to meet someone. It won't be where Ell is being held, though. They wouldn't keep her in the same place."

Clint cursed softly beneath his breath. "So we're no closer to knowing where she actually is?"

"Or where Kat is," Dean added.

Fox took out his phone. He wasn't sure what to do, but the anxiety inside him demanded he do something, as if the answer would suddenly appear with an internet search.

The icons on the home screen on his phone met him, but one caught his attention. The locator app, the one Ell had refused to authorize on her phone.

What if…

He opened the app out of blind hope more than anything, because when there was no path ahead, sometimes going into the weeds was the only option.

The app opened, and the words on the screen made Fox jump to his feet.

App connected to Eleanor Hayden's phone.

She'd approved the tracking app sometime the night before, which meant…

He clicked on her name, and a map came up on the screen. "I know where she is," he said so softly, no one heard. They kept talking amongst themselves.

He repeated it in nearly a yell. "I know where she is."

When everyone finally looked his way, Fox turned the phone around to show them the map, the pin dropped on a motel on the edge of town, the sort of place that didn't ask for ID and had people pay in cash.

Everyone was up so fast, it was like a whirlwind took over the conference room.

Then again, they needed to go save the woman they loved before they lost her a second time.

* * * *

The light that poured in through the window spilled across the floor. It showed just how thin the dingy brown curtains were.

Jerry sat at the table, having spent a good amount of time on his phone to different people. The longer Ell listened, the more she realized how much trouble she was in.

Jerry wasn't some small criminal. Given what Ell overheard, he had a lot of people who reported to him, lots of people who seemed to defer to him, and they weren't people Ell much cared for having anything to do with.

Kat had come to, though beyond a few hushed whispered, Ell hadn't talked much to her. The last thing they wanted was to piss off Jerry or say something they shouldn't have.

Jerry finished his latest phone call as he walked back inside the motel room, his gaze landing on Kat for the first time since she'd woken. "You are quite the handful, aren't you?"

Kat didn't flinch at all as he stared at her. Then again, from what Ell knew, Kat routinely played with some of the scariest Doms that Sanctuary could find—it meant she didn't frighten easily. "You should ask your buddy that."

Ell cringed at the comment. Annoying the man who had captured them wasn't a good idea.

Then again, Ell understood it as well. These men had stolen them, had taken Ell and Kat against their will, had taken all their freedom and power. It wasn't uncommon for someone, when confronted by that, to try to regain some of their own power.

While not uncommon, it was also rarely helpful...

Jerry let out a laugh, as if amused by Kat's behavior. "And here I thought this would be boring. I expected to get Ell here, to use her to get what I wanted, and that's it. I didn't expect to be nearly this amused. What's your name?"

Kat narrowed her eyes but refused to answer.

Jerry laughed again. "Katherine Grant, isn't it? You live at 6235 Oak Drive. A woman's purse can reveal a lot about her, and I found myself curious enough to go through your things. Going into anything blind is foolish, and I prefer not to do foolish things. Don't worry, I left your phone at your friend's apartment, so no one will come looking for you here."

"If you knew, why'd you ask?"

"Because I wanted to see if you'd answer me."

Jerry's expression said he enjoyed the back and forth, and it made Ell uneasy.

She didn't care for the way he looked at Kat, for the interest there.

A knock on the door didn't break Jerry's attention, didn't make him pull it from Kat. A second knock made him sigh and answer, "Come in."

The door opened, and Ell's eyes widened when Donnie walked in. His gaze found hers, and the relief that passed over his expression made Ell realize the truth, made her put it together.

They hadn't been blackmailing her men—they'd been trying to force Donnie work for them, to steal for them. It all made sense.

Donnie's fear, how bad he'd felt after her first attack, him telling her about how difficult it was to get out of that world. No matter how much he tried, how far he got, he was dragged back into that muck.

Jerry turned, narrowing his eyes when he spotted Donnie. "This wasn't where you were supposed to meet us."

Donnie pulled his shoulders back, looking far older than his age would have said. "I wanted to make sure she really was okay."

"So you're not just a mole, you've got some actual skills as well? How did you find us?"

Donnie shrugged as he moved into the room, the door shutting behind him and the guard outside staying outside. "It's not that hard, not when you grow up around here. People talk. Doesn't matter who you threaten, people still talk."

Jerry let out a chuckle. "That they do. So, the files?"

Donnie looked in Ell's direction for a moment. "Then you'll let her go?"

"Of course."

Ell offered a slight shake of her head to Donnie, trying to get him to understand her point. Jerry had no intention of letting Ell go, and Donnie needed to save himself. He needed to get out of there and run.

Donnie pressed his lips together, then pulled a file from inside his jacket. He held it out to Jerry.

Jerry took the file, then flipped through it. "Good job. I wasn't sure you'd do it. The more time passed, the surer I was that you'd end up letting her die. I mean, I can't say I really understand the appeal, but I'm glad I was wrong."

"So you'll let her go?" Donnie asked again.

Jerry got to his feet, then tucked the file under his arm. "In time."

"That wasn't our deal."

"Deals change. Besides, I need to review what you brought before we even consider our interaction finished. Why don't you stay here with my friend while I go look over this?"

He took a few steps toward the door that went to the back room before he paused. He peered over at Kat. "I could use some company. Come."

Kat offered a dismissive glare, one that said she didn't give a damn what he wanted.

And yet again, Jerry seemed only farther smitten with Kat, as if that reaction was better than the sexiest striptease a girl could do. He walked over to her and grabbed her by the arm, hauling her to her feet.

Kat yanked, but with her hands bound behind her and her feet shackled with a short length of rope between them, she couldn't get enough reach or strength to do anything.

"Leave her alone!" Ell shouted, trying to get to her feet, to do something. With where she was, however, and how her hands were bound, she couldn't get up.

"Keep an eye on them," Jerry told the guard. "If either of them does anything, feel free to shoot them. We have what we needed."

The door to the room shut and panic enveloped Ell. She couldn't seem to think, couldn't do anything but imagine what might happen beyond that door, but think about Kat suffering all because she'd been with Ell, all because she'd tried to be Ell's friend.

"Stay down," the guard snapped when Ell managed to rise slightly, then shoved her back down. Without a way to brace herself, she hit the floor hard.

"Stop that," Donnie snapped.

The guard turned a hard glare on Donnie. "You heard the boss—I can put a bullet in either of you if I want. Don't push it."

"Calm down," Donnie said, this time to Ell. He held his hands up and passed the guard, the knelt in front of Ell. "Just relax, okay?"

"Relax? Do you understand what he could be doing to her?"

Donnie's gaze moved toward the door, and Ell knew he understood. Still, he let out a sound of frustration. "I know. Just…try to relax. You can't help her if you get yourself shot."

"This coming from you? You should have told me about Jerry, about the threats. We could have done something, could have figured it out before it went this far!"

"I know," Donnie said softly. "I know, damn it. I just…I'm not used to having people in my corner. I thought if I just kept at it, I'd figure out how to get out of it, how to fix it all by myself."

That silenced Ell for a moment, since the conversation sounded eerily familiar to so many that she'd had with Ethan, Fox and Clint. Maybe that was why she got along with Donnie so well, because they both had trouble trusting people or allowing them to help.

A scream came from the bedroom, one that made Ell's skin crawl. She'd heard screams in Sanctuary before, the ones filled with pain and desire, but that wasn't the sound Kat made…

Instead, it was one of fear, one Ell would have never expected from the confident, funny woman.

Before Ell could get up, before she could try to do something again—and she would try, because she couldn't help it—Donnie shook his head once.

His eyes held something serious, as if trying to get her to understand, but what she had no idea. A horn honked outside, and as if waiting for just that, Donnie dove forward and covered Ell with his body.

It startled her so much, she nearly missed how the motel room erupted into chaos. The door all but exploded inward, and bullets were loosed, though from whose gun she wasn't sure.

"You're okay," Donnie told her, and Ell hated herself a little for relaxing at his voice. He was a kid, but in that moment, they were in *his* world.

"Ell?" The sound of that voice had Ell releasing a broken sob. It was as if everything were right in the world, suddenly, as if, if she heard that voice, she would be okay.

Donnie moved off Ell, and it revealed Clint there, his gaze hard, a pistol in his hand. It reminded her that he wasn't just Clint, not the man who had more sweetness than anyone would expect. He was a detective, a man who knew how to handle himself. The point was made clear by Ethan as well, who despite being smaller, looked every bit at dangerous.

Ell remembered then and nodded toward the door. "Kat's in there. Jerry took her in there, and she screamed a minute ago."

One of the other officers nodded and tried the door. When the handle wouldn't turn, he kicked it in. "Clear," he called out.

"Is she…" Ell couldn't finish the question.

Ethan peered into the room, his lips drawn into a thin line. It reminded Ell that while Kat was her new friend, the men had known her for years. "She's alive," he said softly, "but we need to get her to the hospital to get checked out."

Ell sank down, relieved by the fact Kat would live. Maybe that wasn't much, but it was so much more than she'd thought they'd get.

Hands touched her cheeks, and she flinched before familiar blue eyes met hers. Fox stared into her eyes, then patted along her arms, her legs, as if searching for injuries. "Are you hurt?"

Ell shook her head, even if that didn't feel true. She hurt, just not physically.

Fox leaned in and pressed a kiss to her lips. "I have to check on Kat."

She didn't want him to go but understood it. Still, as she looked around the room, as she recognized that it was over, that she'd somehow survived, all that adrenaline that had kept her going disappeared.

Ell couldn't stop herself from shaking, and only Clint gathering her up into his arms made her feel as if she'd ever be able to stop.

Too bad she already knew she'd just lose them again…

* * * *

Fox thanked the nurse as she passed him, after having given him a rundown of Ell's condition.

Basically?

She was fine. A few bruises, but nothing major. Mostly, just shock and PTSD. It would be a rough road to recovery, especially since no doubt this event would have just dug into wounds she already held.

Fox entered the room, Clint and Ethan waiting inside. Clint sat on the couch and Ethan had pulled a chair up beside Ell's bed. It was funny, since the two men rarely ever came to the hospital. In fact, it took a small act of god to get either to go, even when they were seriously hurt, yet there they were without complaint.

If that didn't prove just how much the loved the woman, nothing would.

Ell lifted her gaze to Fox when he entered, so much uncertainty on her face.

Who could blame her, though? She'd gone through hell, and just before that? They'd managed to break her heart and abandon her. No wonder she stared at each of them as if not sure where they stood.

"You'll be released shortly," Fox said. "Your tests all look good. No serious injuries, so no reason to stay here."

"And Kat?"

He hesitated. He wasn't Kat's doctor, so he didn't have any issues with confidentiality. He just didn't want to upset Ell any more than she already was. Still, he wasn't the type to lie. "She'll be okay. She got hurt, but she's tough."

Ell dropped her gaze. "It's all my fault."

Clint frowned. "What?"

"It's all my fault," she repeated slowly, as if Clint really hadn't heard her. "Kat would have never been there if not for me, and if Jerry hadn't tried to use me,

Donnie wouldn't have gotten involved either. All of this is because of me."

"It's all because of Jerry," Ethan said. "He decided to blackmail Donnie, and he decided to abduct you, and he chose to hurt Kat. None of that was you."

She sighed softly. "And you three had to get involved. I'm sorry."

"Sorry for what?"

"For dragging you into this. I know you were done with me, that you didn't want to see me anymore."

Fox flinched at the words, at how deeply she believed them. They really had hurt her, hadn't they?

"That's not true," Ethan said.

"You made it pretty clear to me." Ell's tone said she wasn't hearing them at all.

Which meant Fox had no issue sinking low to get his point across. He came over and leaned his hip on the edge of her bed, then leaned in so his face was inches from hers. "Listen carefully, princess." He made sure to use the nickname, to offer it up like breadcrumbs for her to follow.

And Ell did what she always did—she leaned into him, into the moment, as if she knew what she needed even if she didn't understand or accept it.

So Fox took the chance. "We were wrong, okay? Jane came over and talked to us last night, set us straight, and I realized that I pushed you away because I was afraid. I was afraid of not reading the situation right, of doing something wrong, of getting hurt or hurting you. I know that isn't fair to you, and I'm willing to accept responsibility for that, but I need you to listen."

Ell licked her lips, especially as Fox moved back to give her a little space. "You're just saying that because I'm hurt, and you feel bad."

"We realized you were missing because we went to your new apartment this morning to apologize," Ethan said.

That seemed to hit home for her. She paused, frowning. "You did?"

"Yeah, we did. Come home, baby girl."

She dropped her shoulders. "How do I know you won't change your mind again? How do I know you won't end up deciding it isn't working for you again?"

"Because we're here," Clint said. "I was terrified when you went missing, when we found blood. I've done this a long time—I know exactly where this sort of thing can end up. It made me realize that I don't want to do that, anymore. I thought about you not coming back, about never falling asleep with you there again, and it made it clear that isn't what I want. I want you back. I want you home again. I want you to be *mine* again."

Ell stared back like she couldn't believe the words, like they were too much, like they were what she'd wanted to hear but never really believed she would. "You're sure?"

Fox smiled, that sweet hope in her tone telling him they hadn't lost her entirely. She might be afraid, but she *wanted* them still.

Fox set a hand on her cheek. "Yes—I'm sure. I've never been as happy as I have been with you in my life. I want to go back to setting up your mornings, to praising you when you're a good girl, to help you with whatever you struggle with. Without you in my life, my day feels empty, and I don't want that anymore. Whatever it takes, I want you back."

Ell took her bottom lip between her teeth, then peered at Ethan as if fearful he might not agree.

Ethan huffed a laugh. "You know I love you, baby girl, more than I thought I was capable of. People think I laugh my way through everything, that I'm not serious about anything, but you know what? I'm really damned serious about you. Come home, please, to where you belong, and I swear I'll take every damned day from now until my last making damn sure you know how much I love you."

Ell didn't say anything right away, just moved her gaze from one man to the next, as if trying to judge if they were telling the truth, if she was willing to take the risk, and all Fox could do was sit there and wait. It was all any of them could do.

Finally, she nodded. "I was terrified to give up control of my life. I thought that I had to do everything myself, that I had to control everything. I grew up in so much uncertainty, never knowing what would happen, if I was safe, so I thought I had to hold tight onto everything or my world would fall apart. You guys taught me that I don't have to do that, that it's okay to let other people help me, that I can trust you. I don't know if I've ever really trusted anyone like this."

Fox couldn't help the way his lips curled into a smile at her admitting that. She loved them. It was in each word she spoke, in the flush on her cheeks, in the way she looked at them. It was so much more than he thought he'd have.

"So you're going to come home with us tonight, right?"

She nodded.

"And you'll stay with us?" Clint pressed.

"Yes," Ell said.

Ethan caught her chin so she looked at him. "Yes what?"

She let out a thin whine, one that said she'd missed them all. "Yes, Daddy," she whispered.

"Good answer," Fox said back. "Let's take our girl home and show her *exactly* how much we missed her."

And Fox knew there was nothing he wanted more than that.

Epilogue

Ell laughed as Ethan pressed a kiss to the back of her neck. "I'm trying to cook," she said as she elbowed him. Not that she did it hard — she was used to Ethan's moods. He tended to ignore the future, like appointments or plans, in exchange for what he wanted in the moment.

And judging by the way he slid his hand around her front, the way he traced the line of her bra through her shirt, she had a good idea of *exactly* what he wanted right then.

"I'm hungry for something else," he whispered before he nipped at the back of her neck.

Ell moaned, the sound leaving her on a rush when the heat he inspired inside her roared to life. How did he do that so easily? One little touch, one little kiss, one sultry look and Ell just melted for him.

"Company will be here soon," Ell argued, though she didn't try to move him again. All she could do was squirm when he danced his fingers over her breasts, when he teased the bare skin at her chest, where the button-up shirt revealed cleavage. She leaned her head back against him, giving in.

"There's a good girl." Ethan scraped his teeth over the side of her throat, then latched his lips to the spot. The sting told her he was leaving a mark, that she'd wear a bruise on the side of her neck.

Which was no doubt his exact point.

Despite Ethan enjoying others watching him, watching Ell, he still could be the jealous type.

Especially when it came to Dean…

"If you burn the food, we'll never hear the end of it." Clint took the spatula from Ell and scraped it over the pan.

Which was when the scent hit Ell's nose, a reminder that it had nearly burned, all because Ethan had distracted her.

She went to turn, to glare at Ethan, but as soon as she moved, Fox took the opportunity to trap her between them. Fox set his hand on the front of her throat, then took a kiss without a word.

And *damn* he could make a woman forget herself with a kiss like that. He wasn't aggressive, but he wasn't hesitant either. He was thorough and dominating, taking her as he pleased, adding fuel to the fire Ethan had started.

When he broke the kiss, Ell had completely forgotten why she'd been annoyed in the first place.

"You two are impossible," Clint said as he removed the bell peppers and onions from the pan and slid them into a bowl.

"I recall you being late for work last week because you couldn't get out of bed with our baby girl," Ethan said. "I'm not sure you get to complain about us."

Ell's cheeks heated as she recalled the morning in question. She'd been the one to make the first move, to wake early to find Clint sleeping so peacefully, his bare chest tempting her until she'd decided to have some fun. He'd woken to find her lips trailing down over his stomach, and yeah, he hadn't made it to work on time that day...

Not that she was sorry about it. It was those little moments that she cherished the most, the times when life didn't go the way she'd expected it to. She'd spent so long trying to organize her life, to control it, and that had only made her miserable.

"What's going on in your head?" Fox asked as he tilted his head. That was always Fox, though, quick to see through her defenses, to force her to confront whatever was going on so he could help and they could move forward.

The desire to say nothing hit Ell, as it still did each time. It was less than before, though, and Ell pushed it away herself. "I was just thinking about how chaotic my life is now."

Fox paused, as if unsure how to react to that.

It made Ell realize what it sounded like. She shook her head quickly. "I didn't mean it bad. I was just standing here, thinking about how things would have been before. I would have had dinner already done..." Ell offered Ethan a slight glare at that. "I'd have the table set, the time all worked out, and I'd be busy trying to scrub corners until someone showed up and I had to pretend not to be anxious. I mean, if I even had anyone over, since I didn't have anyone to invite before."

Fox's hesitation slid away, and he offered his trademark calm smile. "And here we are, distracting you, making you not stress about every little detail. What monsters we are."

Ell narrowed her eyes as she recognized…they were right…

She'd stood there, worrying about one of their first dinner parties since being together. She'd thought about everything that could wrong, about if the food wasn't good, if the people didn't get along, if they thought there was something wrong with her apartment.

Had Ethan known that? Had he seen it in her eyes? Was that why he'd done what he'd done?

A smirk from Ethan said yeah…that had been exactly what he'd been doing.

Clint caught her chin and made her look at him. It was funny how often the men did that, when they didn't just order her to look at them but when they forced her too. And yet each time it felt special, made her feel important and cherished by them. "I told you we'd always take care of you," he said. "That includes stepping in when you're spiraling. Now, the elevator went off, so I expect the guests will get here soon."

That once again set her anxiety soaring.

He shook his head, then pulled her closer to steal his own kiss, to press her against his front and wipe every other thought from her head. Before she realized it, the doorbell went off, waking her up.

Clint pulled back and offered her a rare, playful smile, as if calling her on the fact he'd managed to distract her yet again.

Her cheeks were heated and her breath rapid. A part of her wanted to ignore the party and go back to having time with her men. "You three are trouble," Ell said before pulling away to answer the door.

A sting to her ass made her yelp, and she turned to find Ethan smiling even wider. "You shouldn't be so rude, baby girl. I have no problem making them wait a little longer to make perfectly sure you know your place."

Ell sputtered, but no actual words came out. She rushed from the kitchen before any of them could distract her farther.

She smoothed her hair down just before she answered, hoping that would make her look like nothing had just happened, like she wasn't flustered.

Of course, the grin on Dean's face, especially when his gaze dropped to her neck, said he was fully aware of what had just been happening.

"Elly," he said on a laugh, but went no farther. The reason was clear when just behind him stood two other guests.

Donnie and his grandmother, Marlene, were there, both looking unsure.

"Come in," Ell said, waving everyone into the apartment. The dinner party was going to be large, so they'd moved the furniture around to make room for it all. She'd invited not only the three who had shown already, but also many of her new friends from Sanctuary, as a sort of housewarming party, so everyone could meet everyone else.

Clint took over the rest of the cooking, which would give Ell the time to meet the guests and entertain. Ethan came up beside her, all too willing to chat with everyone. Fox came out from the kitchen as well, probably kicked out by Clint when he kept offering advice and getting in the way.

"Thank you again," Marlene said to Fox when he said hello to her. "The apartment is so much more than I could have every hoped for."

Fox nodded, a kind smile on his lips. "Not a problem. Donnie's been incredibly helpful at the station, so I'm glad you two are in a better area."

Tears glistened in the older woman's dark eyes, and Ell understood the feeling perfectly. It had been years of her striving to take care of her grandson, trying to do her best, and years of knowing they were still right in the middle of a very dangerous area. She carried the weight of the problems he'd gotten into, knowing part of that was due to location.

Which was why the day after Ell had been abducted, Fox had called Marlene personally to offer her an apartment on the ground floor at a severely reduced rate. He'd understood how important that was to Ell, how much Donnie meant to her, and he'd done what he could to help, to take care of the situation. It was yet another time when Ell fell harder for him — for them all.

Since the attack, Donnie had finished his community service but had taken on a job at the station, where he could build experience and make some money until he turned eighteen, when he planned to apply to become a cop. It was a future Ell wanted for him, one she'd do what she needed to to help him achieve.

And now he had not only her but three overly protective men who had no issue stepping in to ensure he was safe and had anything he needed.

I almost feel bad for him…

Once the rest of the guests showed, everyone sat the large table, piling in close to make room. Clint sat to one side of her, Fox to the other, with Ethan across the table. The food rested at the center of the table, so people could get more whenever they wanted, and the conversation flowed easily. It was funny, because Ell had always assumed anyone who went to a BDSM club would be a horrible conversationalist with normal people.

Those normal people included Olin, the officer who had been one of the people to rescue her and Kat. He'd come when Ethan had invited a few people he knew from the station. From Sanctuary, they had Dean, Sunny, Garrison, Trent, Connor, Toya and Jane—who by some miracle Ell had become friendly with, despite the awkwardness of the situation.

"Have you heard anything from Kat?" Olin asked, his voice low as if he didn't want to spread that across the entire table.

Ell shook her head. "Not much. She hasn't been by..." Ell paused, unsure what to call Sanctuary in front of regular people.

Fox chuckled softly. "Olin has been there before," he whispered. "Just call it the club in mixed company."

Ell nodded. "She hasn't come back to the club since. I've talked to her on the phone a few times, but that's it. I think she's trying to just put herself back together." The reminder spread fear through Ell, the fact that Kat had suffered.

Worse, she'd suffered and Jerry hadn't actually been caught. He'd escaped through a window, slipping past the police line. Amazingly, it hadn't bothered Ell much. She felt safe with her men around, and now with Donnie living there as well, it seemed to her that she'd closed ranks.

However, Kat was a different story. No one knew exactly what had happened—she'd been mostly silent—but there was no doubt she'd suffered.

"I invited her here tonight," Ell continued. "She never responded."

Dean gave her a subtle side-eye, the look he always had when he wanted to hear something but didn't want to make it obvious. It made Ell wonder if there was something between Dean and Kat? Or was that just general concern for a friend?

Olin nodded after letting out a soft sigh, telling her he wasn't happy with the answer.

"She'll be okay." Clint took Ell's hand, squeezing it tightly. "Kat is one of the toughest women I've ever known. She'll get through this."

Ell allowed Clint to offer her the comfort, clung to it as she took a deep breath and nodded, letting the topic drift away. There wasn't anything she could do right then, so she might as well enjoy her time.

And enjoy it she did. The folks from Sanctuary mingled perfectly with her friends, with the men's other friends, and by the time she shut the door, by the time she'd said goodbye to every person, Ell leaned her back against the closed door and let out a long exhalation.

It had been a good night. A busy night, but a good one. When had been the last time she'd just relaxed and enjoyed time with friends?

She peered at the table, at the plates sitting there, at all the work that needed to be done before she could relax and go to bed.

"Not a chance," Ethan said, throwing her off.

"What?"

"You're not going to stress and spend the next two hours cleaning up."

"But it needs to get done."

"And it will. *Later.*"

"I won't be able to relax until it's done."

"Too bad," Fox said as he left the kitchen. "The leftovers are put away, and we'll do dishes tomorrow."

"I can't sleep here knowing it's dirty," she pressed.

"Good point." Clint came over and before Ell could even guess his actions, he'd lifted her.

"What are you doing?" she all but shrieked.

"If you can't sleep here, I guess you'll have to sleep at my place."

Ell let out the loudest sigh. "That won't change that I'll be thinking about it."

A hand ran over her thigh, then her ass, then stroked right over her slit through her slacks. "Oh, if you can think about the dishes while we play with you, I'll be impressed." *Ethan.*

The world passed her by as Clint moved, and before she knew it, he'd taken her to his apartment, the doors closing after them telling her that the others had followed. Sure enough, Clint dumped her onto his large bed, and Ell was confronted with the three men.

And she knew exactly how much she loved them each. She loved Ethan's humor, Fox's laid-bad care and Clint's honesty. She'd never felt as if she belonged, as if she could trust the world or anyone in it. She'd struggled for so many years trying to hold it all together, trying to make sense of everything, but it had only slipped from her fingers the tighter she held.

Until she met these three, until they showed her that relying on others wasn't so bad.

In fact…she rather liked it.

"What are you thinking?" Fox asked as he pulled his shirt off.

"That I love you," Ell admitted.

That earned her a pause from each man, followed by slow, surprised smiles.

"You sure about that? Because I don't think you addressed us properly," Ethan scoffed.

Ell glared for a moment before giving in. "I love you, Daddy," she said.

Fox crawled onto the bed before her until he was a few scant inches from her. "That's better, princess, and don't you forget it."

"You are *ours*," Clint added, the bed dipping when he sat on it beside Ell. "Doesn't matter how difficult you want to make it, or what happens, we aren't letting you go, not ever again."

The words washed over Ell, and these were the only men Ell would ever truly believe such a promise from.

"Besides," Ethan added before he held up cuffs as if to make a point with them, "if you want to question it, if you want to doubt it, go ahead. I have no problem proving that you belong to us just as often as you need it."

Ell was surrounded by these men, by the only men who had ever made her feel safe, who made her feel wanted and needed. She'd been terrified of everything before, terrified of the world, of losing control, of herself. She'd been buried by her past, by her fears, by the doubt that had run her entire life.

And it was these men who had broken her out of it, who had dug past all her defenses. She had a home and a family and a *life* for the first time ever, and it was all because of her Daddies.

Want to see more from this author?
Here's a taster for you to enjoy!

Larkwood Academy: Silenced
Jayce Carter

Excerpt

Eyes forward — just ignore the werewolf.

I repeated that to myself as I quickened my steps. It wasn't hard to identify the shade who crouched over a trashcan, rifling through whatever he could find inside. Even if he hadn't been wearing the law-required bright yellow band on his wrist to identify himself, there was just something about shades that made it easy to spot them.

They had this *danger* in them, this bone-deep hesitation they provoked in normal humans when a shade crossed our paths. They had a feral quality to their movements and an emptiness in their eyes, as if everything that had been real about them had drained out when they'd become infected by source.

It meant that this shade, despite appearing young for the change — he couldn't have been older than eleven — could have torn me apart if he lost control.

Though, the fact he was out on the street, even identified, meant he had to have been a weaker specimen and on the proper medication to treat his affliction. Otherwise, he would have been properly secured at an academy.

"Don't stare, Hera," my friend Moa said.

"How can he be out on the streets?" I asked, keeping my voice low as we passed by the shade. "I thought we had groups to keep them out of sight."

Moa gave me a sharp look, one that reminded me just how different our lives were.

Moa wasn't privy to reality, to the danger shades posed. She got to live in ignorance, to pretend the world was a safe place while I watched as people were slaughtered by uncontrolled shades. Then again, her family ran a little consignment shop whereas my mother was a senator and headed the committee for shade control, and my father ran one of the largest pharmaceutical companies in the country.

I was Hera Weston, the only child of Zachary and Regina Weston, which meant I didn't have the luxury of not knowing.

Still, I played along, pretended I had no idea what her censure was for because there was no reason to have this fight again. A nonchalant sip of my water bottle helped to sell that. "What?"

"He's just trying to get some food. Do you have any idea how many shades are kicked out of their homes when they change? How many can't get hired after that?"

"They don't *change*. They're infected and they die," I countered, but kept walking so she couldn't give me another long winded, politically correct explanation about how they didn't really 'die.'

Moa was one of those who thought that shades were just altered, that they were still the people they'd been when human. It wasn't true, of course, and if she paid any attention to the news or in school, she'd have known that.

Source — a substance that leaked through invisible tears between our realm and the darkness — could infect some humans. When it happened, that infection caused mutations so dramatic that only a fool would consider the resulting shade to be the same person as the human they'd been. The infections seemed random, since the tears could be neither tracked nor stopped.

It was just part of life.

"Besides," I added, trying to offer the next words like an olive branch as we passed the shops that lined the outdoor mall, "that's why we have academies set up, to take care of them safely and determine how best to treat them."

"Those academies are prisons," Moa snapped, tugging my arm to stop us, drawing the same line in the sand we'd danced around for years. She faced off against me as if we were engaged in some battle instead of standing in front of a high couture boutique shop. "Kids are stolen from their parents and thrown into the institutes. They're often experimented on, drugged and who knows what else."

"You need to stop reading the tabloids. Have you ever even *been* to one?"

"No," she admitted softly. "Have you?"

"Yes. Two years ago, I went with my mother to see Jasmine Academy. I can promise you, *none* of what you're talking about was going on there. The shades were happy, healthy and unable to hurt themselves or others. Isn't that the goal?"

Moa shook her head. "You are naïve, Hera. Do you think places like that want people to know what's really going on? Do you think they're going to just show all the bad things they do when the VIPs come around? It's all a publicity stunt so people tell the government to keep sending them all the money they want. It's just about creating enough fear so we don't pay any attention to the atrocities they do there."

I sighed and let the conversation drop. I could argue with her all day — and I had before — but Moa had no idea about the real world. I wasn't angry with her about that — I envied her some of the time.

It would have been nice to fall asleep each night with no idea of what lurked in the shadows. I still remembered my first time seeing a fully changed werewolf, the horror as it had pulled at the silver chains wrapped around it, as it had roared. My mother had brought me with her, had worried when I'd become enamored with shades as so many teenagers did.

The power, the rebellion, the danger of something so powerful was intoxicating and most people went through a phase where they thought they could change them. Why we women felt the need to do that, to find fixer-uppers who we had to work on, I didn't understand anymore.

Not after witnessing the bone-deep terror at coming face-to-face with a shade that could rake its claws through my throat in a heartbeat. I'd realized that day that the world was far more dangerous than most people knew.

Moa still had that fascination because her parents were bleeding hearts who hadn't taught her better. She'd learn, eventually. Everyone did, because the world didn't let people keep their illusions for long.

So, instead of furthering that line of thought, I pointed at a kiosk up ahead. "Let's look at the necklaces up there."

Moa let out a long breath, as if reining in her own temper, as if *I* were the difficult one to deal with, then nodded. "Sure. Maybe we can get matching ones."

The selection wasn't great, but it offered the perfect distraction. We were only weeks away from the new academic year starting, and we hadn't gotten into the same schools.

Moa had gotten into a local state school, something that would work well enough for her to get the business degree she wanted so she could help and eventually take over her family's shop.

I, on the other hand, had the acceptance letter on my desk from one of the premiere colleges in the country. I'd had good grades, but the fact that the building had a 'Weston Wing,' and my last name was Weston had gotten me in. In fact, I hadn't even filled out an application. One call from my father and the doors had sprung open.

Moa had held the letter in her hands, staring as if it were the holy grail. Me? I'd tossed it to my desk because fuck that. Going across the country to some university sounded dreadful to me. It felt like another nail in the coffin of my future, the one my parents had laid out for me before I'd ever been born.

The right education, the right career, the right husband. It was all a path to the perfect little Weston life they wanted me to have. And I'd trudged along that path because what other choice did I have? Even now, at nineteen years old, I was stuck. An adult by age but a child by freedom.

An arm wrapped around my waist, spinning me before lips pressed to mine. Aaron swallowed down my startled gasp, then only laughed when I smacked his chest.

"Don't sneak up on me," I snapped.

He offered a crooked smile. "Don't stand there looking like you want a kiss then. You never know who might just take you up on it."

I shook my head, grinning at his playfulness.

The right spouse. That had my smile disappearing.

Aaron was that. The son of a business associate of my father's—our parents had basically planned the wedding when we were still toddling around the playground in diapers. I'd grown up knowing what was expected of me, had fallen into line before I'd gotten old enough to question it.

Besides, Aaron wasn't that bad. He was charming, handsome, rich. The sex was tolerable, and he never treated me badly. I didn't have butterflies, or head-over-heels nonsense, but I was pretty sure those things were only in cheesy books and movies.

In the real world, 'not bad' was the best a person could hope for.

"What are you looking at?" he asked as he tugged me against him.

"Necklaces," I explained. "Moa and I were going to get matching ones."

"What about me?"

"What about you?" Moa asked with a smile. She'd always liked Aaron, probably more than I ever had, but she'd been respectful of our relationship no matter what.

"Well, I mean, we've been running around together all this time. I should be part of the whole necklace thing, too."

I rolled my eyes. Aaron could be awfully clingy at time, but he wasn't wrong. He'd been friends with Moa and me, like some weird love triangle, for most of our lives.

"I'm not wearing two necklaces."

Moa reached out and picked up a small white paper that had hung on a hook. A silver charm dangled on it, and she held it out to me. "Why don't we do chains?

Then we can pick the charm we want each of us to have, and we'll all have those matching charms wherever we go."

"That is cringingly sentimental, and I *love* it." Aaron snatched a charm from the wall of product. "Look, a bear — this one is perfect for me because I'm big and tough and super manly."

Moa smirked and grabbed a rat. "Or this one because you're constantly shoving cheese into your mouth and are rather annoying."

Aaron put a hand against his chest as if she'd struck him with her words. "Fine, you don't get a charm from me. Good job."

I laughed at their antics as I scanned the available options. What was for me? What would represent me enough that I'd want my two best friends to wear it?

Aaron settled on a racoon, which seemed fitting. He was hard to ignore, stayed up way too late and was rather entertaining. Moa chose a paintbrush, because of her love of art.

My gaze landed on one, and I knew it was perfect to represent me. A silver music note, something elegant and simple and so intertwined with who I was that it felt obvious.

I'd sung my entire life. In fact, my mother said I hadn't learned to speak sentences so much as verses. The headphones hanging around my neck were a testament to my love of music, to the fact I couldn't fathom a few hours without putting on the large earcups and disappearing into the sounds, into how they took away everything happening in my life I couldn't control.

Music made me feel as if I still had a hold of something, and singing was my way of putting my voice into a world that always felt too loud, to make a mark when the world didn't want to hear me.

"That's perfect." Aaron took all the charms and chains to the salesperson to pay for them, Moa now complaining.

Aaron or I always paid for things, since our parents were far better off than Moa's. What was a hundred bucks between friends?

After Aaron handed them over, we hooked the charms on the chains, then put them on. It was a surreal feeling, like an acknowledgment of how much our lives were about to change, with all of us going to different schools, on different paths of life that would take us different directions.

Aaron and I would come back together—we didn't have much choice there—but I wondered what would happen to Moa. Was this the end of our little group?

The three charms sat next to one another, cool against my warm skin, and I had a moment of wishing things wouldn't change.

Unfortunately, I had a feeling nothing could stop that from happening.

* * * *

"I need to get home," I complained to Aaron three hours later.

Moa had already abandoned us, since she was by far the most responsible. She'd taken off around ten, but Aaron hadn't been ready to turn in, and I was easily bribed with a caramel macchiato.

"I'm leaving tomorrow." Aaron's voice lost some of its humor.

"You're only going to be a few hours' drive away from me," I reminded him. "And we'll talk on the phone all the time."

"It won't be the same. Come on, Hera, can't you at least pretend you'll miss me?"

I blew out a breath, sick of that question. He hurled it a lot, and it had taken me a while to understand why.

In the end? I just didn't think I was an affectionate person, not like he was, not like he wanted me to be. He wanted someone who called in the morning because I just couldn't stand not hearing his voice. He wanted someone who couldn't imagine life without him.

And I tried, I really did. I set alarms on my phone to remind me to text or call him, and I did everything I could to play the part he wanted me to, even if I never felt it.

"I will miss you," I lied. "I just think you're being a bit dramatic. It isn't like we're never going to see each other. We can visit every weekend, and we'll have all summer together. But I *can* say you're going to have a miserable flight tomorrow if you don't get some sleep."

He let out a slow sigh, and the lines in his face, the ones put there because I wasn't living up to what he needed, hurt.

So I slid my arm around him, trying to be and do what he wanted. "I'm sorry," I offered. "I think I'm just nervous about the move, about how everything changes, you know?"

He nodded, but a shadow in his eyes said he probably recognized the change of subject when he saw it. "Yeah, I know. It'll be good, though. We'll get out of this town, out on our own. And, who knows? Maybe I can get my classes on the right days and split my time between your place and mine."

I smiled even as I cringed at the thought. I wanted my own space, my own life, and I wouldn't get that if Aaron was my shadow the whole time. Still, I'd upset him enough, so I nodded. "Yeah, that would be nice."

He nodded, as if it had been decided. "Why don't we—" A yawn broke his statement.

"That's it—you're exhausted, and you have a long day tomorrow. You should go home and get a few hours of sleep before you have to leave."

"No goodbye sex?" He lifted an eyebrow to pair with his smirk.

"That would defeat the whole purpose of going home to get sleep. Classes don't start for two weeks. What if I agree to fly out to you Monday? We'll spend a week together at your place, then I'll fly to mine. It'll give you a few days to get set up."

"Then we'll christen my new apartment?"

"Sure." I didn't have to fake a smile at that. Sex might not have been mind-blowing, but like most things, I had a feeling that pretty good was the best a person could hope for, and Aaron's enthusiasm went a long way.

He offered me a ride home, but I said no. If we did that, he'd talk me into ignoring the things about sleep. Besides, I'd driven myself, and I didn't want to leave my car.

Once Aaron left, I was able to sip my coffee in silence, a benefit as my headache hadn't gone away.

Over the past year, I'd gotten more headaches—stress, my father had told me. Getting ready to move out for the first time, to a place across the country—that was a big deal. I was preparing to leave everything I'd ever known, the people, the places, the familiarity of it all and branch out.

That would make anyone lose sleep.

It felt like something more, like something deeper, but when I couldn't figure it out, I chose the easy answer.

The crowds had thinned, now that it was past midnight. There were those celebrating and those mourning, all drunk and stumbling and far too loud. Their voices lacked harmony, grating on my nerves, making my head pound worse.

Still, I pushed through, crossing the large outdoor shopping area with lights strung everywhere, toward the parking lot. I had a spot up on the top level. My father leased it every year so when he came for dinner, he never had to worry about finding a spot. Since he rarely came, I happily used it.

I got into the elevator, my hand shaking, my head throbbing. When the doors shut, I closed my eyes and pulled in a breath, trying to ease that tension inside me, a reaction to panic being my only guess. These attacks had kept getting worse, and even the pills my father had given me hadn't done much to help. The only thing that seemed to help were my headphones drowning out the noise.

The elevator moved quickly, and I held the railing to keep myself steady as my stomach churned.

Relax. Deep breaths, nice and slow. I coaxed myself through it, as I had before, as my therapist had taught me. The idea I had anxiety annoyed me. I had *nothing* to be anxious about. It made me feel like every other rich kid who didn't realize their life was damn near perfect so they came up with pointless little problems and blew them out of proportion.

I hadn't ever been that person before, but it seemed I was now.

Still, I refused to let myself remain that way, so I forced my body to relax and grabbed two ibuprofens from my purse, swallowing them with my coffee even though taking pills with hot drinks wasn't the easiest thing to do.

By the time the doors to the elevator slid open, I'd mostly gathered my wits. My head still ached, but the world seemed sharper again and nothing spun. I told myself a good night's sleep would do the trick, that I was just up too late and dealing with Moa and Aaron had just been overwhelming.

I walked the large parking lot, toward the back where my car was. Many of the spots were filled because the floor was also used for residents who lived in the condos just across the small path. It meant the cars were all expensive, since it wasn't a cheap place to live.

I turned the corner and froze.

Three men stood there in dark hoodies, one with a slim-jim already inside the window of a car. Their faces all turned toward me at once, and the curl of one's lips made all that panic I'd had inside the elevator rush back into me.

This wasn't good…

About the Author

Jayce Carter lives in Southern California with her husband and two spawns. She originally wanted to take over the world but realized that would require wearing pants. This led her to choosing writing, a completely pants-free occupation. She has a fear of heights yet rock climbs for fun and enjoys making up excuses for not going out and socializing.

Jayce loves to hear from readers. You can find her contact information, website details and author profile page at https://www.totallybound.com

Home of Erotic Romance

Sign up for our newsletter and find out about all our romance book releases, eBook sales and promotions, sneak peeks and FREE romance books!